PRELUDE

My Love,

I love you dearly and I adore the woman you are. I have had the pleasure of watching you grow from a girl to the wonderful woman you are today. You are my soulmate Jewels. I know when He created me He already had you in mind as my wife. Baby, I promise to love, protect, and provide for you until I take my last breath. You are a special gift to me from Him, and I will cherish His gift for life. I love you Jewels and am ready to continue this journey with you and hopefully add occupants as well. For life baby.

My heart is fulfilled, thank you baby.

♥♥♥You are my good thing baby, I love you.♥♥♥

Love,

Tony

Forever My Jewels

CHAPTER ONE

TOGETHER AT LAST

The ground is still wet from the rain that watered the Earth all night. The only sound there is in the neighborhood are birds chirping as the sun rises. The entire neighborhood is still asleep waiting for their alarms to wake them.

Hearing the birds, Jewels wakes to the sun shining in her eyes and smiles. She immediately smiles because she is thinking of how good it feels to be back in Jacksonville lying in her bed. She smiles even more when she rubs Tony's muscular arms wrapped around her as he sleeps.

She meditates a moment on her Father. As she meditates, she recites a few verses from the Book of Psalm, Chapter Seventeen in her mind. She continues to rub Tony's arms as she meditates and thinks about their time spent in CaliforniA. She is still in disbelief that her and Tony have been married for a year and a half. She also thinks and smiles at the fact that Tony came to her two weeks ago saying,

"Baby I know I have six months left, but I think I am going to call it quits now. I know you are ready to go back home, I am too. I have talked with my old job and they have a part-time position for me. I am going to take it and continue to sell my artwork on the side. What do you think?"

"It sounds good to me, but have you reached your goals?"

Smiling, Tony said to her, "Baby, I surely have and I am staring at her now."

Jewels blushes as she thinks of this moment as Tony wakes and kisses her on the cheek, rubs her arm, and says, "Good morning baby."

"Good morning", she says as she rises to walk to their bathroom.

While in there, she lifts her head to the ceiling and spends more time with her Father. Thanking Him for being back home safely and for continuously filling her with joy. She begins to wash up while humming the song Lovely Day.

As she finishes up, Tony walks in, hugs her from behind, and kisses her cheek. He rubs her stomach while smiling. Jewels looks at him through their mirror and says,

"Tony, you have been caressing my stomach like this for the past two weeks. Why do you keep doing that?"

Laughing, he kisses her cheek again, and responds, "Baby you don't know?"

Looking confused, she asks, "Know what?"

Rubbing her stomach again he says, "Baby you are carrying my seed."

Laughing, she turns to him, and says, "What? How would you know that, especially before me?"

He walks to the sink to begin brushing his teeth, but first says, "Baby, we are in the middle of the month and your period hasn't come on yet. And we have been making love everyday since it ended last month. Your period was supposed to come on the first part of the month and it hasn't. And baby, I have noticed little changes about you before we came back to Jax.. You are carrying life and don't know it."

He turns on the water as he stands at the sink and begins brushing his teeth when Jewels says, "But Tony, I have the rest of the month. Shouldn't you wait until the end of the month before jumping to that conclusion? And I have no changes, no morning sickness, or anything in that nature that are signs of pregnancy, so what changes did you see?"

He is in the middle of brushing his teeth and does not respond verbally, but shakes his head no. He finally gargles, spits out the water, then says, "Baby, remember you started throwing up out of no where before we came back. You thought it was food poisoning, but I never got sick and we have been eating the same food. You had no fever or aches. You just threw up the whole day."

Jewels walks to their bathtub to hang her washcloth to dry, saying, "But yea baby, that only lasted a day. I thought morning sickness lasted longer and only in the morning. I threw up all day, until nothing was left on my stomach and felt better."

As she turns, Tony is standing in front of her drying his face and shrugging his shoulders with a smile on his face. Staring at him, she asks, "Tony, is something wrong?"

He laughs as he sits his wash cloth down then pulls her to him and begins kissing her passionately. She kisses him back and he picks her up to walk her to their bed. As he walks to their bed, he says, "Baby, you are carrying my seed though", he laughs and continues to kiss her. She giggles too and kisses him back.

After their love session, he holds her and says, "Baby, I love you."

Rubbing his arm, she replies, "I love you too."

He smiles and says, "I love our baby growing inside you too."

Jewels laughs at his remarks, then stands to walk to their bathroom to shower. He soon follows to shower with her.

After they shower, they make a quick breakfast and eat it on their patio. They cook themselves an egg sandwich on toast, with a side of grits. Jewels has ginger tea for her drink, while Tony has a glass of orange juice. As they eat, they discuss a wedding they were invited to in Miami. It is in a few weeks and Jewels wants to make sure Tony still wants to attend. She also double checks their hotel reservations. He still wants to attend and asks,

"This is your friend right? Y'all were roommates?"

Shaking her head yes, she asks, "Yes, is something wrong?"

"Naw, just seeing who we are traveling to Miami for."

She laughs and they hear their doorbell ring. Shaking his head, Tony says,

"Now, who is at our door this Saturday morning? I mean, we just got back to Jax. Wednesday night."

As Jewels shrugs her shoulders, Tony checks their doorbell ring's camera he installed, shakes his head, and says, "I should've known", he looks at Jewels and continues, "it is your friend Kellie. I swear she does not like me being alone with you. Always interrupting us, since we were kids", he laughs at this as he watches Jewels walk to the front door.

As Jewels walks to the front door, he walks to their bedroom and closes the door. Jewels walks on their front porch and says, "Hey Kell, how are you?"

"I am fine, just came by to see you and to see if you needed any help?"

"Awwwweeee, but no, we do not need any help. We just have a little more things to clear out of storage for him, thanks though." Jewels pauses then asks, "Hey, are you going to Justice's wedding?"

"Yea, Brandon and I will be there."

Smiling, Jewels says, "I have not seen Brandon in a minute. He is always out of town working. How is he?"

"Oh he is fine. I think he is finally getting tired of it. He has been looking for local work lately. He asks about you and Tony all the time. When I told him y'all finally tied the knot, he would not believe me." Laughing, she continues, "I had to actually show him the picture you text me of you two on your wedding day at the courthouse and speaking of that, I am still salty for you not telling me or inviting me."

Laughing, Jewels asks, "Why didn't he believe it? And Kellie, everything happened so fast. I was wrapping my mind around becoming a wife and moving to L. A., we just decided to have our parents, Jacob, and his wife there. You know Tony was just ready to become husband and wife, but you know we are planning a wedding and I want you in it."

Tilting her head, "My guess, he assumed you two would play, 'cat and mouse', with each other for life and stick to friendship. But yes, I know, I am ready for my bride maid's duties as well."

Jewels laughs and responds, "Oh, he probably is not the only one who thought that. And you probably won't have much to do, you know Zee loves that stuff."

Kellie hugs her and says, "You are right. I remember her marrying off the neighborhood kids." They laugh and Kellie continues, "Well, I'ma leave. I just stopped by to see if you needed any help. I know Tony is waiting for you and ready for me to go."

Jewels hugs her back while ignoring her last statement and says, "I love you Kell and I will talk to you later."

"I love you too", Kellie says as she walks to her car.

Jewels walks back in their house and sees Tony lying in their bed working on a digital sketch on his Tablet. She lies next to him and asks, "You need any help?"

He kisses her cheek and says, "I'm good baby, thanks."

She rises while saying, "Okay, I will be up front doing some yoga if you need me."

He sits up and slaps her butt as she stands, "Alright baby, thanks."

She retrieves her cell phone and starts a Gospel melody playlist to begin her yoga routine. She turns on her portable waterfall that has lights all over it, lights an incense, and begins her yoga routine with, I Told The Storm beginning her playlist.

~~~~~~

Later in the day, Jewels and Tony gets dressed to clear out his storage. After she gets dressed, Tony stands in their doorway examining her with one hand resting under his chin while his free arm is propping it up. Looking at Jewels, he says to her,

"Baby, I think those shorts are little to short to wear outside."

She models them in their full sized mirror as she says, "Baby, you think so? I am just trying to be comfy to work."

He walks to her and hugs her as he says, "I know. But baby, you are waaaaay to sexy for those shorts. I already have to check a few dudes with a death stare who look to hard. Most do a quick peep and keep it moving, but a handful get a little bold. With these shorts on they probably will zone out looking. And you know I am not having it."

She looks at him, rolls her eyes in laughter, and swaps her cheerleading style shorts for some stretch capri pants. Tony smiles as she changes and says, "Thank you Jewels."

She laughs some more at him and blows him a kiss.

An hour later, they finally make it to his storage. Although they have been clearing out his storage slowly for the past year, it still feels like they are clearing out a four bedroom home. As they gather Tony's items, they decide on what to keep and what to give away or throw out. As they gather things Jewels come across a few shoe boxes, and of course, she opens each box. Not to her surprise, there are no shoes in any of the boxes. As she begins to go through the boxes, Tony hugs her and says, while showing her something, "Look Jewels. Baby, do you remember taking this?"

Laughing, she responds, "Yep, it was the first day of school for us. I did not know you still had it."

Smiling as he looks at the picture, "My mom had it. When I told her you and I were in a relationship she gave it to me, messing with me too."

He chuckles while still looking at the picture, and says, "My momma had jokes too, saying she did not think I would ever get the courage to ask you to be my girl." They laugh and he continues in his deep voice, "Talking 'bout, 'look at how you are looking at her in this picture. Trying your best to focus on the camera, but your eyes kept looking at her'. She was right though, my eyes kept looking your way", he laughs at himself.

Jewels laughs some more as he goes back to gathering his things and she continues to go through his shoe boxes. One box is filled with artwork and an unfinished comic book. Opening her mouth, Jewels asks, "Tony, why didn't you finish this comic strip? I did not even know you were working on this", she flips through the pages, "they are amazing baby, why did you stop?"

He walks to her and looks at it. He smiles at first flipping through the pages, then stops smiling as he continues to flip through more drawings and says, "Baby, I just lost focus. It wasn't important to me anymore, then I got the Cali job offer and put it away."

Looking at him in disbelief, "Tony that is not like you, you always finish what you start. What made- you- lose---", she stops talking and looks at him as he looks at her with his head tilted, and continues, "never mind."

Laughing and shaking his head, "Yea baby, you know why I lost focus", he smiles, "I got her back though", he kisses her cheek and continues working.

Laughing at him, Jewels opens another shoe box that is filled with memorabilia from his life's journey. She sees certificates from academic and athletic accomplishments. There are acceptance letters from a few Universities along with scholarship offers. As she goes through these, she smiles with joy and pride.

She finally closes that shoe box and opens another. As she opens it she shakes her head and asks, "Tony, what are you doing with a shoe box full of condoms?"

Stretching his eyes, he drops his head while shaking it, and says, "Baby, those are old, why do you think so many are in there. I forgot I even had them. You know we didn't use condoms."

"Yea whatever Tony", she checks the expiration date and sees they expired four years ago. She continues, "You have a whole shoe box filled with condoms, Tony were you having sex with that many women?"

Laughing he responds, "No Jewels, but my dad always taught me to stay overly prepared. It is better to be safe than sorry", he laughs.

Shaking her head she responds, "Whatever Tony."

He walks to her, hugs her, and kisses her cheek, "Baby, you know I was waiting on you my whole life, but baby, I had urges too and had to protect myself until you were ready to 'receive' me." He kisses her cheek, "I love you baby, you know I ain't go through that many women though."

Laughing, she responds as she looks at him, "Whatever Tony."

Smiling, he kisses her cheek and says, "I love you too", and continues working.

A few hours later, they finally decide on what to keep and what to give away. They keep all of his artwork, including, the unfinished comic strip that was slowly turning into a comic book. They also keep some patio furniture, a set of car rims he has, some clothes and shoes he left behind, and all of his trophies and awards from his school years.

They give some of his furniture, a dining table and sofa, to friends. There parents do not want anything and neither does her brother. What is left are, clothes, shoes, luggage, and an area rug, which they give to their parents' neighborhood church that always give back to their community in one way or another.

After, they return the storage key and ends Tony's contract with them. They then travel to a church that is in their parents' neighborhood. While at the church, a familiar face greets them saying, "Hey Tony and Jewels, my bad, it is Mr. and Mrs. Ellison now."

They pause, smile, and Tony says, "Heeeeeyy, man. How are you, what are you doing here?"

Shaking Tony's hand, the familiar voice responds, "I work here now."

Looking shocked, Tony asks, "What? You work here? You live in Jax. now?"

"Yea man, I am back. My wife is having our second child and I decided not to reenlist and come back home where our families are."

Nodding, Tony says, "Baby, you remember him from middle school?" Jewels nods yes and shakes his hand as Tony continues, "But you said you work here? What do you do at a church?"

"Right now, taking donations for the neighborhood. But I usually run our youth center for the kids and the pastor recently asked me to teach bible study."

Looking shock, Tony asks, "Bible study? Are you a pastor as well?"

"Yes I am."

"I would have never thought you would become a pastor, congrats man. I am proud of your evolution." He pauses and looks at Jewels, "You know my baby and I are planning a wedding, do you think you would want to officiate it for us", he looks at Jewels and asks, "are you okay with that baby?"

She nods in agreement and the pastor says, "I will love too. Here is my contact info, just let me know."

They exchange information. Tony and Jewels finally leave there items then travels home to rest.

Sunday afternoon arrives, Tony and Jewels decides to do yard work. As they work, Lenny walks over to speak to Tony. As he walks on their driveway, Lenny waves and says, "Hey Mr. Tony and Ms. Jewels. Welcome back."

They stop what they are doing and walk towards Lenny.

"Hey Lenny", they both say with smiles, "how are you?"

"I am fine. I was just coming over to let you know that Bernard and I are leaving the lawn business."

In a shocked voice, Jewels asks, "What? Why? I thought you two enjoyed it."

Laughing, Lenny continues, "Oh we do, buuuttt", he looks at Tony, "thanks to Mr. Tony, we both made the Junior Varsity basketball team and will not have time for our lawn service anymore."

Smiling, Tony says, "Congrats to y'all. I didn't even know y'all were trying out."

"Yea, we kept it low. The coaches were really impressed too. One of them wanted to put us on Varsity, but the others were like, no, we are just freshmen and need to get a better feel of the court first. We saw all your pictures too, you played almost every sport. We didn't know you were basketball and baseball captains either. When we told them we knew you and you taught us, they smiled and understood."

Smiling from ear to ear, "Ah man, this is nice to hear, and I can't believe they are still there. But yea man, I was captain for a year in baseball and all four in basketball. Good times", he laughs as he thinks of high school memories.

Laughing, Lenny says "Yea, they are and had a lot of stories too."

They laugh and Lenny continues, "But my lil' bro and his friends are taking over the lawn service. If y'all want their services let me know. The first few months will be discounted, so y'all can see if y'all like the work or not. If it is acceptable, than we can go back to the original pay."

Smiling at this, Tony says, "Alright, sounds good. We will give them a try next week. Will they be available?"

"Yes they will. I will let them know."

"Okay", Tony says as he gives him a pound and Jewels hugs him.

Tony and Jewels spends the rest of the day doing yard work. After Tony clears debris and walks their yard looking over their home, making sure nothing else needs his attention, he helps Jewels prepare an area that she will use for a vegetable and herb garden. He politely moves her to the side to complete the task of removing the grass then waves to her to get the water hose. As Jewels soaks the ground, Tony removes the grass and other debris and places them in the trash.

Monday arrives and Jewels wakes happy, singing, and humming. When Tony wakes, he joins in on the singing. They sit and eat breakfast, not talking much. As he indulges in his scrambled eggs, toast, and grits, Tony is busy scanning over the news while also making sure everything is in order for his first day back at his old job. Jewels, is busy looking at job listings that are in education in some aspect. From career counselors at public schools to teacher's aids.

They finally finish breakfast. As Jewels sits their dishes in the kitchen sink, Tony kisses her cheek and says, "Thanks for breakfast baby."

Kissing him back, Jewels responds, "Anytime."

Smiling, he walks to the door and Jewels follows him. He kisses her cheek again, squeezes her butt, and says, "I love you, see you in a few hours." Finally, Tony leaves for work and Jewels watches him with a smile. While Tony works, Jewels spends her morning still searching for work. During a small break she takes, she decides to call her doctor to schedule an appointment for a pregnancy test. Her doctor's secretary schedules her for the next morning. It is an open appointment that someone canceled. Jewels takes it with a smile because Tony will be at work and she does not want him to know she is taking it.

After she schedules her appointment, she decides to stop her job search and start dinner. While in the middle of cooking, Tony comes home. He hands Jewels a yellow rose that is placed inside of a card and says,

"Hey baby, it smells good in here", he kisses her cheek and continues as he hands her the card, "this is for you."

Smiling, she says, "Thank you baby, I appreciate it", she takes the rose and cuts the end off. She plants it in a pot sitting near a window in their living room, with all the other roses he has brought home since they have been married. She walks to and sits at their kitchen table to read the card while he showers. The card reads on the front:

Forever

My

Love

The inside:

You are Awesome

Tony's handwriting:

I love you baby.

Thank you for being you.

And for putting a smile on my face every morning I wake up holding you. Thanks for bringing sunshine back into my life baby, I Love You.

Just as expected, his words puts a smile on her face. She checks dinner and sees that everything is done then joins him in the shower.

After they shower, they prepare for dinner.

As they eat dinner, Tony tells her how his first day went and Jewels does the same. Tony lets her know, that much has not changed at his workplace and that his transition back should be smooth. She lets him know that she has not found work yet, but is still looking. She continues,

"Tony, my job search is harder than I thought. I just knew I would have work by now or at least top prospects."

Smiling he says, "Baby you know we are good financially, take your time. This may be a sign too."

"A sign for what?"

Looking at her, he asks, "Have you ever thought about being a stay at home mom?"

Laughing, she says, "No I have not, but you really believe I am pregnant?"

"Baby I know you are. I mean, look at you, your glow is even different."

Blushing from ear to ear, she responds, "Tony, please do not get your hopes up, but would you really want me at home? Are you trying to make me a, 'barefoot, pregnant, and in the kitchen', type of woman?"

Bursting into laughter, he says, "No Jewels, you know that is not me. But what I am saying, is that we both were lucky enough to experience that. Not many kids on our block had that experience, and I did notice the differences. You know how they were always at our houses getting some of that motherly love from our moms. Not because their moms did not give it, but their moms had to work a lot. I will like for our child or children to experience what we did."

Smiling, she responds, "Tony, you have a great point. I must admit, I loved coming home from school seeing my mom on the porch waiting for me, then walking inside and smelling dinner cooking."

He smiles, blows her a kiss from across the table, and they continue dinner.

The next day, Jewels sees Tony off to work after breakfast. She tells him that she will stop by with his lunch. He smiles, kisses her, and slaps her on the butt before leaving, something he cannot seem to stop doing. After he leaves, she gets dressed to go to her doctor's appointment. She drives in silence thinking over their conversation during dinner.

The appointment takes no time. Her doctor laughs and agrees with Tony about Jewels' glow. After her appointment, Jewels drives home to prepare lunch for Tony. She packs it and places an inspirational card in the bag with it.

The card reads on the front:

The Best

Jewels' handwriting:

You are the greatest husband ever, I love you. I hope your work day is going well, *kisses *

She checks the time and notices she still has a couple of hours left before he takes his lunch break. She decides to stop by her parents' home to say hello.

As she arrives at her parents' home, she sees her mom sitting out talking to Mrs. Ellison, Tony's mom. Jewels exits her car smiling and says, "Hey moms. How are you two today?"

Smiling back at her, they both say, "Fine, how are you?"

"I am fine. I stopped by to say hi because I have some downtime and I have not been able to see you all much since we have been back. Where are my dads?"

As she leans in to give them hugs, Mrs. Ellison says, "Jewels they are fishing. We cannot keep them off the boat, I enjoy the fish though.

Laughing, her mom says, "I do too." She looks at Jewels and says, "Baby girl, what are you using on your skin? You are just glowing like I have never seen before."

Laughing, Jewels responds, "You know Tony has said my glow is different too, I have not changed my skin regimen either." Looking at Mrs. Ellison, she continues, "You know your son thinks I am pregnant."

Both their moms look at each other and agrees with Tony. Jewels shakes her head with laughter and sits to talk with them until it is time for her to leave. They tell her how everything in their neighborhood is the same and asks when is the last time she has been to the gun range.

She lets them know, that she has not been since she moved to and from L. A.. Jewels also tells them how she is having trouble finding work. They give her advice, tell her to not get discouraged, then Mrs. Ellison asks, "Are you guys' bills okay?"

"Yes ma'am. Tony has that covered. He has actually been laughing at me wondering why I am looking for work, but he knows I like my own source of income and better yet, I need something to do."

They laugh at this and Mrs. Ellison says, "Jewels, you know Tony was still paying your bills when you left him, you know he will always look out for you financially."

"Yea, I know, he is a provider in that sense, but I need something to do as well."

Laughing, Mrs. Ellison says, "Yes he is, just like y'all's dads", they all laugh, and Mrs. Ellison continues, "but you know you are the only woman he has ever spent his money on like that, even when y'all were just friends. You know he can be a little tight at times, but with you, he did not care. He has always loved you like that.

His high school girlfriend could not stand it. I remember once, he bought some school supplies for you because they were out and came across an unbeatable sale. So he picked up things for all three of y'all and she went off on him, but he still got your stuff." Laughing at the story, she continues, "Jewels, when he told us why she was mad, his dad was like, 'Tony, you can't do that. That was wrong.' Tony did not care and was like, 'Dad, Jewels is my friend, that's it. I know she has not been school shopping yet, so I helped. Tika will get over it, she knows how tight our friendship is.'"

Jewels bursts into laughter while shaking her head, "See this is why that girl never liked me, but he was right, she did know beforehand about our friendship."

Mrs. Ellison laughs along with Jewels' mom, "He was still wrong for it, but he always looked out for you."

Jewels nods in agreement and sees her mom nodding too. She drops her head and laughs at the both of them. She receives a notification on her cell phone. It is a text message from Tony reading,

"Hey baby, I am taking my lunch earlier today, in 30 minutes, do you think you can make it? If not, I will just grab something from a restaurant, love you, <kiss>."

She responds,

"Yes baby, I can make it. I'm on my way, love you too <kiss x3>"

She looks at her moms and says, "Well, that was my baby texting, he is taking lunch early. I have to go, I love you two though."

She hugs them then leaves. As she walks away, they laugh at her and she hears her mom saying, "Look at my baby trying to act like a wife, I bet you are pretending to cook too."

Jewels bursts into laughter at her mom's remarks, but continues to her car.

She makes it to Tony's job and sits in the front for a few minutes because he is in his office talking to one of the firm's clients. He stands, looks out his window and sees Jewels. He waves at her then motions for her to come into his office.

As she walks in she hears Tony say, "No, she is my wife, but I want to introduce you two."

Jewels waves at the gentleman as she walks to Tony smiling, hands him his lunch, and says, "Hey baby, here you go", she kisses him and continues, "I hope I did not interrupt."

He kisses her back and says, "No you did not baby, but I want to introduce you to Jermaine." She waves and shakes his hand as Tony continues, "He is a customer here, but he is also one of my clients. I do a lot of design work for him, for years, and I think it is time for you two to meet. You know you help me sometimes and are better at personal details, so meeting some of my clients in person can help with that."

She smiles, "Yes, it surely can, nice to meet you Jermaine. What is your business?"

He smiles and responds, "Nice to meet you too. I make signs for store fronts, but I am a terrible artist. I just put the pieces together, but that is where your husband comes in. He draws me a great piece for my client and I have yet to have one of them not like it, then I create the sign from his design."

Smiling proudly at Tony, Jewels says, "Yea, he is an amazing artist."

Smiling at her compliment, he kisses her and says, "Thank you baby."

She smiles and Jermaine says, "It was nice meeting you and you two make such a lovely couple. I hope to find this one day."

Tony hugs Jewels and says, "Thanks man, I love my baby too."

Jewels blushes and waves at Jermaine as he leaves. Tony shuts his door and Jewels says, "He seems like a real cool dude, I see why you have worked with him so long."

"He is. I started working with him right out of college. Even when I was in L.A. I was selling him designs", he sits, sanitizes his hands, and sees the card in his bag. He reads the card Jewels has accompanied with his lunch. He smiles while reading it, then blows her a kiss as he places his card next to a picture he has of Jewels on his desk. He sanitizes his hands again and begins eating. He licks his fingers as he enjoys the chicken salad Jewels made accompanied with crackers and sweet black tea. He looks at Jewels and says, "Thanks for lunch baby, its delicious too. You are so good to me."

"Anytime baby. Thanks and it is a pleasure, you know I got you." She laughs, "Oh and my momma has jokes, I stopped by there before I came and you text. I told her I was leaving to bring you lunch, she yells to me as I walk to the car, 'you acting like a wife'."

Tony bursts into laughter, and Jewels continues, "She really believes you have me so spoiled, that you do everything and this is not a team sport."

He laughs some more, "But baby you are spoiled. Between your dad and me, you know you never wanted for anything."

Laughing while nodding in agreement, she says, "That is true, and I am both grateful and thankful, but baby I do my part."

"Exceptionally well baby. But I enjoy spoiling you, it is nothing better than seeing a smile on your face put there by me. And I am def not about to leave any room open for another man to slither in."

Smiling, she says, "Thank you baby, you know I appreciate you too. And you know you have no worries there."

"I know", he blows her a kiss.

They talk more as he continues to eat. He stops eating, sits back in his chair, and says in a low voice, "You know my boss quit yesterday, so we have a temp boss right now. You know he and I were cool too, but I do not know why he quit. They asked me to apply for the position, but I declined, it is not my career path. The only titles I care about are ours", he laughs, "just run me my check."

They both laugh and Jewels asks, "How do you feel about the change?"

Still speaking low, he responds, "Indifferent, baby it's just a job. It does not make or break me. I know who my Rock is", he looks up, "and baby, He gave me you. I am good."

Jewels laughs, "Baby, I love this attitude."

He smiles. After he finishes his lunch, he walks Jewels to her car, kisses and hugs her, helps her sit, and says, "Thanks again baby, I love you", he rubs her stomach, "and you. Drive safely baby, see you in a couple of hours."

"Love you too, baby", she says as she starts the engine.

\\

Saturday is here again. Tony wakes to a knock at their door and the smell of breakfast cooking. He looks out the bedroom's window to see who is at the door and listens as Jewels answers. He quickly realizes it is Lenny's little brother with his friends to start the yard work.

As they begin to work, he makes his way to the bathroom to start his morning. After he finishes, he walks to the kitchen smiling as he sees Jewels singing and dancing as she finishes cooking breakfast. When she sees him, she smiles, and says, "Good morning baby. I made us some pecan pancakes and scrambled eggs. I made enough for Lance and his friends as well."

"Thanks baby", he says as he kisses her cheek, "good morning too."

They eat, then Jewels places the lawn workers' pancakes in a to-go box. She and Tony decide to sit on the porch and watch them as they continue to work. As they sit, they notice Lenny and Bernard are standing in the driveway monitoring the work of the new lawn crew.

They see Tony and Jewels walk out and decide to join them on the front porch, "Good morning", they both say as they approach the front porch.

Waving, Tony and Jewels, responds, "Good morning."

Grinning, Bernard takes out his cell phone to show them a picture. It is a picture from their high school yearbook. It is the senior prom. Taking his cell phone to look closer at the picture, Tony grins, and excitedly asks, "Bernard where did you get this picture from? Maaaaan this feel like ages ago", he shows Jewels and she bursts into laughter.

Bernard laughs, "One of my teachers had us in the library doing research for a paper. I was done and went looking around and came across old year books. I did the math, to figure out y'all's graduation year and went through the yearbook laughing the whole time."

Laughing, Tony asks, "What was so funny about our class?"

Still laughing, Bernard says, "Everything just look so different. Man, y'all pants were so baggy, I wondered how y'all walked", he laughs, "Y'all had some cute girls though."

Tony chuckles while saying, "We managed, but we wonder the same about y'all in these tight skinny jeans, like y'all not even giving yourself room to move and breathe. Ain't going to give your parents no grand kids when the time comes."

Tony and Jewels laughs, and continues to listen to Bernard as he continues, "We manage too." Bernard laughs, then says, "But I came across this picture and was shocked, because I thought y'all didn't date in high school. But here y'all are, hugging like a happy couple for this photo. It even looks like you were trying to kiss Ms. Jewels' cheek."

Laughing still, Jewels says, "We were not a couple then, just went to the prom as friends. We were both single and decided to go together. And he was trying to kiss my cheek, but I moved my head and reminded him who my dad is."

Smiling, Tony says, "Yea baby, that worked out perfectly. We both became single right on time. We had so much fun that night, even after your dad sat the gun on the table and said, 'Don't try me Tony, my baby girl better come back as she left. I know your reputation at that high school'."

Bernard and Lenny laugh so hard at this, tears roll down their faces. Tony looks at Jewels, "Baby, your dad was dead serious too. Knowing I was not gone try you like that, but I guess he had to make sure."

Laughing too, she says, "I know. I heard the convo, he talked with me too and said, 'Don't let Tony run game on you Jewels'. Tony I was laughing so hard thinking, 'Dad, you are worried about the wrong one, the last dude was the problem'."

They all laugh. The new yard crew walks to them to let them know they are finish. Tony, Bernard, and Lenny look over their work. Lenny nods and gives them two thumbs up. Tony and Jewels are satisfied with the work, pays the discounted price, then Tony says, "We are satisfied with the work young men. I will see y'all next month", he looks at Lenny and Bernard, "Thanks for the discount, but if the work is good next month, I will pay regular price."

"Thanks, Mr. Tony", Lenny looks at his little brother, "Y'all make sure, your work stays great. You heard what he just said. Him and Ms. Jewels are great customers, do not slack."

Tony laughs as Lenny talks. He gives them all pounds and returns to the porch with Jewels, who is sitting holding their food she kept warm for them. They watch as they gather their equipment then hands them their food and watches them as they walk home.

Jewels kisses Tony on the cheek, and says, "Baby, I love you, you are so warmhearted."

He smiles, "Thanks baby, I love you too. And you know I know about the kid hustle life. I used to be all over our neighborhood selling my artwork for one dollar, five for a special design. The adults always supported me and bought one too. Now it is my turn to return the favor in a way."

Jewels smiles as she listens to him. They continue on their front porch a couple of more hours and converses about whatever crosses their minds.

CHAPTER TWO

THE WEDDING

Tony and Jewels are walking back and forth to their car putting their luggage in the trunk. It is a nice sunny day, in February, where the temperature is seventy degrees. The wind is no where to be found, but the weather is delightfully pleasant. As Jewels skips back and forth to their car, she sings every song she can think of from all eras and music genres.

After everything is in the trunk of their car, they walk their house making sure no electronics, lights, or appliances are turned on. They make sure all their windows are down, locked, and double checks their patio doors. As they walk towards their opened front door Jewels receives a phone call. She sees it is her doctor's office and answers it nervously,

"Hello", Jewels says.

The voice cheerfully asks, "Good morning, may I speak to Jewels Ellison please?"

"This is she", Jewels responds with one hand placed on her hip.

"Hi Jewels, this is Janice from Dr. Penn's office. I was just calling to tell you the results of your test."

Looking at Tony, she says, "Can you hold for one second please? My husband is standing here and I will like him to hear it too, so I am going to put you on speaker phone."

Not sure what is going on, Tony looks at her in confusion but puts his listening ears on once he hears the voice on the other end. Janice continues, "Are you two ready?"

"Yes we are", Jewels says.

"Well, I am happy to tell you two that you are expecting. Jewels you are pregnant."

Dropping her mouth in disbelief, she looks at Tony who is grinning wide, and Janice continues, "Jewels, I am making an appointment for you so we can start this journey of new life with you. What is a good time for you two?"

"Janice we are on our way out of town, so when we get back I will call you and we can go from there."

"Okay, sounds good. Talk to you soon."

"Okay. Bye, enjoy your day."

As she ends her call, Tony rushes her and picks her up saying, "Baby, I knew it!" Laughing at this new revelation, he continues, "You did not even tell me you were taking the test, man Jewels this is a lovely surprise."

Smiling, while he is still holding her, she says, "Tony I really didn't think I was and didn't want to get your hopes up."

Looking at her, still smiling, he says, "Dang Jewels, you really have my seed inside you growing. Baby, dang, I am just so happy right now. I love you."

"I love you too", she says grinning.

He kisses her for a moment then puts her down. He closes their front door and locks it. Smiling, while knowing what is on his mind, Jewels says, "Tony we do not have time for that."

Embracing her while grinning, Tony says, "We do baby, I just need a few minutes."

Laughing, she says, "When have you ever needed just a few minutes? And you know you usually want seconds."

Smiling as he listens to her, but steadily unbuttons the buttons to her knee length dress, he nods in agreement. Once all her buttons are undone he begins to passionately kiss her while caressing her at the same time. Jewels stops protesting and undo his shorts as well as he whispers in her ear, "Dang baby, I love you so much", and continues kissing and caressing her.

After their love encounter, Jewels walks to the bathroom to shower. Watching her walk away with love in his eyes, Tony retrieves his cell phone to call their hotel. He tells them they are running behind, but are still coming and asks them to hold their room. After he makes the phone call he joins Jewels in the shower. Laughing as he pulls the shower curtain back, she says,

"I knew you were coming."

Smiling, he says, "I know."

"Did you call the hotel?"

He shakes his head yes as he enters the shower with her.

Finally, they hit the road to Miami. While traveling, Jewels calls their hotel to check their room again. Everything is fine so they spend the rest of their drive talking and listening to non stop love songs.

As he drives, Tony says, "Baby, I still can't believe you are carrying our baby."

Laughing, she responds, "Me either, what a change."

"A great one. When do you want to tell our fam?"

Bobbing her head from side to side, "I think we should wait a couple of months. You know, give the baby some time to grow."

He nods in agreement, "I agree. Do you want a boy or a girl?"

"Baby, I do not care. I just want a healthy baby but I know you are praying for a boy."

Laughing, "I surely am, but I will be just as happy with a daughter." He laughs and says, "I can see myself acting like your dad too, if we have a daughter."

She giggles as he leans over and kisses her cheek. As he continues to drive he passes some billboards, and says, "We have to visit there one day so we can relax with no interruptions." He laughs and looks at her, "And you know who I mean when I say no interruptions."

Laughing hard, she replies, "Yes I do, and I will love to visit here. I will get to see more of nature as well."

He nods and continues to drive while serenading Jewels to Shai's Comforter hit song.

Close to six hours later they make it to their hotel, tired. They check-in, sanitize their room, and rest for tomorrow's wedding. Before he goes to sleep, Tony kisses Jewels on the forehead and says, "Good night baby." He kisses her stomach and says, "Good night Little Jewels or Little Tony."

Smiling at this, Jewels says, "Good night baby", as Tony wraps her in his arms to go to sleep.

The next day, they both rise early enough to see the sunrise over the beach's water. As he holds her while watching the sun makes it appearance for the day, he says, "Baby this is always such a beautiful sight. I have to make time to see it more. His artwork is just so beautiful."

Jewels nods her head in agreement and continues to enjoy His beautiful artwork while resting her head on his shoulder.

As the sun places itself in the sky, they head down to the dining area for a quick bite to eat, then hurries back up to get dressed for the wedding. They have both decided on the color blue. Jewels has on a solid sky blue pencil skirt with a white blouse that has a blue flower on it, accompanied with a silver belt and silver pumps. Her hair is plaited in single box braids that she pulls into a high pony tail to show her silver studs, Tony gifted her a month ago. As she wraps her silver belt around her waist, Tony holds her and squeezes her butt while saying, "Dang baby, this skirt is really hugging you just right. You gone have my neck on swivel making sure no man is staring to hard."

Jewels kisses his cheek while giggling and rolling her eyes at Tony's comment.

She turns and checks out his outfit while blushing. He has on white slacks with a white care free top accompanied with a solid sky blue blazer. He accessorizes it with a silver watch he has and a blue belt Jewels bought him while in California. He was going to let his Locs hang, but Jewels pulls them back in two big twists and lets the rest hang then says, "Baby, you need to show your goat tee and bone, it looks really good."

Laughing, he says, "Thank you baby, but I don't want to look tooooo good and have these women I do not know staring and you looking at me like I'm creeping. You know your man is fine", he laughs at himself as he rubs his beard.

Bursting into laughter, she says, "Whatever Tony, you know these women do not care how you look, they always stare. So look your best boo, I love it, you are coming home to me. And yes, you are", she smiles and winks.

He smiles, "Come home with a huge smile too baby." He laughs and asks, "You ready?"

"Yes."

He takes his camera out of his pocket and says, "Smile baby", she does with a sassy pose. He then holds her and takes a picture of them two together as he smooches her cheek. As they leave for the wedding, they pass a full body mirror on the way to the elevator. Tony stops, holds Jewels, and says, "Dang baby, we look good together."

She laughs and says, "I wonder if our baby is going to be as cocky as you."

He shrugs and laughs, then says, "It is the truth baby, we do."

Jewels laughs and continues to the elevator. While on it, he takes more pictures of them and nibbles on her cheek.

They make it to the wedding thirty minutes later and sees that it is packed. There is barely sitting room. Tony and Jewels sits on the bride's side, close to the back. As they sit, Jewels sees Kellie and Brandon sitting to the front. Jewels text messages Kellie who turns around looking for her and waves at them, Tony even waves back. Brandon then turns around and waves too which prompts Tony to lean over and ask,

"Jewels is that Brandon?"

"Yes", Jewels says as she nods and pats his thigh.

"I have not seen him in a while, I didn't even think they were still together."

Jewels is about to respond, but sees the groom and his best man walk out. Quickly after she hears, Case's Happily Ever After, begin to play and the bride's party begin to walk out. Not long after, Jesse Powell's You plays and everyone stands to see the bride make her way down the aisle with the beach as the back drop. As she walks the ocean is beautifully calm with waves rolling slowly and periodically. The birds are chirping non stop, reminding Jewels of the singing birds in the old Cinderella movie.

The ceremony is beautiful and there are barely any dry eyes in the room. The groom sings, Babyface's Everytime I Close My Eyes, to his bride who cannot stop crying. The little flower girl almost drops the rest of her flowers because she almost falls asleep standing there. A woman, who turns out to be her mom, gets her and sits down with her to enjoy the rest of the ceremony.

After they exchange their vows, everyone stands to watch them leave smiling with happiness and holding hands. Finally, the guests leave and walks next door where the reception is being held. Tony and Jewels begins to dance as, Let's Get Married by Jagged Edge plays. As Tony dances with Jewels, he whispers in her ear,

"Baby, baby, baby. My love, my love, I can't wait to do this at our wedding", Jewels smiles as she listens to him, then looks at him when she hears him do an irritating sigh accompanied with a deep breath. She turns her head to look in the direction he is looking and sees Kellie walking towards them. They stop dancing and leave the dance floor to talk to Kellie and Brandon.

As they meet up to talk Tony shakes his head at Kellie, but grins when he sees Brandon. He walks over to Brandon as Jewels walks to Kellie. Tony and Brandon catches up while Jewels and Kellie talk.

Giving him a pound, Tony says, "Heeeyy Brandon. Man I haven't seen you in a while, how you been?"

Brandon replies, "It has been a minute, but I have been busy. Just working a lot, you know Kellie is always spending my money like she does not have a job."

Tony laughs, as he continues, "I think this is my first time seeing you two since y'all got married. Congrats man, how is married life treating you?"

Tony looks at Jewels who is laughing while talking to Kellie and says, "Wonderful man. I couldn't dream of a better wife."

Brandon nods and says, "Hopefully I will find me one, one day too."

Tony shakes his head, looks at Kellie, but says nothing. Then a song comes on which leads Brandon and Kellie to the dance floor. As they dance, Jewels says to Tony,

"Baby, I will be back. I have to use the restroom."

He looks at her and says, "Baby, you know I am coming with you."

"I am good. I need you to stay here and watch our things."

"Okay baby, it is a lot going on out there so stay alert."

She kisses him and says, "I will."

He watches her as she walks away, until she disappears from his sight. Not long after, a few women walks up to him and asks, "How long have you two been married?"

"A year and a half", Tony says while looking at them with a straight face.

"She is a lucky lady. I hope to find a man to look at me the way you look at her", one of the women says.

Shaking his head with laughter, he responds, "Naw, I am the lucky one. I found her and wake up every morning smiling holding her in my arms."

Kellie sees the women talking to Tony and walks over to them. One of the women then asks, "Do you have a single brother?"

Kellie interrupts as she clears her throat and says, "No. He is the only child, but he does have a wife."

The same woman says, "We know."

Tilting her head, Kellie responds, "Well, y'all need to get out of his face---." As Kellie continues to talk to the ladies, Tony checks his time smiling, thinking, "Dang, I have never been happy to see Kellie before, but I am happy she came over." He continues to look at his cell phone and sees nearly fifteen minutes have passed and Jewels is not back. He grabs their things and walks towards the restrooms.

Meanwhile, Jewels exits the restroom and sees someone standing on the wall waiting. She avoids eye contact, but as soon as she exits the person says, "Hey beautiful."

Recognizing the voice, Jewels freezes as he walks up to her and asks, "You are not going to speak to me Jewels?"

Trying to walk away, he steps in front of her and says, "Jewels why don't you want to talk to me?"

In an angered voice, she responds, "We have nothing to talk about Jesse, now move out of my way."

"Jewels, yes we do. You just left me. You never told me why. You just said it was over, through a phone call. You even blocked me. Don't you think I deserve closure? Why did you leave me? My daughter still asks about you."

"It just did not work out, now move. And tell her I am fine and hello for me, now move!"

Not moving, but still wanting answers, he asks, "Why? What went wrong? I thought we were happy."

Looking a little scared, she asks, "Are you following me? How did you know I was here?"

"No, I am not following you. We are at the same wedding. The groom invited me and I saw you walk in, with your ex by the way. Are you two back together? Is he why you left me? Where you cheating on me?"

"Jesse, you know I am not a cheater. Were you? You know what, I do not care, now move."

She tries to walk pass him, but he holds her to stop her. As she struggles away, he sees her wedding ring and says, "Jewels, you are married? We have been broken up a little over a year and you are married. You wouldn't even move in my home, but you are now married."

Ignoring his statements, she begins to raise her voice and says, "Let me go", repeatedly.

As Tony walks to the restrooms he notices there are three different events going on at this beach front hotel. There seems to be a birthday party, a bachelor's party, and a retirement party. There is a lot of noise, from music and chatter, along with the smell of an array of foods. Ranging from Soul Food, Chinese, and Mexican. As he gets closer to the restrooms he hears voices coming from that direction, but cannot quite make it out because of all the music playing. He begins to listen closer and picks up speed. He finally realizes he hears Jewels saying, "Let me go." Once he hears this he takes off running to the restrooms. Running down the hall he sees a man holding someone and knows it is Jewels from the voice.

He finally makes it to them, grabs the man holding Jewels, and forcefully throws him to the ground while placing Jewels behind him. As he stares down at the man, he quickly recognizes him and says, "Jesse what the hell is wrong with you? Don't you ever touch my wife again! Do you hear me Jesse, don't you ever touch my baby again!"

While still looking at Jesse, he asks Jewels, "Are you okay baby?"

Holding his blazer tightly, she says, "Yea baby. Lets go, I just want to leave."

He takes her hand and they walk pass Jesse. Still watching him the whole time, Tony sees him stand and hears him shout, "I'm sorry Jewels."

Jewels shows no response to this, but holds Tony's hand tighter. As they travel back to their hotel, Jewels text messages Kellie to tell her she and Tony left.

"Hey Kell, I am just texting to let you know Tony and I left."

She replies,

"Is everything okay, why did you two leave?"

"Jesse is there, but everything is fine. I will talk more about it later with you."

"Okay Jewels, y'all drive safely and I will talk to you later, love you."

"Love you too."

After she sends the text messages, she looks at Tony and he is still heated. She rubs his arm and asks,

"Tony, are you okay?"

"Yea baby, I'm good. I just can't believe what just happened."

"Me either."

He looks at her while they are stopped at a red light and asks, "Jewels, has he ever put his hands on you?"

"No, I never even seen him mad before. I do not know who that person was."

He continues to drive and says, "I am glad you did leave him because that behavior just does not happen all of a sudden. He was to aggressive with you. It took everything in me not to hit him."

"You are right about that."

They make it to their hotel and park. Tony turns the car engine off as he looks at Jewels with a serious face and asks, "Jewels, how did he know you were there?"

With a shocked look on her face, she replies, "Tony, he did not. He said he was invited by the groom and saw us when we walked in."

Dropping his head and shaking it in disbelief, he asks, "Jewels, were you having a conversation with him? Is that why you went to the restroom?"

"Tony no. When I walked out the restroom he was standing there and immediately begin to block my path as I tried to get away from him."

Looking at her with a straight face he says, "But baby, if you were just trying to get away from him how do you know why he is here?"

Looking at him still in shock and disbelief, she responds, "Tony, as he was blocking me and I continually told him to move I wondered if he was following me or something and asked him how he knew I was there? He told me he was invited by the groom and saw us when we walked in. Tony, are you implying that I am sneaking around with him or something?"

He sits back in his seat, looks up to the roof of the car, and says, "No baby, just trying to figure out what happened."

Looking at him, still in shock, Jewels exits the vehicle and Tony quickly follows. While on the elevator he tries to put his arm around her, but she moves away from him and folds her arms. Not caring, he moves next to her and hugs her until they make it to their floor. Once in the room, Jewels quickly heads to the shower without saying anything. Knowing he will want to join, she locks the door.

After she showers, she walks out and sees him sitting on the foot of the bed looking into space shirtless with his arms resting on his thighs. He looks at Jewels and asks, "Baby, why did you lock me out?"

She looks at him, but says nothing and lies down. He wants to say more but decides to shower first. He stands and looks at her. Wearing his slacks and socks with his Locs hanging, he stares at her as she lies down with her back turned to him. As he looks at her he rubs one hand over his face while taking a deep breath. Hearing it, Jewels rolls her eyes. After he showers, he walks out and asks, "Baby, why aren't you talking to me?"

She sits up, looks at him, and says, "Because you basically just called me a liar and a cheater."

Sighing, while sitting on the bed, he responds, "Baby, I did not. I am just trying to figure out how deranged Jesse is and how high my alerts should be." He holds her, kisses her forehead, and continues, "I know you are neither of those things."

She says nothing but lies back down. He continues as he rubs her back, "Come on baby, we vowed to never go to sleep mad at each other. Baby you know I did not mean it in that way."

She sits up again and looks at him, "Tony, I am not mad, just want some rest."

Leaning back as he looks at her, he asks with a semi hoarse voice, "Why did you lock me out then?"

Laughing, she says, "Well, I was mad then, but I am not now."

Laughing while shaking his head, he kisses her and says, "I love you baby."

She kisses him back and says, "I love you too."

Tony turns on a slow jams playlist he has, lies down, wraps Jewels in his arms, and falls asleep with her.

The next morning they travel back to Jacksonville. For the first time, or second time according to Tony, Jewels begins throwing up. Between the motion of the car and the baby growing inside of her, Jewels' body decides to get rid of everything in her stomach, even water. Their five hour drive turns to seven and Jewels' stomach finally settles. They are both happy they decided to leave before the sun rose. When she finally stops as they make it closer to Jacksonville, Tony caresses her cheek, and says, "Baby, I'm sorry."

"Sorry for what?"

"For your throwing up."

"Baby, what are you talking about?"

Laughing, he says, "Your pregnancy. You know I do not like seeing you sick and all I can do is hold you."

Smiling at him, she responds, "Awwweee, baby that is all I need you to do and keep putting a smile on my face."

Grinning, he says, "Oh, that just comes naturally."

She blushes and kisses him on the cheek as he continues to drive. They finally make it home. He walks her in the house so she can lie down on the couch. He begins to make her soup. As it cooks he takes their bags out of the trunk and sits them in their wash room. After, he checks the soup and sees that it is ready then brings it to Jewels.

Smiling, she says, "Oh, thank you Tony."

He kisses her cheek and says, "You are welcome baby. Call me if you need me, I will be in the laundry room."

She nods as she begins to sip her soup.

After he starts a wash and dinner, he rejoins Jewels who is still sipping on her soup, eating a turkey sandwich. He sits next to her, rubs her cheek, and asks,

"How are you feeling baby?"

"Better, thanks."

Smiling, "I'm baking chicken breasts for us, what vegetable do you want?"

"Uhhhhhh, do we have any squash left?"

"We do. I will make that."

Smiling, "Thanks baby."

"You are welcome."

He kisses her cheek then turns on the television and channels surfs until he sees a program on the history station about Egyptian empires. He finishes his sandwich and lies in Jewels' lap as he begins the show. As he watches, he corrects some of their knowledge, including some of the physical descriptions they have given to some of the Kings and Queens. Jewels sits and happily takes in his knowledge, but laughs at him becoming a professor to the television screen.

A few days passes and Kellie stops by to pick up Jewels for a lunch outing they are having with some old classmates. As they drive, Kellie asks, "Jewels, why did you two leave the reception? Did something happen?"

Shaking her head, "Kell, when I walked out of the restroom, Jesse was waiting for me and held me so I could not leave. But Tony walked up and got me and I was ready to leave after that. I am still in disbelief. And it is crazy how we ended up at the same wedding, just crazy."

Shaking her head, Kellie responds, "Wow. Do you think he still likes you?"

"I am not sure, he said he just wanted closure."

Listening attentively, Kellie asks, "Do you still like him?"

"Not at all. What made you ask that?"

She shrugs her shoulders and says, "After you text me, I did see him walk into the reception. You know, I wonder if he sent those women over to talk to Tony as a distraction? But I asked just to be sure, you were with him for a few years and I know how emotions can get caught up sometimes."

She responds, "Oh I understand, but naw, there is nothing there. Tony has my full attention and my heart. BUUUUTTTT", holding her head back, she asks, "what women? Tony did not say anything to me about women."

Laughing, Kellie responds, "It wasn't serious Jewels. When you walked off they came up asking him if he had a single brother and stuff like that. I interrupted them and he left."

Laughing, Jewels says, "I swear, he cannot go anywhere without one woman trying to get his attention." Shaking her head, "That's my baby though", they both laugh.

They finally make it to their destination and enter a sports bar, where they meet up with three friends from high school. They also attended college with a couple of them. As they eat, they catch up and one of their friends asks, "So Jewels, how is Tony? And married life?"

"Great, I will let him know you asked about him Ciara."
"Thanks, how is your job search?"

"Not good, but I think I am going to stop and focus on our home."

"What", another friend asks?

Jewels laughs as that friend continues, "You are going to stop working and depend on his income? Whose idea was this?"

"It is mutual."

Shaking her head, that same friend continues, "Jewels isn't two incomes better than one?"

"It depends. In our case, it does not matter. We are comfortable enough were I am able to not work and take care of home, like our moms did."

"The third friend, Tina, says, "Jewels that will make you happy? I have never known you not to do anything."

Laughing, Jewels responds, "Taking care of home is doing something, especially if we begin having kids. I mean, don't you have a maid? You pay someone to take care of your home and I am deciding to do it myself. I enjoy it as well and being able to greet him when he walks in from work, working hard by the way, to make sure I want for nothing. We were going to blow my money anyways, it is not needed." She laughs, "I mean, even when we were just dating he was paying the major bills at both of our places and we would use mine to vacation. I mean we always had a bond like that, even as friends."

Ciara chimes in saying, "Jewels, you know that is a control move right? Now you will be dependent on his cash, it is not 1920."

Shaking her head, Kellie finally speaks, "Don't try that Ciara. I have known Tony since we were kids and he is not like that. And I def know he cares about my friend, he loves her to much to try and control her."

Jewels looks at Kellie and says, "Thank you Kell! This is a mutual decision. We are married, his cash is mine anyways, but, if you really believe it is control shouldn't you be more concerned with when I am leaving. Working or not, you should not want me to be with a controlling man. I would have never married him if I thought he was controlling."

They all look at Jewels, nods, and Kellie says, "Exactly."

Ciara adds, "You have a point, I would not want you with a controlling person at all. He did not seem like that in high school either, but you know we only want the best for you. We are just making sure."

Jewels responds, "I understand and appreciate it. But know, some woman are okay with staying home as work."

They all nod in agreement, finishes lunch, talks a little more, then travels to their local mall. They use the mall trip for exercise, shopping, and more conversation. Jewels buys some work shirts for Tony and a few items for herself at a local retailer's shop. As they walk the mall, she notices a new store and says, "I worked at a store similar to this in L. A.."

Shocked, Kellie says, "Jewels, I did not know you were working out there. You never told me."

Laughing as she remembers her time there, Jewels says, "It was only for three months and part-time. Tony thought it was hilarious and would burst into laughter every time I walked through the door with bags in hand after 'a hard's day of work'. I really liked the clothes and put in an application after I visited their store. It was a fun job---."

As she continues, she hears a voice saying, "Hey Ms. Jewels."

She turns and looks. She sees a young man, who is waving at her friends but leaning in to give her a hug as well, "Oh my gosh, hey, how are you", Jewels asks in an excited voice?

"I am great. How are you and Mr. Tony, my mom told me you two got married and it broke my heart?"

Laughing uncontrollably, Jewels says, "Yes we did. We are fine, but how are your parents? How old are you now?"

"My parents are great. I will let them know I saw you too. I am nineteen now and a sophomore at an HBCU, at Loward University. The business is still good, but my dad stepped down and finally started his car detailing business."

Smiling with pride, Jewels says, "That is great to hear, I always knew Mr. Johnson would do that one day. He talked about it non stop, but what are you majoring in?"

"Business management", he says while taking out his cell phone to show Jewels his dad's business. As he shows her a young lady walks up and says,

"Babe, are you ready? They did not have what I am looking for."

He smiles, and says, "Yea, I am ready, but I will like for you to meet Ms. Jewels and her friends. She used to work with my parents", he looks at Jewels and says, "Ms. Jewels this is my girlfriend. She is now interning with my mom."

Smiling, Jewels shakes her hand saying, "Nice to meet you."

"Nice to meet you too", the young lady responds.

Smiling, he gives Jewels one more hug and says, "It was nice seeing you. I hope y'all enjoy the rest of your day", he and his girlfriend waves bye as they walk away.

Kellie looks at Jewels and says, "You and his girlfriend favor."

Laughing, Jewels looks at Kellie and asks, "You think so? She seems sweet, but I know he is good catch, so she better not play around with him."

They all laugh and continue shopping. They shop in a few more clothing stores, where Jewels purchases slacks for Tony and blouses for herself. While her friends focus on bags and stilettos. They end their outing with hugs then Kellie drives Jewels home.

The next day, a cloudy one, Tony leaves work at One to take Jewels to her first doctor's appointment concerning her pregnancy. While there, he watches as Jewels has her weight and all her vitals taken. Her doctor takes blood to check for any health issues.

While traveling home, Jewels asks, "Baby, how was work?"

"It was fine baby. How was your day?"

"Great. You know I do not need you at every appointment, you can stay at work."

He looks at her and says, "Baby, this is our first child, being at your appointments are a joy. You know I have my time worked out too so I can be on the scene when needed."

"Okay baby. Just making sure because I don't want you to overwork yourself."

He laughs, and says, "Never Jewels. My family is my first priority, my job will be there."

She smiles and listens to the music as they travel home. He looks at her and asks, "You want a smoothie?"

She nods yes. He stops at their local smoothie place and purchases them a smoothie then detours to a local park, where they sit and watch the river as the sun begins to peek. They drink their smoothies and talk until the sun sets. He smooches her cheek in between him telling her how his work day went and how excited he is to become a father.

CHAPTER THREE

Four months have passed and they have finally decided to tell their families about the pregnancy. They stop by Lowds' house first and plan to walk to the Ellisons' after.

It is a bright day and a little humid. The birds are chirping non stop. Before they leave, Jewels does a little garden work and the humid weather has her sweating like she is running a marathon.

She has decided to work on her vegetable and herb garden, but she has also planted flower seeds nearby and are attending to them as well. From tulips to elephant ears. She wants to see how green her thumb is, so she has been planting an array of seeds. Some of her seeds do nothing, while others grow rapidly. So far, her herbs, that include basil, rosemary, and thyme, are growing wonderfully. She has already used them in meals. As she finishes, Tony walks up and says,

"Baby, it looks good. You may be ready for the cannabis business. They have been making big money, since it has been becoming legal. It is about time for us to cash out with it as well."

Laughing, she looks at him and says, "You are right and you did 'invest' in it as a teen. It is time for you to see a return on your 'investment'."

Dropping his head in laughter, "Baby you are right. That is one disadvantage for working for someone, you have to follow their guidelines. I had to stop and replaced it with alcohol, but I rather have had my herb. I had to let that go too though", shaking his head, "you know why too."

Jewels laughs at him as he continues, "You know I was actually allowed to smoke it in L. A., but you know I only trust my man here for it." Laughing at himself, "I remember our bro used to mess with me, after his business took off and he ain't have to work for no one. He would look at me laughing, like, 'Alright Tony, I gotta go.' He would blow fake smoke from his mouth while he walks off saying, 'No contact high for you', Jewels all I could do was shake my head at him and laugh."

Shaking her head at him, with a few giggles, Jewels pats his back and says, "I am going to go shower, then we can head to our parents' houses."

He laughs with her, then kisses her, "Okay, I'ma shower with you."

She laughs as she walks in their house to shower with him following behind her singing an array of songs by the group Silk.

After they shower they travel to their parents' neighborhood. To their luck, everyone is at the Lowds' home. Tony gets out first and waves as he walks to open the door for Jewels. As they walk up, their parents say at the same time, "Congrats you two", while smiling. Tony and Jewels look at each other and laugh wondering how they knew, but remembers Jewels now has a small belly bump?

Tony's dad looks at him, and says, "Son, I didn't think you were going to make me a grand dad." He laughs and continues, "I am glad you waited for the right time and person though."

They all laugh, then sit around and talk for an hour. Tony and Jewels listens as each parent gives them pregnancy advice. Each one has an old wives tale as well, from telling Jewels not to hang clothes to not riding bikes. From their knowledge, both activities can cause the umbilical cord to wrap around the baby's neck and strangle him or her. They both listen as they look at each other trying not to laugh, but nods and agrees with their parents. Their moms tell Jewels to use raw Shea Butter on her stomach to help with stretch marks. As they continue to give advice, Tony checks his time while laughing at all the advice, and says,

"Oh man, I gotta go. I am supposed to meet your brother and some friends in thirty minutes to play a pick up game."

He hugs and kisses Jewels, then says, "Baby do you mind staying here so you won't be alone?"

Looking at him, then seeing concern in his eyes, she thinks about the Miami incident and says, "Yea, baby I will stay here. How long will you be gone?"

Smiling, he says, "No more than two hours."

She walks him to their car where they hug and kiss again. Before he gets in, he squeezes her butt, laughs, and says, "I love you sexy."

Jokingly rolling her eyes, she says, "I love you too."

As she says this, their dads walk up, and Mr. Ellison says, "Hold up Tony, we are coming with you."

Jewels walks back to the porch with their moms and they all wave bye to their husbands.

While the men are at the park, the women decides to walk the neighborhood. Both of their moms ask if Jewels wants a baby shower. She responds, "Not really. I doubt that we will need anything, you two know Tony will have the finances together. I plan to sew some things as well."

Mrs. Lowd responds, "Baby girl, this is both y'all's first baby, you sure you want to skip a shower?"
"It isn't important to me, but I will double check with Tony."

"Okay, let us know so we can start planning."

"Yes ma'am."

They continue to walk and Kellie passes them. She stops and parks on the side of the road near them. She gets out and runs to Jewels saying, "Friend, you did not tell me you were expecting. Is this why you decided to stay at home and not work?'

Laughing at her, Jewels says "Yes, but I wanted to tell our parents first. Where are you headed to?"

Her mom cuts in, "Jewels I didn't know you decided on this. I never thought you would want to stay at home."

"Yea ma. Tony and I talked and decided it will be best for our child to experience what we did."

Their mothers nod in agreement and continues to listen as Kellie talks.

Kellie continues by saying, "Well, I was actually on my way to your parents' house", she pauses and finally hugs Mrs. Lowd and Mrs. Ellison, then continues, "to talk to you. I stopped by your place and you weren't there and figured you were probably over here."

"Oh, you figured right." Jewels laughs, "What's up", Jewels asks?

"Nothing, just came by to chill. I took off from work to spend time with Brandon, but his job called and offered him a bonus to do an emergency run and he took it."

"Oh okay. Well we are just walking the neighborhood for some quick exercise then I will go back and wait for Tony to pick me up. I want to make a quick meal for us too."

Mrs. Lowd cuts in again, "I got it Jewels. I will make enough for you two and you can pretend to cook tomorrow."

Jewels drops her head in laughter, "Ma I do not pretend, I actually cook and he enjoys my meals. I bake cakes sometimes too, from your recipes."

Her mom laughs, "Yea, I hear you baby girl. Tony probably thinks your boiled water is amazing."

Everyone laughs at this and Kellie says, "I'ma park at your parents' house and meet you all back 'round here and walk too."

"Okay."

‸‸‸

As Tony drives to the park, he and their dads converse the whole time. On the drive, Tony's dad jokingly says, "Tony, I did not think you were going to ever be a dad" he laughs, "but are you ready for this responsibility? It is a big one."

Smiling with glee, Tony says, "Dad, I surely am ready, but you know I was not trying to plant my seed in any random either. Like you said, it is a big responsibility. You know my baby is the only one I ever wanted to share this joy with anyways. It feels good too, y'all should know the feeling."

They both say, "Yea we do." Mr. Lowd continues, "I was nineteen and scared as ever, but happy at the same time. We were married for like three months, then five years later Jacob came. By that time, I was extra ready", he laughs.

"Your 'baby', Jewels almost did not make it."

"What", Tony asks in a shocked voice!?

Laughing, Mr. Lowd says, "Yea, after we had Jacob, we decided two was enough. But my wife did not want to tie her tubes and I did not want to get snipped. So we went back to condoms, but one night we forgot the condom and nine months later Jewels was here."

"I am thanking the Lord y'all forgot that condom. I can't believe I almost not had my baby", he looks in his rear-view mirror at Mr. Lowd and says, "I thank y'all though."

Their dads looks at Tony and cannot stop laughing. In a serious tone, he says, "I am serious." They continue to laugh.

Mr. Ellison stops and joins in saying, "Tony, your grand dad, your mom's dad, wanted to shoot me."

Tony looks shocked, but bursts into laughter and asks, "Why?"

He laughs, "Tony, you know we were seniors in high school when we found out she was pregnant with you. Your mom told me during a gym class we had together, man I was soooo scared and nervous. I know she was too, but she hid it well. Mine was showing like a neon light in the dark. But after school, we asked all our parents to meet at her house because we needed to tell them something. After we told them that she was pregnant and we want to get married, man your grand dad, jumped up and came at me, but your grand ma caught him and held him with the help of my dad.

They all asked us to wait until we are twenty one for marriage, but I was ready to marry her then, I always loved her. We waited though, but on her twenty first birthday we were at the courthouse and your grand dad was happy for us." He looks at Tony, "You know your mom is the second and last woman I have ever had sex with. I do not know where you get it from."

Tony drops his mouth in shock and says, "Really dad? I know the stories of both my grand dads, so you know. I know grand ma cut your dad once too", he looks at his dad laughing, "yep, dad I heard the stories. But that is old and gone. I got my baby back. These women can't do a thing for me."

Mr. Lowd says, "Yea, it better be gone."

Stopped at a red light, Tony looks in the backseat and says, "Mr. Lowd, you know it is. I love my baby."

Shaking his head, Mr. Lowd says, "Tony when I found out what you did and my baby girl left you, I was so mad. I am talking to Jacob saying, 'What, he did what?' To be honest, I did not want Jewels to leave you, but I knew she was----."

Interrupting, Tony asks, "Mr. Lowd are you serious? You wanted Jewels to stay with me after that? I would have never thought that", Tony says in a shocked voice.

Mr. Lowd continues, "Yea, Tony. I really did believe it was a mistake, more importantly, I know how much you care about my baby girl. I knew I could go to sleep at night and not worry about her safety. I am a dad until I take my last breath, you will understand that soon. My childrens' safety is important to me, no matter the age. And you always treated my baby like the princess she is."

Tony smiles as he listens to Mr. Lowd, and Mr. Lowd continues. "So Tony, when Jacob told me, I am shaking my head thinking, 'Now I gotta vet some new man'. Tony, I wanted to jack you up, asking Jacob, 'What was he thinking? He knows how Jewels is'. Jacob was like, 'he wasn't thinking. His emotions were.'"

Shaking his head at himself, Tony looks through his rear-view mirror again and says, "Dang, it's no excuse, but Jacob was right." He shakes his head some more at himself and says, "I'm sorry Mr. Lowd."

Mr. Lowd laughs and jokingly waves him off. Tony glances at his dad and sees him nodding in agreement at his apology. They continue to the park as they continue to discuss the pregnancy and pregnancy stories.

While at the local park, Tony is playing exceptionally well and is very happy. Every three point shot he has attempted, he has made. He has stolen a few balls from the opposing players as well. Jewels' brother notices and during a break he says, "Tony you are in a really good mood. What has you so happy?"

Smiling from ear to ear, he looks at their dads then at Jacob, Jewels' brother and says, "Man, I am", he rubs his hands and continues, "your sister is pregnant."

Grinning, Jacob says, "What! Congrats! Man I am finally going to be an uncle!"

Still smiling, Tony nods and Jacob continues, "How far along is she? When did y'all find out?"

"Near five months. We found out like four months ago, right before we went to her friend's wedding."

Still smiling, he hugs Tony and gives his congratulations again. After hearing about the wedding he then asks, "How was the Miami trip?"

Tony stops smiling, which prompts Jacob and their dads to do the same. Their dads walk closer and Mr. Ellison says, "Did something happen in Miami?"

With an angered face, Tony shakes his head and says, "Man, y'all, I thought was going to catch a case there."

"What? Why", Jacob says in a concerned voice?"

Looking at them, Tony says, "Jesse was there."

"Who Jewels dated", Mr. Lowd asks?"

"Yes."

"What happened", Jacob asks?"

Shaking his head while remembering, Tony explains, "This dude is crazy. He has my alerts extra high looking out for my babies. We are at the reception and Jewels went to the restroom. I notice it is taking her longer than usual, so I went to check on her. Man as I am walking I start hearing my baby say, 'Let me go'. So I take off running to the restrooms and see Jesse holding her and stopping her from leaving.

Maaaaaannnn, I wanted to whip his----", he pauses, looks at their dads, and continues, "man y'all know. But I did not want to risk getting locked up and leaving my babies alone. I know he knows where Jewels' house is too, I wish I never sold mine now. I do not like leaving her there when I leave for work now. I am glad we have nosy neighbors and I know Mrs. Dubois is always locked and loaded."

Shaking his head, Jacob says, "I knew Jesse seemed a bit controlling and Jewels thought I was gone leave her there after you called. I'm so glad you called too because she would've never told us."

Folding his arms, Mr. Lowd says, "When were you going to tell me this? Tony, I know my baby girl is now your wife, but bring her to my house while you are at work. I don't care if she says no, tell her I said she is coming to her parents' home until this is all straightened out."

"Thank you for saying this. I have been trying to do this since we have been back. You know she always hit me with the, 'you are not my dad', when I am just trying to protect her. And she didn't want me to tell y'all. It has been eating me up. I know she will be mad, but she will have to be mad on this one. She will start reaching the point where she can't move as fast and easy."

They all sit and think about what was said. Play a little longer, once they see the other players are ready. Tony continues to play exceptionally well. After, they all go back to the Lowds' house where Jacob hugs his sister and playfully rubs her stomach, while singing, "I'm gone be an uncle."

```
''''''''''''''''''''''''''''''''''''''''''''''''''''''''''''''''''''''''''''''''''''''''
```

Friday rolls around and it is date night for Tony and Jewels.

Every month they set a day to the side to specifically date each other, like they did before they were married. Tony always book a hotel room on the beach. Every date night, he leaves to get dressed there and drives to her to knock on their front door to take her out. He never comes empty handed and Jewels never knows what he will have, besides the yellow rose he never forgets. She is really excited about tonight's date because they have not 'dated' each other since the Miami trip.

This particular day, Tony lounges around the house. At one point he walks to their closet to lay out an outfit for their date night. Noticing this, Jewels asks, "Baby, you are not getting dressed at the hotel?"

"Not this time. Baby we will leave from here together. Jewels I am just not comfortable leaving you solo after what happened in Miami. You are constantly on my mind and I am calling you non stop just checking on you."

Laughing at him, she says, "Tony, I will be fine. I have done it this far and you will only be gone a couple of hours. I am not afraid of him Tony, we are good."

"Yea baby, I know you are not, but I don't trust him."

"Baby, I know, but I just want to enjoy our date night like we usually do. I mean, in a few months we will have a baby and will not be able to do this as often. We have already missed a couple of months so you know when the baby arrives we will have less nights like this."

Reluctantly, Tony agrees and decides to do their usual date night activities. He asks his neighbors to be watchful because he will be gone for a couple of hours. They do, because they now all know about the Miami incident.

He makes it to Jewels a couple of hours later. As he knocks on the door at Seven in the evening, Jewels smiles showing all her teeth when she hears his, 'Computer Love' tune knock.

She opens the door in a yellow knee length fitted dress, accompanied with embellished gold pumps. She has big gold hoop earrings to go along with her gold cuff bracelet, Tony gifted her nearly five years ago. As she stands to the door Tony smiles from ear to ear, and says,

"Good evening baby. This is for you", he says as he hands her a yellow rose, a teddy bear holding a heart, and a gift box. She opens the box and bursts into laughter because it is pink and blue pacifiers. He laughs with her and says, "We will need these soon, but I don't know what color yet though."

He then takes her hand and watches as she locks the door. They walk to the car and wave bye to their neighbors. He opens Jewels' door, helps her sit, rubs her belly, then kisses her forehead. As he drives, he says, "Baby you know you look beautiful right?"

Blushing, she says, "Thank you baby, you do too."

She leans over and kisses his cheek which makes him smile. They pull into a Soul Food restaurant momemts later. Tony parks then opens the door for Jewels. They walk in and see that it is pretty crowded. They have to wait to be seated. As they wait, Tony is constantly hugging Jewels, kissing her cheek, and rubbing her belly. Not long after, someone comes over to seat them and they quickly place their orders. Jewels orders fried chicken wings, mustard greens, and pan fried cornbread. Tony orders smothered chicken breast, cabbage, and yellow rice. They both decide on water to quench their thirsts and converse while they wait for their food to arrive.

As the waiter leaves, Jewels says, "Tony, I am shocked you did not order pork chops."

Laughing, Tony responds, "Yea baby, I thought I told you I am eliminating pork from my diet."

Smiling, "You did, but I did not take you seriously."

"I am baby. You do not cook it either, so it makes it easier too. I actually feel better as well."

"I told you, you would. I am proud of you", she stands to kiss him as he stands to meet her leaning across the table.

"Yea you did baby", he says as they sit.

The waiter brings their water, they say thanks, and begins to sip it as they continue to talk.

At one point, Tony sits back and stares at her. He smiles and says, "Baby, our baby is really giving you such a radiant glow. I mean you always have a glow, but since you have been carrying our baby it is popping more or something."

Jewels blushes and drinks a sip of water. Noticing he is still staring she asks, "What Tony?"

"Nothing baby, just thinking how I can't believe it has almost been two years since we've been married. Baby, you are finally my wife, finally baby."

Smiling she says, "Yea, I can't believe it either. It feels good too."

Smiling, he says, "Yea, it does. To be real, I remember the first day I saw you. I knew you were my wife then, I was just to young to articulate it."

Jewels bursts into laughter and says, "Tony, we were only eight."

"I know, but I still knew." He says while laughing and continues, "The neighborhood put together a block party so we can all meet and get to know each other better. Your parents were walking around with y'all, introducing themselves, man Jewels when they got to us I could not stop looking at you. I am staring at you like, 'She is beautiful. I am going to marry her when I get older'. My dad noticed and when y'all left he kept messing with me, saying, "'You like that little girl don't you? Tony has a crush already'. I'm feeling embarrassed and saying, 'No I don't', but thinking, 'Yes I do'."

They both laugh and the waiter brings their food. They say thanks and grace over their food, with Tony giving it. He then continues, "Then me and your brother became friends. He was always like a big brother to me too, but Jewels I knew we would be together one day. Especially as our friendship started to grow. You are the closest person I have ever been to. I mean I could always tell you anything and not feel judged."

He laughs, "I remember that time we were sitting on your parents' porch talking. I was getting advice from you about what college I should attend and I made the mistake of laying my head in your lap, just out of comfort nothing sexual. But your dad walked up and saw it and was like, 'Tony if you do not get your bleeping head out of my daughter's lap I will bleep your bleep bleep ' and some more stuff he said. Jewels, I rose up so quick apologizing letting him know I did not mean any disrespect, it just happened."

They both laugh hysterically, "Jewels that is the first and last time I think I have ever heard your dad curse. I understood though. I don't know why he always thought I would try you like that though, I respected you and our friendship to much for that."

Jewels continues to laugh while saying, "Yea, I didn't quite understand it at first, but my dad sat me down and was like, 'Baby girl, don't let these boys lay in your lap like that. Even friends, they are trying to take it to another level'. I was like, ohhhhhh...."

He takes a few bites as he laughs at this, looks at her, and says, "Baby, yea, your dad was right. But you know I wasn't coming at you like that. I am just always so relaxed around you, you know. You are just comforting." He pauses and stares at her, then says, "Baby, I really believe He made you for me. Do you know what I mean?"

Laughing, she says, "I think I do."

He takes a few more bites and continues while laughing, "I'm serious, we really compliment each other. Baby, we were together for five years. Five years baby", he holds up five fingers and continues, "making sweet love with no condoms and I know you weren't putting that poison in your body, but you never became pregnant. Fast forward, right after we become one in the eyes of the Lord, boom, you are carrying my seed. I am wondering if it is a gift from Him to us?"

"Tony, you know, I never thought about it like that. You never know."

He smiles and blows her a kiss while eating. He laughs, and Jewels asks, "What's funny? I want to laugh too."

Still laughing, "Having this convo made me think about a convo I had with my lil' cousins a few days ago. They stopped by my job last week asking me to do some artwork for a fashion show they are putting together. You text me as they were telling me the details to see how much it would be. I told them, 'I will do it for free, but be ready to babysit for free as well.'

They laughed at me so hard, but was like, 'Cuz we will babysit for free, but this is a paying gig. We are getting paid and so are you.' As they continue to talk, I start to read your text. I guess as I am reading your message I was smiling and one of my lil' cousins was like, 'Man, big cuz', why are you so rare?' I asked, 'Huh, what do you mean?"

She continues, 'I bet you were just reading a text from Jewels.' I nodded yes and she continues, 'I knew it had to be because your smile said it all. You have always looked at her like that, these dudes barely want to pay for dates. I know you probably still pay on dates now.'

Baby, I laughed and was like, 'Of course I do. She's my heart, BUT, y'all know no other woman got the Jewels' treatment either. She has always been special to me. So if y'all really want that, you need to be more selective. I knew Jewels was my wife from jump. Pay attention to their actions, eyes do not lie either. My baby can have whatever she wants. If I got it, she got it, if I ain't got it I will get it. But the funny part is that out of ALL the women who have been in my life, Jewels is the only one who can have anything she asks for, but she is the only one who never has her hand out. But I make sure I stay gifting her things though. She deserves it all.'

I stopped, looked at them, and was like, 'But guess what my baby was asking me though?' They were looking like, what? I smiled and was like, 'She wants to know what I want for dinner? My baby is at home, with a smile making sure we are good and I appreciate her for it and will continue to make sure she knows it, even if she decides to go back to work'. You know I had to mess with them and was like, 'I bet y'all still don't cook and ramen noodles don't count'."

They burst into laughter at his last comment while continuing their meals.

Looking at him as she eats and listens, Jewels is smiling while blushing the whole time as she listens to this story. She stops eating then says, "Baby, I can't stop smiling listening as you say this. You know I love you and appreciate you too."

"I know baby". He smiles and continues, "But as I am telling her this, her male 'friend' calls asking what she is doing and if he can stop by. Stuff like that. When she ended her call, first thing I ask, 'Why are you sleeping with him with no title if you want a relationship?'

Baby she was so shocked at my question and finally asks, 'How do you know if I am sleeping with him?' I did not even respond to her question, she knows I know what is up. She finally admitted she does because she likes him a lot. She told me some other stuff. I'm like lil' cuz', 'You like him a lot. He is not taking you out. He just stops by for pleasure, but you are wondering why you are not his girlfriend? I guarantee, he either has a girlfriend or someone he is working hard to get. You are probably his distraction until he gets who he wants, lil cuz' close up shop. I thought I had the sex talk with y'all at eighteen. Every girl I laid down with knew what the deal was though and I paid for dates. I can't believe you letting this man touch you and he ain't even taking you on dates. I gotta fill your brothers in because I know they don't know.'

I could tell she was a little aggravated saying, 'Tony, y'all did. I protect myself, bu---.'

I cut her off, like stop with this foolishness, 'Ain't no buts, lil' cuz. If you want a relationship, stop having sex before you get that. Def, stop having sex with him and see if he still contacts you. If he doesn't, you have your answer. Move on and pay attention to the next dude's actions.'

One of my other lil' cousins, was like, 'You need to listen to him. You and this man been at it for two years. If he wanted a relationship, y'all will be in one by now'. I was like, 'Two years??? You been laying down with him for two years??? I ain't touch my baby until we were in a full blown relationship, months in, and had no problem with it because I always cared for her. Lil' cuz, you need to stop now and I'm calling your brothers after work. I can't believe you are allowing this.'

Baby, she looked at us and was like, I'm out, and left my office. All I could do was laugh with my other cousins and told them to talk some sense into her head. They hugged me and was like, 'Tony, you know how she is, but I bet she takes your advice'."

They both laugh at the story, and Jewels says, "Baby, I am glad she is comfortable talking to you. She is still trying to find her way. She always had a good head on her shoulders though, this dude just has her caught up right now. She probably loves him, but I hope this man is not taking advantage of that. I am surprised she did not learn who to dodge just based on your actions."

Laughing at her last statement, he replies, "Whatever Jewels, you know I never played these women. They all knew what was up. They wanted it just like I did. But baby, I guess I have known you to long and you do not play around like that, talking about, 'caught up', she better wake up. I shoulda told her to come talk to you."

Laughing, Jewels responds, "Whatever Tony, but you know everyone is different. I bet at least one of those women still wanted more than just sex with you, but just took what they could get. Sometimes, people's desperation, emotions, and/or low self esteem gets in the way of rational decision making."

"I hear you baby, but you know I ain't lead no one on either. It was always a mutual exchange."

They laugh and continue eating. Tony vibes a little to some music he has playing on his cell phone sitting on the table. A few minutes pass and he stops the music.

Looking at Jewels, as she continues to eat, he says, "Baby, you know I finally told our dads and brother about the Miami incident."

Sitting back in her booth seat, she responds, "Tony, I knew you would eventually. So what is the verdict?"

"Well, your dad agrees with me and does not want you home by yourself until we are sure Jesse is not a problem. So Monday, when I leave for work, you are leaving with me to go to your parents' home."

Shaking her head, she says, "If that will make you all feel better, I guess I will."

Looking at her, he says in a concerned voice, "Of course it will baby, especially with you being pregnant now. I mean this is your first pregnancy, you do not know how your body will react. Baby, if something was to happen to y'all, baby I would not be able to forgive myself. You know I have been protecting you since we met, just naturally. Baby, we just want you safe. You know people can snap."

"Baby, I know you all do and that way I can start walking more to help with this baby weight", she laughs.

Laughing with her, "Baby, you know you will be fine with it. Plus I know your mom and have met all your aunts on both sides and they all have a regular weight. Even your aunt with ten kids still look like she has zero."

Laughing and looking at him with squinted eyes, she asks, "Tony you been looking at my momma and aunts?"

Laughing hard, he says, "Not like that Jewels, but I do know between your mom's genes and your dad's, you were bound to be the beautiful array of thickness you are." Laughing and whispering to her as he stretches his eyes, "Baby, you just don't know."

Blushing, laughing, and dropping her head, she says, "Tony, you are just a whole trip sometimes. I just do not know what to do with you."

"Just love me baby."

"Forever."

He smiles and blows her another kiss. Jewels stands to pull her dress down, to feel more comfortable because it rose a little. As she tugs on her dress, Tony watches while laughing, and says, "Baby you look fine, no need to pull on your dress like that. This is like your fourth time."

He continues to smile and laugh at her as she sits back down. He glances across the room and immediately stops smiling, tilts his head to the side with a straight face, then shakes it. Noticing this, Jewels asks, while looking in the direction he is looking, "Tony what? Why are you looking like that?"

Still shaking his head, "I told you women can be just as bad as men. As you were sitting, I saw those two women over there just staring hard at you. Like I am not sitting here. I know they have to know we are together and you have a pregnancy bump."

Laughing, she responds, "Tony, now you have a glimpse of what I deal with, with you. Women are forever staring at you, like I don't exist."

He drops his head laughing, "I guess, at least most of the dudes glance quickly and keep it moving."

Rolling her eyes in laughter, "Yea, but baby you know you are always touching me in someway if your hands are free. You are either holding my hand, hugging me, or have your arm around my waist and they do not care. Even when your hands are full, you still try and steal a kiss or two, you know, you are very affectionate with me, which I love. But they look pass all that and stare you down. Most of the time, you do not even realize it."

Shaking his head, "I don't baby. I focus on you, but I told you about some of these women out here. A lot of y'all in our neighborhood had me fooled until we made it to high school. And Jewels, some of the stuff I heard and saw in the locker room shocked me, but it taught me too", he shakes his head and laughs at the memories.

Jewels laughs with him and they continue their date night dinner.

As they eat, he asks her, "Baby have you decided if you want to be a stay at home mom?"

Smiling while taking in his question, she happily responds, "Actually, I have and have decided to take on that task. I think it will be best for all of us."

Grinning, he responds, "Thanks baby. I agree too."

"Tony, I was out to lunch a few weeks ago with some old high school and college friends who were in town, oh yea, Ciara Thompson asked about you too." He nods at this as Jewels continues, " I told them how I was thinking about doing this. And do you know they all tried their best to talk me out of it. I just do not understand why? I told them that your income overly takes care of us and that my income would have been throw away cash anyways.

They hit me with, 'He is trying to control you', 'don't you think you will be bored', 'it is twenty nineteen not nineteen twenty', and stuff like that. Like they were really trying to convince me not to, because they chose not to. Even Kellie jumped in to defend you when they brought up the controlling narrative---."

Tony cuts in and shockingly asks, "What!? Your friend Kellie defended me? I am shocked", he laughs as he continues to listen.

Jewels laughs and continues, "Yes she did, but I told them that this is a mutual decision, both our moms were at home so it was bound to happen that we will follow in their footsteps. Both our moms enjoyed it too, they, and the other at home moms mothered the neighborhood. I am like, 'If you all think it is truly a control move shouldn't you all be more concerned with, when am I leaving this controlling man? And I would never share my body with him if I could not even trust him with our finances.'

When I asked that, they shut up because they knew it was a hail mary attempt to get me to change my mind. But I honestly do not know why they are against me doing it. They know I am not one of those, 'independent woman' or feminists types. To each her own, but that was never me. We are a team and I truly appreciate you heading our household the way you were created and raised to do. I am not trying to be an independent wife", she laughs at her statement and continues to eat.

He laughs too, "Baby, I am not surprised at all. I work with and have worked with women like that. I never understood why some, go out of their way to get other woman to live that way. Everyone is different. I always thought that movement was about women having choices and options anyways."

He drinks a sip of water and continues, "I remember when I first moved to Cali. It was this co worker of mine, who always seemed down and tired. She started talking to me a lot and finally told me that she was starting to regret coming back to work after giving birth. I asked her why she did and why is she even comfortable talking to me about it? But she was like, some of her friends and other women co workers talked her into it. She was like, seeing how I talked about you over the past couple years, she knew I would be real and caring with my response."

Jewels cuts in, shocked, and says, "Tony, you used to talk about me? Seriously, you risked your chance with other women?"

Tilting his head, looking at her, "Whatever Jewels, you know I was missing you and I never played where I worked either."

Jewels laughs and Tony continues his story, "But my co worker said both her and her husband wants it. I told her to do what is best for your family and not your friends or co workers. Do they go home with you to cook, do your laundry, clean, or anything else? She just laughed and agreed, but a year later, she became pregnant again and quit."

He laughs, thinking of this, and stares at Jewels, "But baby, I am glad you know this is not a control move. I would never try and control you. Heck, I couldn't even get you to your parents' house, your dad had to step in."

Jewels laughs, "Yea, baby I know it is not. I know you to well for that, you still think you are my dad at times though", she laughs some more.

He laughs, "Whatever Jewels." He laughs some more then says, "Baby, maaaannnn some of my male co workers, the day after you brought me lunch, was like, 'Man how did you get this? A woman who does not mind being home as a job and bringing you lunch with a smile'. I told them, 'I am blessed, but she is looking for work. But if she decides to stop looking she knows she can. She knows she will not have to worry about one bill, worry about nothing. You know, my baby knows she ain't got to worry bout stuff like that. I got her. Some women don't feel they can count on their partner in that way, my baby knows she does not have to worry about any of that. What is mines is hers and vice versa'.

They looked at me and was like, 'Tony you have a rare woman'. One said, 'I pay all the bills, even daycare, so she can work and use her check for bags and shoes. I love her though'. Jewels I fell out at his last statement, like do you or are you trying to convince yourself?"

Jewels burst into laughter hearing this and adds, "Baby, this made me remember how I told them that I am happy with this arrangement and so are you. No one else's happiness on our decision matters. And how I appreciate how hard you work to make sure we are okay."

Tony nods in agreement and laughs at their friends.

After dinner they go back to the hotel, where he has a beach front room. They sit out on the room's patio, watch the waves, and looks at the night's sky while relaxing in each others' arms.

The next morning, Jewels rises before him. She cleans her teeth and face. Freshens up, prepares some hot tea, and sits out on their room's patio to listen to the calm waves as the birds sing glorious Praise as she continues to read a book she started two days ago. An hour later, Tony walks out there with breakfast, kisses her cheek, and says, "Good morning baby", as he hands her the breakfast sandwich.

He sits next to her and they both begin to eat. Jewels looks at him and says, "Good morning and thanks for breakfast."

Smiling, he responds, "You welcome baby." He watches the waves for a minute and says, "Babe, is there anything you want to do today?"

Shaking her head no, she says, "Uhhh, not really. I just want to relax, but is there something you want to do?"

"Naw, I was just checking before I start on this design."

"Okay, design away. I am going to try and finish this book. Let me know if you need any help."

Smiling, he says, "You know I will. What are you reading?"

"They Were Her Property: White Women as Slave Owners in the American South, by Stephanie E. Jones-Rogers, and baby it is a hard read too. I want to invent a time machine just to go back and handle her."

Laughing, he looks at Jewels and says, "Baby you might need to stop reading that book."

Laughing with him, she says, "I'm good, I will make it through."

He laughs, kisses her, then walks in the room, for his Tablet, sketch tablet, and pencil to start his artwork.

While sitting next to Jewels, he first sketches her as she sits reading and rubbing her belly while making sure he has the beach etched in as well. After he finishes that drawing he gives it to Jewels who lights up at the drawing, not realizing he was sketching it. Like always, her smile makes him smile then he begins the work on a logo a company wants him to design.

They spend the whole day out on the room's patio. They order take out for lunch and dinner. He repeatedly flirts with her after he finishes his design by constantly hugging her and singing non stop love songs. He tries to get her to the beach's water at one point, but she declines. So, they both watch the sun as it sets then go inside to prepare for bed.

The next day, they both rise and immediately start packing to check-out and go home. With smiles on both their faces as he drives home, Tony begins his music playlist with the first song being, Jodeci's Forever My Lady, and of course as the tune starts, he looks at Jewels while blowing her a kiss.

CHAPTER FOUR

GETTING OUR HOUSE IN ORDER

One Wednesday afternoon, Tony is home and while there he decides to empty the rest of his boxes from his storage. They have not had much time to complete this task, but he wants it done before the baby arrives. He first, flirts with Jewels some as she prepares dinner for them. He walks in the kitchen, slaps her butt, then hugs her as he kisses her cheek, saying, "I love you baby."

Laughing at him as she unwraps a block of sharp cheddar cheese, she blows him a kiss and says, "I love you too."

He slaps her butt again then walks to the sink to wash his hands. After, he cleans and seasons smoked turkey legs for her to help. While she boils noodles and cuts sharp cheddar cheese for their macaroni and cheese. He notices that the black eyed peas are already soaking in a bowl of water then looks at her and asks, "Baby, do you want me to start cooking the smoked turkey for you? I have cleaned and seasoned them already, but I don't want to mess up your flow."

She walks to him, kisses his cheek, and says, "Thanks baby, but no. I got it and you can rest up."

He holds her and says, "You know I don't mind, but if you need me I will be on the patio going through the rest of my boxes", he kisses her forehead and slaps her on the butt once more as he walks to their patio.

As Jewels cooks, he begins the task of going through three boxes he has left from his storage. As he opens each box, he notices they are filled with books and movies. When he sits, he notices an extra box in the corner. He walks to it and sees that it is filled with things from California. He laughs at himself wondering how long this box has been sitting there?

He returns to his chair and begins his task. The first box is filled with 'how to' books. From topics like computer programming, website designs, animation creations, and more. He decides to keep them all and places them on their book shelf.

The second box is filled with comic books, biographies, and autobiographies. He sits three of them on their table to re-read later and puts the rest on their book shelf. The three he decides to read again are biographies about, Tupac Shakur, Martin Luther King Jr., and Malcolm X.. As he sits the books on the table he shakes his head thinking how all of these men had different approaches but believed in the betterment of their people and still all died the same tragic death leaving lasting impressions.

The third box is filled with movies. He has VHS tapes and DVDs packed in the box. The movies range from, Boyz In The Hood, Tales from The Hood, Boomerang, The Wood, Love Jones, and more. He leaves all the movies out to ask Jewels which one she wants to watch later? He places the movies on a table then breaks down the three boxes to put them in the trash. Next, he gets the extra box he saw and sits it next to his chair.

Before he goes through it he checks on Jewels to make sure she needs no help. As he walks in the kitchen, he grins as he sees her swaying her hips while singing, No Diggity by Blackstreet, as she stirs a mixture in a bowl. He stands behind her, holding her saying, "Baby, what are you mixing? Whatever it is, has you dancing and calling me and you don't even realize it."

She laughs and half twerks for him as she says, "I had a sweet tooth and decided to make us some brownies with chocolate chunks. My sweet tooth is craving chocolate, I even want some chocolate ice cream", she laughs at herself.

He kisses her cheek, laughs, and says, "Thank you baby, you know I appreciate you", he squeezes her butt while laughing some more and says, "all of you too. But I came in to see if you needed any help?"

Smiling as she looks at him, she says, "Nope, everything is cooking. I am waiting for the mac and cheese to finish, then I will bake the brownies and be done. How is it going with your boxes?"

"Okay baby. I am done with the three from storage, but I saw an extra box in the corner that I missed filled with stuff from Cali. I'ma go through that, then I am done. But I found some old movies and sat them on the table. When you are through in here, you can come pick out a movie for us to watch after dinner."

"Okay, sounds good. You always had a good selection. But make sure you don't have any you were watching with your Cali women though."

Bursting into laughter he responds, "Well that will leave all of them because you know I was not entertaining women like that in Cali.." Kissing her cheek, he continues, "I am serious baby. After experiencing the art of making love going back to casual sex just was not that easy."

She laughs as she shrugs her shoulders and says, "I guess", as he walks back to their patio laughing at her.

He opens the final box, sits, and begins going through it. He smiles as he sees pictures of them goofing around in the pool at his L. A. home. He smiles even harder when he sees a few pictures from their wedding day at the courthouse. He laughs looking at the pictures remembering how they had to catch a flight back to California right after because he had to be to work the next day. He looks to the kitchen and says to himself, "Dang we didn't even make it to her bedroom once I carried my baby across the threshold." He laughs some more and smiles as he thinks of this memory.

He continues to go through the box and sees his old name tag from his job there. Accompanied with them are two certificates he was awarded along with a bonus for winning two art contests there.

As he continues to look he sees more pictures of them. One is of him and Jewels at a co-worker's birthday party. Looking at the picture makes him laugh. As he laughs, Jewels walks in and asks, "What has you laughing", as she sits in his lap?

He looks at her and says, "Baby, I am looking at this picture and just noticed the woman in the far left giving us a mean unit."

She looks at the picture and laughs, "Oh wow, I never noticed her before. I wonder why she's looking at us like that?"

Bursting into laughter, "Baby she used to like me but I did not like her back and you see how I am just loving on you in this picture. You know I was loving on you the whole night. We were finally official, official. I mean, not only were we back at one, but we are One. I'm like 'My baby is my wife now. She is Mrs. Ellison now'. We were a month in at this time and you know I was still on an extra high about it. Even in this pic, I'm holding your left arm out fiddling with your ring and kissing your cheek. And baby, look at how you were looking up at me. We were just in a whole zone to ourselves that night. I'm wondering why we even went? We should've stayed home and love on each other."

He stops and laughs at himself then continues, "So she was probably mad and baby she used to try hard too. You know I was never into women who threw themselves at me and she just wasn't my type either. All them Cali dudes thought she was a dime too and thought I was crazy. I'm like, 'I am good. She does nothing for me and I am not into 'ambiguous' women sort of speak'."

Laughing at that situation, he continues, "I mean, baby I really had to tell my co worker, like tell your friend it is a no for me. I don't think she was used to hearing no either but it is a first time for everything. My co workers really thought I was crazy and you kept dissing me at that time too. They were like 'You passing up on these women---'"

Jewels interrupts, "Whatever Tony, I did not diss you. I was just a little distracted at the time."

Bursting into laughter, "Naw baby, you were dissing me at that time. I forgive you though."

She laughs as she shakes her head at him and he continues, "But baby, they were like, 'Your girl back home must be everything'. I'm thinking to myself, 'She is'."

She blushes to this as Tony blows her a kiss, saying, "You are baby." He continues, "But I think this was their first time seeing you too. Jewels, the next work day they coming to me like, 'We understand now'. Baby the look I gave them was like, 'Y'all better stop there to y'all my baby better look like Freddie Krueger mixed with Jason'. They recognized that look though and moved on."

As they burst into laughter, Jewels glances in his box and sees an envelop. When she sees it, she widens her eyes because she recognizes it, opens her mouth, stands as she picks up the envelop saying, "Oh my gosh! What are you doing with this? I mailed this to my brother." She shakes her head at herself, "Now I know why the money never left my account."

Tony says nothing, but looks at her laughing. She continues, "Tony why do you have this? I told my brother not to tell you."

He sits her back in his lap and says, "Jewels you know your brother couldn't keep that from me, he tried though. I know Jesse was late on a couple of payments." He pauses and looks at Jewels, "And I know he did it on purpose too. Hoping you would come to him begging for cash."

Shaking her head as she listens, she asks, "Why did you think that?"

"Because he is an insecure man. I know how they roll."

Jewels laughs as he continues. Tony then says, "But baby, I was talking to our brother one day and he was telling me how he was looking for a part-time job. I asked him why, and he was like, 'My business isn't banking like it was. We are slow now and I need extra cash'. I am still not understanding because this is how his business flows every year and he never needed extra work. So I'm asking him if everything is okay and he knows I will help if he needs it? He was still like, 'Naw we are good. I just need some extra cash'. So we talk a little more, but it still wasn't adding up to me, but I eventually asked about you and if you were home? You know, you would never tell me if you were back in Jax. or not so I used to get it from our bro and I still couldn't catch you. Waiting until the night before to tell them you were coming home."

Laughing at herself, "Yea it was usually a 'spare of the moment' thing for me. That's why."

He laughs looking at her and says, "Now you know I don't believe that. I know why."

She bobs her head while rolling her eyes at him, and continues to listen to his story, "But baby, Jacob got a little quiet and started talking in circles just from that question and I'm like, 'Is my baby okay? Do I need to travel to D.C.------?'"

Jewels interrupts and sarcastically asks, "And do what Tony?"

Looking at her out of the side of his eyes, he does not answer that question, but continues his story, "But finally, he was like, 'Naw, she's okay. Jesse is just late with her full payment and she needs help with her mortgage payment. I'm trying not to touch my savings right now, so I am looking for a quick temp job to help my baby sis. Ain't no way I will have her begging this man for anything'.

I'm looking at the phone, like, 'What, I just talked to her last night and not one time did she mention this to me. She knows I will help her'.

Jacob said, 'Yea she knows, but didn't think it would be appropriate asking you when she is in a relationship'. I'm saying to Jacob, 'Man forget him and his emotions. I'm 'bout to call her and let her know I am putting the money in her account. How many months?'

Our bro was like, 'Tony she was thinking it would be inappropriate to expect you to pay this bill. She wasn't thinking about Jesse's feelings'."

Jewels says, "Yea, I felt that way. I know I would look crazy at you if you were asking me to do something your girlfriend should be doing."

Laughing, Tony says, "I know Jewels, but you know I got you regardless. There is no way I will sit back and watch you struggle. I will have to whip my own ass if I let that happen." He laughs at himself and continues, "But our bro was like, 'Tony don't let her know I told you either because she will be mad.' I'm nodding, like okay, 'But how many months? I'ma wire you the money so you can pay it for her.'

He told me it was two months. I wired him the money, then a couple of months later this was in my mail box. I'm shaking my head looking at it, thinking, 'He knows I do not want this check', but I kept it as a reminder though."

"A reminder for what?"

"That Jesse wasn't about nothing, you deserve better, you had better, and that you will get the best again."

Laughing, Jewels says, "I am still trying to figure out how I fell in love with such a cocky man?"

He kisses her cheek and says, "Because I am good to you with all my cockiness added."

She kisses his cheek, "Well there is no argument there. You are good to me."

"It's my top goal too baby and you make it so pleasurable."

She blushes as Tony blows her a kiss and says, "I am glad I do."

Jewels then walks to the table to look at his movies. As she looks, she smiles remembering scenes from each movie she picks up. She finally sees the movie, Crooklyn, and says to Tony, "Baby I didn't know you had Crooklyn. I haven't seen this in years so lets watch this."

Looking up at her, he responds, "Yea baby, I found it at a store out in Cali, but okay. You feel like setting it up for us?"

She nods yes as she walks to their living room to set up the movie.

He finishes his task and cleans up the area. When he walks back in the house, he sees that Jewels is bathing and joins her with a smile. After, they eat while engaging in a lovely conversation then heads to the living room to enjoy the movie after they clean their kitchen. They rewind one scene where a character is crying over a dog, repeatedly, hysterically laughing at how dramatic the character is.

The next day, they spend time on the porch. While sitting there Tony decides to wash their cars. As he washes them, one of the children from the neighborhood walks up and begins conversing with Jewels. She waves at Tony as she sits on the steps. Her and Jewels begins a conversation. They discuss anything that crosses the young girl's mind, from boys to academics.

Jewels notices that she is not as happy as she usually is and asks, "Brandy, what's wrong? You are usually more upbeat than this."

She sighs, and says "Yea, I know. Ms. Jewels I want to transfer out of my school and attend the neighborhood's middle school, but my mom is making me wait until next school year."

"Why do you want to transfer? I thought you wanted to attend that school?"

"I did, but the kids are constantly teasing me. I am just ready to be around my friends."

Jewels is shocked to hear this because Brandy is a very friendly person. She looks at Brandy with concern in her eyes and asks, "Teasing you about what?"

Touching her hair, she responds, "My hair, and my mom won't relax it. She said I am to young, but when I become an adult I can do as I please with it."

"You don't like your hair", Jewels asks with concern?

"I do. I love it, but I am tired of being teased too."

Jewels hugs her and says, "Sweetie, they are really messing with you because you are usually tougher than this. But do not let anyone shame you about what grows naturally out of your scalp. If you just want a change, change, but because you want it and not to please others."

Jewels pats her low ponytail afro puff, then does the same to Brandy's ponytail and continues, "The hair that grows out of your scalp is apart of our Creator's beautiful artwork. Sweetie, take a look around." Jewels points to all the trees, bushes, and plants, then continues, "You see how the leaves on the trees grows towards the sky and bushes out as well? Without these wonderful trees we will lack oxygen right? What happens when the tree becomes lifeless, the leaves droop towards the ground. The hair that grows from your scalp, mimics these life saving things of nature. Your hair grows up and out just like them. Gravity can't hold it down. It is growing towards Heaven and the sun. Be proud. Only see the positive in your hair no matter what someone says."

She smiles while touching her hair saying, "Thank you Ms. Jewels. That means a lot, but I am still ready to transfer."

Hugging her, Jewels responds, "I understand sweetie, but don't' be surprised if you see me pop up to your school one day to say hi and show you some love. I am going to talk to your mom too and give her the number to one of my friends who braids. She is reasonably priced, that way you can keep your natural hair and wear box braids until you transfer. Hopefully, that will make you more comfortable."

Still smiling, Brandy hugs Jewels and says, "I won't and it will. Thanks."

They talk a little longer, then some other children come outside and Brandy leaves to play with them. By this time, Tony is drying their cars. He has them shining like they are on a show room's floor. After Brandy leaves, he walks to Jewels and kisses her cheek, saying, "Baby I love you. You are so positive and uplifting. You had me over there feeling good and you weren't even talking to me", he laughs and kisses her cheek again.

He finishes his car cleaning task and puts his tools away. He finally rejoins Jewels. They relax on the front porch a little longer, then go inside to prepare for bed.

A few days later, Tony and Jewels are out in the neighborhood walking. They notice all their neighbors are out and has small talk with each one they pass. At one point on their walk, Tony hugs Jewels and kisses her cheek. Out of no where Jewels starts crying. Tony looks at her in confusion and asks, "Jewels, are you okay? What's wrong? Why are you crying baby?"

Still crying and sniffling, she says, "Yes I am fine. I do not know why I am crying, but the tears won't stop."

He looks at her, still confused, then looks at her belly and laughs as he wipes her tears. Looking at him as he laughs, Jewels asks, "Why are you laughing at me?"

"Baby, it's not that I am laughing at you, but I realized why you are crying for no reason."

Still crying, she asks, "Why?"

Rubbing her stomach he says, "Your hormones baby. Our baby messing with you." He picks her up and carries her home saying, "I got you though so cry your eyes out."

"Thank you Tony, but I hope this doesn't last long though."

He kisses her cheek then says, "I know."

As they walk into their home, with Tony still holding her, he smooches her lips and says, "Baby, I love you."

Kissing him back, "I love you too."

He smiles and smooches her cheek as he wipes her tears then walks to the couch after standing her up.

They sit on the couch as Tony holds her and continues to wipe her tears she is crying for no reason.

The next day he takes Jewels to her parents' home before he goes to work. Before he leaves, he talks with their moms and gives them a laugh with the crying story. Mrs. Lowd says, "Tony, her aunt was the same way with her first pregnancy. She cried nearly everyday, even certain scents brought her to tears. But when my nephew got here, he barely cried, I guess he had enough from his momma."

They all laugh hysterically at this then Tony leaves for work.

Their dads are out fishing and misses the story, but both their wives fill them in when they make it home.

As the day progresses, Jewels stands outside and watches as her mom does garden work. Jewels is talking non stop. Telling her mom every detail about her pregnancy journey and how she is enjoying every moment. At one point, her mom notices Jewels has stopped talking. She looks up from her task and sees Jewels on the ground. She rushes to her daughter's aid shaking her and screaming her name. She runs to get her cordless phone to call an ambulance. As she talks, she checks for a pulse and finds one. Her neighbors run over to assist as they wait for the ambulance.

The ambulance arrives and quickly loads Jewels, places an oxygen mask around her nose and mouth, then speeds to a near by hospital. As the ambulance drives Jewels to the hospital, Mrs. Lowd calls Tony and Mr. Lowd. When Tony answers he hears a lot of noise and fast talking coming from Mrs. Lowd. A client is in his office, but he looks at him in shock while saying in a worried voice, "Ma. Ma, can you hear me? Is everything okay, where's Jewels?"

She finally responds, while breathing hard, "No Tony, it is not okay. She was just rushed to the hospital----"

Abruptly standing, as he grabs his car keys in panic, he says, "What!? What hospital are they taking her to?"

He turns off his computer and points to the door while looking at his client saying to himself, "Dang, my baby, my baby."

He finally stops and says, as he looks at his client, "I have to go."

He rushes out of his office, passes the receptionist, and quickly says, "I gotta go", and continues to walk.

As Tony exits, his client tries to fill the receptionist in on what is going on, from what he was able to decipher from Tony's words and demeanor. The client realizes, Tony's wife is having a medical emergency.

As Tony starts his car, he continues talking to Mrs. Lowd asking, "Ma, what hospital? What happened?"

Crying, she tells him what hospital, and continues, "Tony, I do not know what happened. I looked up and she was on the ground----", she pauses, calls on the Lord, and yells Jewels' name.

Hearing this, as he rushes to the hospital, he says, "MA! MA, what's going on, is she okay!?"

Tony continues to call Mrs. Lowd's name who has gone silent for a few minutes. She finally answers, "Tony, yes, I just got a little worried when I saw some trauma doctors rushing to her room, but they only came as a precaution until they figure out what caused Jewels to pass out. I think they have it under control now. I am waiting for the docs to come talk to me."

He looks to the sky as he parks and says, "Okay ma, I made it. I am parking now. Lord, protect your child", he says as he turns his car off.

He rushes in and sees Mr. and Mrs. Lowd along with his parents sitting in the emergency room's waiting room area. They all stand to walk to him. They hug each other and Mrs. Lowd fills him in quickly as he signs in to go to Jewels' room. As he listens, he takes deep breaths and shakes his head in disbelief, but his face is filled with concern.

He finally places his name tag on his shirt and prepares himself to see Jewels. When he walks in, he sees her sitting there, in bed, with an IV in her arm and notices the baby's heartbeat is being monitored. Jewels is now alert and is sitting up looking at the ceiling. As he walks in he says, "Hey baby", and kisses her forehead as she looks at him.

"Hey Tony." She rubs his arm and continues, "Baby smile, I am fine. We are fine. I just need more fluids."

Holding her hand that is rubbing his arm, he says in a low voice, "Baby, you are in a hospital bed. I'm concerned. What happened?"

Shaking her head at herself, she responds, "Baby, I was dehydrated. I think our baby has been using more fluids than I have been taking in. I have to drink more water than I usually do. They are pumping me with fluids now. I thought I was, but my body and our baby disagreed."

The doctor walks in and introduces himself to Tony. Tony asks about Jewels then asks about their baby. The doctor assures him that they are both okay, but wants to keep Jewels over night to monitor her and the baby. The doctor then says to them both, "I think if it wasn't for the pregnancy you would've walked around longer in this state. Your baby alerted you sooner that your body needed more fluids."

The doctor says a few more things then leaves. After he leaves, Tony rubs Jewels' belly saying, "Our baby looking out for momma already. I know I am going to be a proud dad."

Jewels smiles as she listens to this. Their parents walk in to see her, two by two, per the hospital's rules. Once they see she and their grandchild is okay, the Ellisons leave. Tony leaves as well to get a few items for them while her parents stay with her until he returns.

When he returns, the doctor moves her to a room, where Jewels is still receiving fluids through an IV and their baby is still being monitored as well. While there, Tony calls his job to let them know why he left and that he will not be coming in tomorrow because of it. After he ends his call, he looks at Jewels and sees that she has fallen asleep. He kisses her forehead then begins to work on a design that he and his client was discussing before Mrs. Lowd called.

The next day, Jewels awake and sees Tony looking at her saying, "Good morning baby, how do you feel?"

Smiling at him, "Fine and I am ready to go home."

Laughing at her Tony says, "Baby you ain't even been here for twenty four hours. We gotta make sure y'all good first, then we can go home."

"I know, but I still want my bed."

He laughs as someone from the cafeteria walks in with her breakfast. She looks at it, then at Tony and says, "I'm not eating this."

He laughs, "We knew you weren't. Your momma on her way with something she cooked for you though. You need to eat for both of y'all."

He kisses her forehead as her parents walk in with salmon croquettes and grits in hand. They update her parents about her health then a nurse walks in to take Jewels' blood to test. Everything turns out fine and a few hours later she is discharged.

Once home, Tony runs her a bath so she can soak, rest, and bathe while listening to rain sounds.

CHAPTER FIVE

Six months into her pregnancy, Jewels has been enjoying every moment and laughs hard as Tony continuously buys baby items. She is happy and shocked, because during her pregnancy she has only thrown up five times. She always thought it would be more, but her mom told her she was the same way. Tony has made every doctor's appointment with her and exercises with her as Jewels is determined to stay fit, during and after her pregnancy.

Whenever they exercise, Tony has a gallon of water nearby and constantly says to Jewels, "Baby remember to drink up. I can't get you to sit down, so please stay quenched so you will not be knocked down again."

"Baby I am. My active body helped too with that moment. I gotta keep moving."

"I know baby, we don't need you falling out either ", he says as he rubs her belly then goes back to lifting weights as she walks to their treadmill.

After their work out they shower to leave for a smoothie. After her shower, Jewels looks in the mirror as she rubs raw Shea Butter on her stomach. The shea butter, her mom and Mrs. Ellison told her to use, seem to be working, so she uses it daily after each bath. No stretch mark has appeared yet.

As Tony sees her using it, he says, "Baby, I really appreciate you trying to stay right, but you know you do not have to do all that. I love you and you will forever be beautiful to me. And on top of that, every mark, will only be a reminder of our baby growing inside of you."

Laughing at him, she responds, "Tony, I really appreciate that, but what makes you think I am doing this for you and not me? I mean", she laughs, "one day you may wake up and decide to leave me and get a new woman."

With a serious face, he says, "Leave you????? Sorry Jewels, you said, 'I do', you are stuck with me for life. I ain't going no where", he laughs and hugs her. "But baby, I do appreciate what you are doing though", he kisses her cheek, "I love you."

"I love you too baby."

They get dressed and drives to their local smoothie restaurant. Jewels orders a simple mango smoothie while Tony orders a berry smoothie that has blueberries, blackberries, and raspberries mixed in. After they receive their smoothies, they decide to drink them at the smoothie restaurant. As they enjoy them, Kellie walks in and sees them. She walks over and talks to them. She double checks on Jewels because she knows about the hospital visit and asks if she needs anything. As she talks, Kellie notices the look on Tony's face and says,

"I'm leaving Tony. You do not have to look like that."

He says nothing which prompts Jewels and Kellie to laugh. Then Kellie finally leaves after hugging Jewels and waving bye to Tony. Tony throws his hand up, Jewels looks at him, and says, "Baby, do you have to act like that with her? She was just saying hey."

"Jewels, I waved, but I can't pretend to like her either. You know I don't trust her."

Shaking her head with laughter, she asks, "I know, but do I act like that with your friends?"

Looking at her with his head tilted, he asks, "Jewels, name one", he holds one finger up and continues, "of my friends who flirted with you, just one baby."

Jewels says nothing and he continues, "Exactly. You know if one of them even looked at you to hard we will have problems. But to come on to you, the friendship will be done. Baby you know me better than that." He laughs at himself and says, "I don't even let them across the threshold. I stop them at the porch because it ain't going to be no 'mistaking' seeing you showing to much skin, or take them to the patio when you aren't home from outside. You know you like to walk around our house barely clothed", he laughs some more at himself.

Jewels shakes her head some more as she laughs at this and continues to enjoy her smoothie.

A few days later, they have another doctor's appointment where a sonogram is taken. The doctor re-visits her hospital stay and makes sure Jewels is staying hydrated. Jewels lets her know how she has added more water and sports drinks to her diet which is helping. The doctor orders blood work to check her levels anyways.

While there, Jewels tells her doctor that she does not want an epidural shot. Tony looks at her with concern and asks,

"Baby, are you sure? I hear the pain is so bad it is indescribable. You sure you want to do that?"

She pats his thigh and says, "Yea, baby. I can do it."

Shaking his head, not wanting to agree he sits in silence as she and her doctor talk more. As the doctor begin to prep her for the sonogram, Tony group text messages their moms saying,

"Good morning moms. I need y'all's advice."

Mrs. Lowd replies,

"Good morning. What is it? Are you two okay?"

Tony replies,

"Yes ma'am. We are at a doctor's appointment and Jewels says she doesn't want an epidural during birth. I think she should get it for the pain, what do you think?"

Mrs. Lowd replies,

"I agree with you. Labor pain is no joke."

Mrs. Ellison joins in and says,

"Good morning y'all. But son, talk to the doc privately and ask them to have some on stand by just in case Jewels changes her mind once the pain kick in."

Mrs. Lowd,

"That is a good idea. Take your mom's advice Tony."

"<smiles>, thanks! I love y'all, but I gotta go now, Jewels staring at me."

Mrs. Ellison,

"Love you too."

Mrs. Lowd,

"Love you too."

As he puts his cell phone away, Jewels asks, "Tony who were you talking to?"

"Our moms."

"Is everything okay?"

"Yea baby, I was just updating them."

She smiles and the doctor walks back in the room with an assistant to start the sonogram. The whole time, Tony is smiling and rubbing Jewels' forehead. After, Tony walks out with the doctor and asks her to have the epidural shot on stand by just in case Jewels changes her mind. The doctor agrees and adds it to her notes.

Jewels and Tony leaves soon after. He takes her to her parents, kisses her cheek, and says, "See you later baby. I love you and please remember to stay hydrated."

Kissing his cheek, she responds, "I will and I love you too."

He watches her until she enters her parents' home then drives to work.

They both decide to wait until the baby is born to find out the sex.

As they wait for their arrival they spend time reading an array of books and articles pertaining to childbirth. They have also been studying The Word together to help with names, mostly in the Old Testament. So far they have narrowed the boy's names to Reuben, Samson, Zion, and Joseph. For the girl's names; Ruth, Sheba, Zion, and Mae.

They also begin the task of getting their baby's room ready. They had to turn the once office, back into its original formation, a bedroom. Now Tony's workspace is the patio. They have been debating if they should buy a bigger home or add an extra room to this one. Tony really wants to purchase a bigger home instead, but continues to prepare this room for their baby.

After everything is removed and the floors are protected, Tony begins to work. Starting with him placing drawings and writings on the wall. In front of where the crib will be he has written the, John 3:16, scripture on it. He also adds the alphabet and numbers counting from One to Ten. On another wall, he writes a verse from the book of Deuteronomy, Chapter Twenty Eight. As he does this, Jewels sits in a rocking chair and reads a children's book to their unborn child. This book is actually one her mom wrote and read to them growing up.

It is about a baby who was born a Prince, but became King at the age of ten. During his ten years, as a Prince, he had no clue of who he was. Once he finds out and understands his power, he orders a candy store be built, where no adults are allowed. Only the ones who makes the candy.

Once he becomes king, at the age of ten, and the store is built, all the children party there non stop while making sure the adults stay away. One day, all the children became ill and are unable to move. Groaning and crying on the floor, wishing the adults were there, a father stands over his son and says, "You really thought we left you all to yourselves. You are my child and I will never leave you even when you leave me."

Jewels looks to her stomach and says, "That is right. We will never leave you, but most importantly, our Creator will always be there for you prince or princess."

Smiling as he hears this, Tony takes a break, walks over to Jewels, begins talking to her stomach, and kisses it. Smiling she says, "Baby, our baby is kicking non stop as you talk. He or she is ready to meet their dad. He's a wonderful man too."

Smiling some more, "Baby, I feel it. I bet we are having a boy because these kicks are strong." He stands and kisses her cheek, "Thank you baby, so is his mom."

Laughing, "Thanks, and I guess, it is 'he'."

He smiles, kisses her stomach again, kisses her, and gets back to work. They have both decided on the colors yellow and blue for the room, which are both their favorite colors. After she finishes reading, Jewels decides to look at cribs and bassinets. The crib is for the baby's room and the bassinet will be in their room.

To her surprise, she sees a gold bassinet and adds it to her shopping cart as an option, but continues to look on. She sees a crib she really likes and asks Tony if he wants it too. He shrugs his shoulders saying, "Baby, I don't care. Get what you want. You know I am not picky", he pauses and laughs, "Well untill it came to my wife, then I had to have the best."

She blushes at this as he blows her a kiss and he continues working,

At one point, Jewels looks up and sees Tony has drawn a big tree with beautiful green bushy leaves. The leaves are resembling an afro and are shaped firmly and big. Above the tree, sits clouds and the sun. He has a rainbow with the scripture explaining its' creation, from the Book of Genesis Chapter Nine. He adds more numbers and letters around the tree, but leaves a place empty next to the tree. He turns and looks at Jewels, "I am going to paint our baby here once I see him or her, most likely him though."

Jewels laughs and nods, "Baby, it looks beautiful. It is all coming along so well. Thanks."

He walks to her and hugs her saying, "You know you do not have to thank me for doing my duties. I love you", he kisses her then says, "you puuuurrrrtttyyyy to baby."

Bursting into laughter, "Tony, I swear you keep me laughing. Now I want to watch, The Wood. It's your favorite too. I am going to set it up while you shower and we can watch it over dinner.

Grabbing her behind, he says, "Okay baby, but we probably ain't going to watch most of it", he laughs, kisses her cheek, and leaves to shower.

As he walks away, she rubs her belly while looking at it, and says, "This is your dad and he is just a whole goof troop. I wonder if you will be a jokester like him------ baby Ruth?"

She laughs as she hears Tony yell, "Heeeeee is baby."

After his shower, they eat as they watch the movie. Tony is reciting nearly every line as he laughs as though it is his first time seeing it. At certain scenes, he looks at Jewels saying, "Baby that's how you used to have me feeling." He laughs hysterically at a playground scene and continues, "I used to want to try that so bad, but could never bring myself to do it. I just looked."

Jewels nearly spits out her drink laughing at this saying, "I am glad you did not because my brother would have done what hers did."

Laughing, "I know. It would've been worth it though, but I liked you to much to let that get in the way. Our friendship was to good too, but is was tempting baby."

Shaking her head filled with laughter, he pinches her cheek and kisses it.

As they watch the movie, she looks over their home and their house is pretty much running over with pampers, wipes, bottles, and baby clothes. They both decide on breast feeding, well, Jewels decided first and Tony soon agreed. They have a baby tub and all other baby needs. They have a stroller and bought car seats for themselves and their parents. They also have an abundance of clothes that family and friends constantly buy. Although, both Tony and Jewels have asked them not to, they buy them anyways. Tony and Jewels always laugh at them, but graciously accepts the clothes and thank them for their thoughtfulness. The last things they need are a crib and a bassinet.

One day, while Jewels is at her parents' home, Kellie stops by to talk about a baby shower. Jewels spends the day semi helping her mother in the lawn. She also spends time on a sewing machine Mrs. Lowd passed down to her a couple of months ago. So far, she has managed to sew a few infant sized blankets and shirts. She has also managed to sew a couple of onesies. She always sings a medley of gospel tunes while sewing which keeps her at a steady pace.

Today she is in a happy mood, but the people around her becomes frustrated with her. They are irritated as well, because Jewels does not want a baby shower. She tells them repeatedly how she and Tony are not in need of anything and just does not feel up to it.

Kellie says, "But Jewels this is your first baby. You should have one to celebrate. I will do everything. You and Tony just have to show up."

Sighing, Jewels responds, "Kell, I know, but I just do not feel up to it and being surrounded by people. I love y'all, but I know everyone is going to want to take pictures and want me to play those baby shower games. I just don't feel like doing that stuff. And I do not want to have to repeatedly ask everyone not to post the pictures to social media." She tilts her head at Kellie and says, "You know, like you posted our wedding picture and I had to ask you to take it down."

"Jewels my bad about that. I was just excited for you two. But friend, you know we want to celebrate with you two and gift you things."

"I understand, but we do not need anything. I don't want everyone wasting their money. They have their own homes to take care of. We are good."

"Okay Jewels. I'ma let this go, but I am still waiting to be asked to be the god mom too."

Laughing, Jewels waves her off saying, "Whatever Kellie, you know that is not on our agenda."

After trying to convince her for an hour, Kellie finally gives up and leaves. Mrs. Lowd walks inside to call Tony hoping he answers. He does and says,

"Hey ma, is everything okay? How is Jewels?"

"Yes, I am just calling to see if you know Jewels does not want a shower and why?"

"Yes ma'am. I know. I just don't think she feels like it."

"Are you okay with that?"

"Yes ma'am. It is her decision. You know, I cannot even get her to have a wedding anymore. I am still trying to talk her into that again ma. I think she is a little tired too, so now we have to put our wedding off a couple of years. But you know we are good. We do not need anything, but she does want you all in the room when she gives birth."

"Okay, I hear you, but I am going to try and talk her into one."

Laughing, he says, "Okay ma, good luck, but I think she has her mind made up on this one." He pauses as someone knocks on his office's door and says, "Ma, I have to go. I will see y'all in a couple of hours. Love you."

"Okay and I love you too."

He speaks with the person at his door and sees that it is the receptionist bringing him a note from a phone call she took. He reads over the note and notates some dates that are on there. He then sits back in his chair, thinks over the conversation he had with Mrs. Lowd, and laughs at them.

As he sits at his desk and thinks over the conversation laughing, Tony text messages Jewels,

"Hey baby, I know they are messing with you about a shower. Are you okay?"

Jewels responds,

"Yes, I am fine. I let it go in one ear and out the other. I love you and thanks for checking <kiss> <smooch> <heartbeat>."

"I love you too and you are welcome, <kiss>, see you soon, <heartbeat> ,<heart eyes smile>."

Thirty minutes later he texts her again with a picture attached of him hugging her saying,

"Ignore them, I love you. <attachment, Anthony Hamilton, The Point of It All>."

"<heart smiles>, <heartbeat>, I love you too and I am, thanks for this song, one of my faves."

"<wink>, I know. <smooch>."

Jewels continues to sit on her parents' front porch and vibes to the song. She replays it three times. Some neighbors walk over to say hello and receive an update on her pregnancy. Jewels lets them all know that everything is going good and thanks them for checking on her.

A couple of hours pass and Tony arrives to the Lowds' house. He exits the vehicle smiling at Jewels sitting on the front porch, who smiles back then blushes when she sees him holding one pink rose and one red rose. He also has her favorite candy, Turtles, in hand. When he gets to her he hands her the items, hugs, and kisses her, then asks, "Baby, you okay? Did they bother you some more about having a shower?"

She kisses him back, smiles, and says, "Yea baby, but I'm fine. I do not know why it is so hard for them to understand that I just do not want one. I mean, we can at least start our own tradition, but following someone else's is not that big of a deal to me."

Kissing her cheek, he says, "Yea, I know baby."

He continues to kiss and nibble on her cheek as Jewels blushes when her dad stands in front of them and clears his throat, "Okay son. You can kiss my baby girl later, but are you two ready to eat? Your moms made dinner for us down at your parents' house Tony."

They both laugh and stand to walk to the Ellisons' house. As they walk, Tony cannot help himself and begins to hug Jewels from behind, kissing her cheek, and rubbing her belly, while singing, "I love you baby and baby junior." Mr. Lowd sees it and shakes his head while laughing. As they eat, all their parents try and convince them to have a baby shower. Tony and Jewels listens, but their minds are already made up and the answer remains no.

Mrs. Ellison says, "Jewels, sweetie, you sure you do not want one?"

Dropping her head, Jewels responds, "Yes ma'am, I just do not feel up to it. I am a little tired with all the changes and now preparing myself, mentally, that a whole human will be depending on us."

"Baby", Tony says, "you know you will be an awesome mom. You have already started."

Smiling and kissing him on the cheek, "Thank you baby. I needed to hear that. I must admit, I am a little nervous."

Rubbing her belly, he gives her a warm look and says, "Don't be baby because this will be natural for you."

Cheesing while watching their exchange, Mrs. Lowd says, "You two are just so cute and adorable together."

Everyone bursts into laughter and Tony continues to rub Jewels' stomach.

After dinner, Tony and Jewels decides to walk their old neighborhood for quick exercise. They pass a corner and Tony says, "Baby, you remember when I had to pick you up and carry you home from here?"

Jewels drops her head, "Yea, Tony, I remember. I felt so bad after you told me the reason, but I didn't know and did not mean any harm."

Laughing, he says, "Yea, I know baby. They did too. When I came back to talk to them they weren't mad and understood you were coming from a place of love and concern. But how they looked at me when you were talking was like, 'Tony please take Jewels home, please'." He laughs thinking of it, "Baby you would not stop talking either. When I saw the hurt, shame, and embarrassment in their eyes, I was like, 'I am just going to scoop her up and walk her home'."

"I am glad you did because I had no clue of their circumstances. All I saw was great talent and intelligence being thrown down the drain. It hurt. But when you said, 'Jewels you know I do not agree and hate it. But Jewels, I understand. They are hungry baby'. That went over my head and I was like, 'We all are. Why do you think we work so hard'?"

Laughing, Tony responds, "Yea, baby it did."

Jewels drops her head still thinking of it and continues, "You sat me down though, looked in my eyes, and said, 'No Jewels, they are literally hungry.' You told me how one day you walked home with them, after your parents fixed them a plate of food, and he opened the fridge and nothing was in it. Tony, that really broke my heart and I was soooo mad at myself. I apologized to them when I saw them again, but they were cool and knew I meant no harm. But now, they are running a successful business. Matter of fact, I need to pay them a visit because my feet need some new shoes."

They both laugh and Tony says, "Yea baby, they are. We can stop by tomorrow too if you want to. You know they have been thinking about making their own shoes and want my help with the design."

Smiling, "Baby no, you did not tell me this."

"I know, but it was just a conversation he ran by me a few years back. Something they thought about, not necessarily up to it, but I am ready when they are."

Smiling, she hugs him, and says, "I know you are and it will be amazing."

He hugs her back and kisses her, "Thank you baby. You are always so encouraging. I love you."

They walk a little more and passes a pole all the kids spray painted their names on. They laugh at their childhood foolery and are shocked to see that their names are still there. Pointing at their names, Jewels says, "I cannot remember who added these hearts by our names baby, but they had jokes. We were just friends then."

Laughing, he responds, "Your sister added those hearts. She knew you belonged to me,---"

Jewels interrupts, "I BELONGED to you? BELONGED, Tony?"

Laughing, while kissing her cheek, "You know what I mean, but you were my woman though. You just didn't know it yet." He laughs and continues as Jewels rolls her eyes, "She was letting everyone else know that you were off limits. I appreciate her help too." He laughs some more, "But Omar still snuck in. Jewels I still can't believe you entertained that clown."

Looking shocked, Jewels drops her mouth, and Tony continues, "Yea, I know it was him. It took a minute because he did not go to our high school. You know around that time I stayed after school a lot participating in different sports, but I finally peeped it one day. I told your brother too. As soon as I figured out who it was I called your brother and he was like, 'Ohhhhh heeeeeccckkk no! Is he even still in school because I thought he dropped out? Jewels has lost her mind, but when I come home I will have a talk with him.'"

Listening with her mouth still wide open, he continues with laughter, "Close your mouth baby. I can't believe you did not realize we figured this out."

"Now I know why he was scared to speak to me after Jacob's visit. You two were wrong for that. I did not interfere with y'all's women."

"Baby, it's different though because we were protecting you. We can protect ourselves."

Bursting into laughter, Jewels asks, "Whatever Tony, but how did you figure it out?"

He looks at her and chuckles. "Really Jewels? You do not realize how I caught on to it?"

"No, how?"

Laughing, "Baby, we were at your parents' house one afternoon talking on the front porch. And I noticed your entire body language was different. So I stopped talking and let you do all the talking, but I was observing you. When I saw how different you were acting, I think you even popped your lips one time, I knew. Baby I was so in shock and hurt, like not my Jewels, noooo." He laughs as Jewels looks at him out of the side of her eyes and continues, "But when I noticed that, I knew someone was creeping and trying to get you.

I knew for a fact it was no one at our high school because I would have known. And I started thinking, like, 'She did give me my car keys back a month ago saying she was tired of coming back to get me after practice and will catch the school bus again'. I thought that was weird, but did not think to much on it. I knew you didn't like catching the school bus, but was like, 'Alright, but if you change your mind let me know'.

Remember, I taught you how to drive and everything so you can stop catching the school bus. Remember we had to sneak and do it too because your dad told me not to. But you gave me that sad face you do and it always gets to me." He laughs at himself and says, "I was risking your dad hurting me to teach you how to drive. So when you gave me my keys back, I was surprised. But Jewels, when I noticed the change in your body language, I was like, 'Nope, I am putting a stop to this now'." He laughs as he sees Jewels roll her eyes and shake her head listening to this.

Tony continues, "The next day I skipped practice and drove you home. We stopped at the corner store and he was there. We all spoke, but I saw how y'all looked at each other and knew. He knew I realized it too, because when he saw how I looked at him after y'all did your little, 'quick stare down', at each other, he dropped his head and laughed at me."

Holding her head down, she asks, "Baby why do you think he was laughing at you and not the fact he knew he was busted?"

"Jewels, you know I never liked him and he knew I liked you. You know we fought once too?"

Shocked, she asks, "No, why?"

"Because of you. He was talking sideways when we were all playing basketball one day at the park. He started talking about your physical appearance and I told him to shut up. He wouldn't, but the next thing I know I threw the basketball at him and we started throwing blows. Our friends broke us up though," laughing, "but D'Angelo held them back for a minute, like, 'Naw y'all, let Tony handle this for a minute. He should've shut up when Tony told him to. He knows how he feels about her'." Tony continues to laugh as Jewels speaks.

"Tony, really? You shouldn't had let him get to you like that. But, Tony, the most we did was kiss. But honestly, I did not know you truly liked me in that way then. To me, we were just best friends."

"Yea, baby I know, but he crossed the line. I know you ain't know that I was truly crushing on you, but he knew. All of the dudes in our neighborhood knew. Most the girls did too. You just didn't pay attention", he laughs at this. "And you were only kissing, but he was working his way to more and your body language let me know he was getting close. And you know I don't play around when it comes to you. The stuff he was saying needed a punch or two. Up into the day he joined the military I would see him and tell him not to speak to me because of it. But when I found out he was joining the army I tried to talk him out of it. I don't like him, but I have love for my people. I tried to give him some other options that fit his background, but it was to late because he already signed. I told him to do your four years and get out. I wonder if he did?"

"You know, I have no clue, but you really thought you were protecting me? Nothing like that was going to happen."

"I was, imagine if your dad found out?"

She pauses and thinks for a minute, then says, "Good point."

They walk a little more as they wave at some people gathered on a corner talking and laughing. They recognize a few, but others are new faces to them. They continue walking, then Tony looks over at a playground and points to a big oak tree as he says, while laughing and whispering in her ear, "Baby", he points to the tree, "remember, I taught you how to kiss over there when we were in middle school?"

Laughing really hard, Jewels says, "Oh my gosh, yes I do remember that. I thought we were going to get busted and my momma would whip my tail."

Laughing, "Yea and your brother would have beat mine."

Still laughing, "Tony, I remember you asking me a thousand questions, like, 'What you want to learn that for? Who are you trying to kiss? Your brother know you want to start kissing?' Talking about, 'Jewels don't make me hurt one of these dudes out here. You do not need to be kissing no one because you are to young for that.' Tony when you said that, I was filled with so much laughter, like, 'He cannot be serious. We are the same age and you are kissing girls, but I am to young?"

Doubling down on his then statement, he hugs Jewels, and says, "You were. Them knuckleheads didn't deserve to kiss you. They probably weren't brushing their teeth correctly."

Jewels bursts into laughter then says, "No you just wanted to be the only one kissing me."

"That too." He laughs and continues his story, "Jewels you would not stop laughing though. I'm like 'How am I supposed to show you, but whenever I try you start laughing?"

Laughing, she says, "Baby it did tickle me and how you kept looking at me when I laughed made it funnier."

Laughing, "I told you, you were to young to be kissing."

"Yea, but you finally taught me."

"Yep and it was wonderful. I was like, 'Let me hold you. I ain't gone grab your butt'. Baby I did not want to stop, but a car passed and we got scared."

They both bursts into laughter and Jewels says, "Tony we have so many stories we will be able to tell our child one day."

Rubbing her stomach, "Yea baby we surely do."

They walk back to the Lowds' home, tell their parents goodnight, and drives home singing every song the radio plays.

CHAPTER SIX

IT IS TIME

It is a calm, but cloudy late night and Jewels decides to stay up to finish a movie that is playing on their local television station. She has not seen this movie since she was a child but always liked it. She has never been able to find the movie in stores so it pleases her when she sees it playing on her local television station.

It is about a group of hunters who takes a homeless man from the streets pretending to help him. Instead, these evil men hunt him like an animal. To their surprise, the homeless man is not an easy target and fights for his life. In the end, the homeless man saves his life while ending theirs. As she watches it, she screams, points her finger, and yells at the characters as though they can hear her.

The movie ends around One Thirty in the morning and Jewels turns the television off to join Tony in bed. Before she falls asleep, she says a prayer and kisses Tony on the cheek. She rubs her belly and says, "Goodnight to you too."

A couple of hours later, Jewels begins to constantly toss and turn in bed. She is in her ninth month and is ready to meet their child at any time and walk normally again. It is now raining non stop, which helps calms her mind, but physically, her body just is not able to rest. The sky is constantly talking as thunder roars over the neighborhood with a few flashes of lightening accompanied with them. As she tosses and turns with groans Tony wakes up. He looks at her and asks in a low voice, "Baby are you okay?"

Sitting up, she rubs Tony's hand that is caressing her cheek and says, "Yea, just feeling uncomfortable and can't rest."

He rises, while still looking at her, rubs her stomach, and asks, "Jewels are you in labor?"

Laughing, she responds, "No, I think it is something I ate while watching the movie. I'm not in pain."

Looking at her, not sure to believe her analysis, he responds, "Baby I don't know, but we are going to the hospital to be sure."

Shaking her head no, "Tony, I do not feel like making another blank trip. I am okay. I am going to lie back down and rest."

"Okay Jewels." Still not completely comfortable, Tony stays up and watches sitcoms on his Tablet as Jewels lies back down. She continues to toss and turn as Tony rubs her back for comfort. He watches reruns of the show, Martin as he continues to rub her back and gives her loving smooches on the forehead every time she tosses and turns. Nearly an hour later Tony is in the bathroom when he hears Jewels scream. He runs out and sees her nearly ripping their comforter apart in agony, and says, while rushing to hold her, "Baby, is it the baby? The baby coming?"

She shakes her head yes, in agonizing pain, while Tony puts her flip flops on her feet and helps her stand to walk her to their car. As they walk to the front door, her water breaks and it runs down her legs like a flowing waterfall. She stops moving and holds her stomach.

As she holds it she says, "Baby, I can't move. Oh my God, I think the baby is coming."

Looking a little frightened, Tony quickly helps her sit on their living room's floor and calls the 911 dispatcher for assistance and an ambulance. He grabs some pillows from their sofa to place under Jewels for comfort. As he waits for the dispatcher to answer, he says, "Baby, remember to breathe. It is going to be okay. I love you baby. Lord, we need you right now."

As he says this he hears the dispatcher saying, "Sir, what is your address and we will send an ambulance over?"

Tony tells her the address and says, "I think the baby is coming now. I need help!"

As the dispatcher tries to say something, she hears Tony say, "Oh God. Baby push. I see the head." In an excited voice he continues, "Baby, baby, you are doing so good. The baby is almost out, dang Jewels, I love you baby."

He tries to comfort her by rubbing her leg as he sees the baby working its way out and hears her agonizing screams. The view is really beautiful to him as he watches his baby wiggle out of his wife to take his or hers' first breath. Tony is filled with a host of emotions from shock, excitement, and joy. He is truly amazed with witnessing how life enters the world.

With a few more pushes accompanied with excruciating pain, Jewels finally hears a baby crying and Tony saying in an excited voice, "Baby he's here! Our baby made it."

Smiling with pure joy, he listens as the dispatcher tells him how to handle the umbilical cord, but first takes their son over to Jewels to hold him. He then proceeds to clean their crying baby as he sees the lights of the ambulance outside. He opens the door for them and walks over to Jewels as he waits for them to come in, holding their son, saying, "Thank you baby. How do you feel?"

She smiles, but says nothing and he kisses her forehead then kisses their son too. As they travel to the hospital, Tony calls their parents and tells them what just occurred. He calls her brother as well. They all meet up to the hospital to meet their new family member soon after. Still smiling from pure joy and happiness while looking at Jewels as she lies in the hospital bed, Tony says, "Baby our son is here. Thank you baby. I love you." He kisses her forehead and looks at their son in her arms as he continues, "Dang baby, you did it with no epidural either. You said you did not want it and got your wish."

She laughs and kisses their son, then says, "Yea, I surely did, but if you put another baby in me, I am getting that shot. Tony, those contractions hurt."

He laughs, "Yea baby, the way you were screaming scared me. All I could do was call the Lord." He laughs some more and rubs her forehead, "You know I hate seeing you in pain. Our mommas told me to have that shot on standby too, because once the pain kick in you will want it. I listened and told the docs, but you still missed it", he laughs some more.

As they continue to talk, their parents walk in to see their new grandchild. They all exchange hugs and Tony pulls out his camera to start taking pictures of this moment. Her brother and his wife arrives a little later. Jacob video calls their sister, Zapphire, who is in Haiti, so she can talk to their nephew who sleeps the entire conversation. As he sleeps, a nurse takes more pictures of them as they all throw out names for their new family member.

Their dads want him named after them, either their first or middle name. Tony and Jewels looks at their moms as their moms laughs and suggests the names; Malcolm, Nathan, and Revelation. Jacob has no suggestions, but his wife suggests the name Timothy. Both Tony and Jewels listens to their suggestions but decides to stick with their list.

As Mr. Ellison holds his grandson, he says as he looks at Tony, "It looks like he has your dimples Tony."

Tony smiles and Mr. Lowd says, "Baby girl, we will see what a year brings, but right now it just looks like you just carried him. He looks like the spitting image I saw of Tony's baby picture. Including the head full of curls. Now you know why you always had heartburn", he laughs at himself while looking at his grandson.

She laughs as well and sees her brother whisper in Tony's ear. Whatever her brother says prompts Tony to nod his head in agreement while giving her brother a pound with a little chuckle added. She wonders what was said, but notices their dads seems to know and chuckles with them.

A couple of hours later their family leaves after taking more pictures and playing with their new sleeping family member. After everyone leaves, except Mrs. Lowd, Jewels rests with their son while Tony makes a quick trip to their home to get their car and gather their things he was not able to get before they made it to the hospital. Once he makes it back, he sees Jewels is awake and they decide on a name for their son. Zion Samson Ellison, born November 7.

After they decide on a name, Mrs. Lowd leaves. She hugs them and gives her grandson a kiss on the forehead then heads home. After she leaves Jewels motions to Tony to close the room's door. He does then Jewels looks at Tony and asks, "What did my brother whisper to you?"

Laughing as he looks at his sleeping son, he says, "Baby, he was just saying congrats."

"Whatever Tony. No he did not. He would not whisper that and your grin did not match that statement."

Grinning, he says, "Baby, I am for real. He was congratulating me on our baby being a boy and the fact he looks like me."

Looking out of the side of her eyes laughing, "Why did he whisper that?"

Laughing, he grins and says, "Okay baby, he was congratulating me on a job well done for having a son who looks like me as well, you know, for handling 'business' correctly. It's a man thing baby."

Jewels bursts into laughter, "You two are something else, but are you serious? Just because Zion is a boy and looks like you, for now, that is what he believes?"

Smiling, he stares at her asking, "But baby, is it a lie?" He laughs and continues, "You know you be climbing the walls."

Still laughing but shaking her head no, "Tony I am done with you. You are just……, I can't even explain it." She is laughing so hard she wipes a tear and continues, "You and my brother are a mess, but I love y'all though."

"We love you too, but I notice you didn't deny climbing the walls either", he says while laughing.

Still laughing, Jewels responds, "An answer was not needed."

He smiles as he kisses her forehead then begins to hold and rock their son.

A week passes, Tony and Jewels are at home enjoying their new found parenthood. Although, they are both tired from late night feedings and diaper changes, they cannot stop smiling. Tony is trying his best to fill his time as he patiently waits for six weeks to pass, because he is passionately eager to make love to his wife again. He does a lot of yard work, begins to lift weights daily, does more design work, and work out excessively.

He does some suicides on their street. Practices some lay ups and three-point shots when Zion sleeps. He uses a neighbor's basketball hoop to practice these. He also works on throwing a football to make sure his aim stays accurate. He converses with some neighbors as well while happily showing them pictures of his son that he has in his cell phone. They all agree with their family that Zion looks like Tony. Mrs. Mary jokingly says, "If I did not see it with my own eyes, I would not believe this child belonged to Jewels." They all laugh, then Tony begins his yard work again.

He checks on Jewels' garden and sees that everything is okay. He edges some of their bushes and cuts back some tree limbs that are hanging in their yard from a neighbor's yard. He quenches their lawn with water from the water hose then checks their property to see if there is anything else that needs his attention. Jewels watches him as he works from their bedroom's window while rocking their son.

Also, during the wait he constantly flirts with her like they are two teenagers crushing on one another. He text messages her flirtatious messages and they are always accompanied with a song. Sometimes, he gets bold enough and attempts some dance routines from some of their favorite videos. Jewels laughs the whole time, but enjoys every moment. Especially when he attempts the dance routine from Usher's Yeah video, but starts to add moves from other artists of that music era. At one point, he stands Jewels up to dance with him as he does his version of the dance, 'Thunder Clap', he renamed, 'The Tony Clap'.

Jewels dances with him, but cannot stop laughing at his goofiness.

He happily changes diapers and wakes with Jewels as she does late night feedings. She is glad that they decided to have a bassinet for him in their room, because it makes the late night duties easier. Although, most of the time Zion sleeps in the bed with them. Every time he sleeps in the bed with them, Jewels lies him on her side of the bed away from Tony. One night he asks,

"Baby, why do you always do that? You don't think I can sleep with him laying by me?"

Laughing, she responds, "Tony, you know you are a hard sleeper sometimes. I don't want you rolling over and smothering him."

He laughs but nods in agreement.

Tony returns to work two weeks after Zion's birth and is completely energized, even with all the late nights. Although, Jewels tells him to sleep, he still happily wakes up with her.

∿∿∿

Finally, eight weeks passes. Tony takes Jewels on a lovely date while her parents watches Zion. As they eat, Jewels constantly checks her cell phone, and Tony says, "Baby he is okay. Your parents raised you didn't they?"

Laughing, Jewels says, "Baby I know, but I miss him already."

Smiling, he responds, "I do too Jewels but I miss you too baby. I am glad we have our parents to take care of him so we can still take care of each other too."

Grinning and looking at him, she jokingly responds, "Well, do you miss me or miiiissss me?"

Smiling with laughter, "Both", he laughs some more and continues, "baby, you know I love you and I just want to make sure we can continue to enjoy each other as we raise Zion."

"We will and I love you too."

Grinning, he flirtatiously says, "Yea, my Locs miss you pulling them too." Jewels laughs at him as he continues, "Baby, we have the whole weekend to ourselves. Your parents will spend time with Zion tonight until tomorrow afternoon, then my parents will have him from then to Sunday night."

The waitress comes with their entree. Tony says a grace for them as they bow their heads then they begin to enjoy their meal. Jewels is enjoying a chicken wrap with potato salad as the side. Tony is indulging in fried chicken wings and onion rings. They are both drinking lemon aide sweetened with honey.

Tony stops eating at one point and stares at her smiling. Jewels asks, "Tony, why are you looking at me like that?"

Laughing, he says, "Baby, I am just thinking about how much pumping you did for this weekend and how those", he points to her chest, "are off limits for a while."

Laughing hysterically as she drops her head, "Baby, only you would say something like that."

Laughing with her, he blows her a kiss and says, "I know."

They finish dinner then drives to their local beach to walk the beach's sand. They constantly flirt with each other while they stroll the beach. Tony holds Jewels a lot, kissing her on the cheek, while giving his best redemption of her favorite song, Beauty. He kisses her a lot while squeezing her butt the entire time. Jewels is blushing with love all over her face, which is always his goal.

At one point, Tony picks her up and says, "Baby, you remember me holding you like this to walk across the threshold at my place in Cali after we got married?"

"Of course I remember, you were determined to do it too and was like, 'I'm doing it again when we make it back to Jax..'"

Laughing while still holding her, "Yep because Cali was our temp home. I had to make it official here too. You know we had to rush back because I had work the next day, but I did not want to wait a whole month for another space to open up either at the courthouse." He laughs some more, "Baby we didn't even make it to your bedroom either. Jewels I had your brother rolling when I told him that you would not touch my bed until I got a new one. You made me get a new sofa too."

"I sure did, I was not about to lie in that bed you had other women in."

Laughing while still holding her, "Baby you know I ain't have no women in my bed. You know my bed was reserved for someone I am in a relationship with."

Jewels smiles and laughs at him as he smooches her lips then stands her back up.

They stop to watch the waves and enjoy the night's breeze. They listen as each wave rolls to shore while looking at the moon and notices no stars are in the sky. As they continue to listen and gaze, Tony says, while holding her in his arms, "Baby, this feels good. Being able to love on you knowing Zion is in good hands."

Nodding in agreement, "Yes it does baby."

He kisses her cheek, and asks, "How many more do you want?"

"Babies? However many we can afford financially, physically, and emotionally. But it is not really my call. If we are meant to have more, we will. I mean we did start later than usual too. What about you?"

Smiling, "Baby we can have a basketball team. I am ready, but I can be cool with one too. I guess we did, but it was worth the wait."

"I agree, I can't imagine going through this wonderful experience with someone else."

"Me either baby, but I'ma still work on that basketball team though."

She laughs at him and he kisses her as he squeezes her tight saying, "I'm serious baby."

She squeezes him back saying, "I know."

They stare at the ocean holding each other as the sound of the waves plays as their background music.

After, they go home to give each other what they have been missing for the last couple of months. "I love you baby", Tony says while kissing her and as I'll Make Love To You by the group Boyz II Men plays.

Jewels responds, "I love you too", as he continues to kiss her. Finally, they end their night in each others' arms until they fall asleep.

The next morning, Jewels wakes to the smell of breakfast. The sun is shining bright and she meditates a few moments as she hears rain sounds playing from a recording Tony made her. It has a few thundering and lightening strikes sounds as well.

Before she rises she calls her parents to check on Zion and them as well.

"Good morning Jewels", her mom says in a cheerful voice.

"Good morning ma. I am just calling to check on y'all. How is Zion treating you and dad?"

"Everything is fine. Tony already called too. Did you enjoy yourself last night?"

"Yes ma'am. I really did. I mean it almost felt like our very first date as a couple almost a decade ago."

Laughing, "That's good baby girl, but hey I think your son knows I am talking to his momma. Hold on."

Jewels listens with a smile as she hears Zion spitting bubbles and says, "Hey momma's baby. I miss you and I love you wookie."

As she says this, Tony walks in smiling and joins the conversation.

Her mom gets back on the phone and says, "Y'all, this is to cute. He is really smiling and lighting up listening to y'all."

They smile and Jewels says, "Ma, I'ma let you go. I was just checking on y'all. I will see you tomorrow."

"Okay baby girl and continue to enjoy your weekend. Zion is okay."

She says, "Yes ma'am and thanks", as she ends the call.

After she ends the call, Tony kisses her cheek, and says, "Good morning baby. I made breakfast."

"Good morning. I know. I smell it. Let me wash up and I will be in there, thanks"

She stands to walk to their bathroom. As she passes him, he slaps her on the butt. She looks at him smiling and he blows a loving kiss. As she washes up, Tony continues to set up their breakfast. As she walks out, she sees he has dimmed the lights. When he sees her, he walks to her, takes her hand, and leads her to the dim lit patio. As she walks in, she grins lovingly as she sees a candle lit table with their breakfast sitting on it. Rose petals are everywhere and she sees a huge teddy bear holding a heart that has a picture of them in it on their wedding day.

As she continues to glare around the patio smiling, she puts her listening ears on and hears the smooth sounds of nineties Rhythm and Blues playing. They finally sit as, Weak by SWV plays. Smiling, she says, "Baby, oh my gosh, I was not expecting this. Thank you."

"I know baby. Do you like it?"

"I love it. When did you do this?"

Smiling, "Baby, I started planning our weekend a week after you gave birth to Zion, but I begin getting the patio ready last night as you slept."

Still smiling, "Tony, you really know how to make my heart smile. I hope I do the same."

"Baby, you know you do."

They begin to eat. Jewels smiles as she sees he has made her an omelet with spinach, onions, cheddar cheese, and turkey sausage. He also made her ginger tea with a peach flavor added. She notices he made himself french toast and scrambled eggs. Being a little greedy, Jewels steals some of his french toast. He smiles and feeds her a few bites.

After they finish breakfast he takes her hand to dance to, Run to The Arms of The One Who Loves You by Xscape . They continue as After7, Ready or

Not plays. He sings every word of this song to her as he twirls her and bends her over his knee, like they are the world's best classical dancers while agreeing with every lyric of the song he sings.

As they continue to dance, he whispers in her ear, "I love you Jewels. You know you are amazing and will always be my love. No one has ever made me feel the way you make me feel baby and now we have our son. Thank you baby."

He twirls her some more as Jewels smiles and says, "I do not think I could have asked for a better husband. I love you Tony." They dance to some more tunes, then Tony begins to passionately kiss her as Silk's Meeting In My Bedroom begins to play and their doorbell rings. Looking irritated, he drops his head, then gets his cell phone to check their ring camera while saying, "Wow! Who can this be? I thought I told everyone, you and I were just hanging this weekend."

He checks his cell phone, drops his head again, "And of course, it is Kellie. Baby, why is she always interrupting us? Did you not tell her that this is our weekend? I really believe she does this on purpose, but at some point you have to stop her baby. I know you don't interrupt her and Brandon."

"Baby, I sent everyone a text, but I hope it is an emergency. But you are right. I do not interrupt them. This is starting to annoy me too."

"I doubt it is an emergency. She gets a kick out of interrupting us, but she's your friend."

Jewels shakes her head laughing as she walks away to answer the door and hears Tony say, "Baby please don't let her across the threshold. I do not want her vibes in here messing up ours."

She nods while laughing and continues to the door. Kellie and Jewels talk for ten minutes on their front porch. Kellie apologizes because she forgot it is their first weekend baby free. She wanted to stop by and update her on their friend, Justice, whose wedding they attended nearly a year ago. Looking sad and disturbed, she hugs Kellie then walks back to the patio with Tony.

As she walks in, Tony stands, and says, "Baby, what's wrong?"

Dropping her head, she says, "Tony, do you remember the wedding we went to?"

"Of course, Jesse ass still has me on high alerts. Has he tried contacting you or something?"

"No baby. But remember, Justice's cousin was killed, well she is starting to believe her husband had something to do with it. This is really scary and crazy. Wow, it makes me even more thankful and happy to have you baby. Tony, I love you."

Holding her, he kisses her cheek, "Dang baby, I'm sorry to hear that about your friend." He kisses her again and continues, "I love you too and now you see why I am so protective with you and now Zion. It is some ruthless people out here. I can see myself doing some real time if somebody hurt you or him baby."

Shaking her head in agreement, she says, "Baby, I know and appreciate it."

He holds her as they sit there for another hour as the music plays. They fall asleep for an hour and awakes to, Mary J. Blige's Real Love, playing. They continue to snuggle under each other as the music plays while bobbing their heads to the beat. Tony adds a few smooches to her forehead until they become hungry and makes lunch after cleaning the breakfast away.

Sunday evening arrives. Tony and Jewels goes to not only pick up Zion, but to enjoy Sunday dinner at the Ellisons' house. While they eat, Jewels tells their parents about her friend Justice's situation. Her dad looks at her and asks, "Didn't you two say the groom invited Jesse?"

"Daddy, yes, he told me he was invited by the groom."

With a serious face her dad continues, "I wonder how well they know each other because you know birds of a feather flock together?"

Tony says, "That is a good question. I wonder that too." He looks at Jewels, "Baby, have you met the groom before?"

"No, the wedding was my first encounter with him. I do not know how well they know each other."

Looking at her, her dad says, "Baby girl I am taking you to the range tomorrow and your mom can watch Zion. I need to see if your aim is still good." He looks at Tony, then asks, "How is yours?"

"Okay daddy, I have not been in a while."

Tony says, "Mine is good. I got a few rounds in after Zion was born. Gotta stay ready. You know if you stay ready, you do not have to get ready. Protecting my babies is part of my job."

Their parents all nod in agreement with their moms adding a prayer.

Not long after, they finish dinner and hug their parents goodnight. Tony gathers his family and they travel home. As they drive, they notice Zion is fast asleep and is resting like he is sleeping on clouds. Mrs. Ellison has bathe and fed him. She has him smelling like fresh cotton and baby powder. His aroma has the car smelling like a baby oil factory, very lovely and soft.

As they continue drive, Tony turns the radio on. The song that is playing sends him into silence and deep thought. Jewels notices and listens to the song. As she listens, she sees Tony shake his head. She rubs his cheek and asks, "Baby what's wrong?"

He looks at her, smiles, and says, "Nothing baby. This song just brought back some memories."

"Do you want to talk about it because you seem bothered?"

He checks his rear-view mirror to see if Zion is still asleep, and continues, "I am not bothered, but it is that this song is a song that I had on constant repeat after you left me. This is my first time hearing it since we been back together. Baby I was even playing it non stop in Cali, still crying over you." He shakes his head at himself, "Maaaan, Jewels our dads sat me down one day, like a couple of weeks after you dumped me and was like, 'Tony stop soft core stalking her before she blocks you and puts up a 'No Trespassing' sign on her gate to keep you away. She needs time. We know you miss her, but chill'. Jewels, baby, I know I was calling non stop and I'm sorry 'bout that, but baby I missed you. Then I remembered this song and played it on repeat. But I am glad I listened to them and stopped hounding you."

Shaking his head still remembering, "Baby, you wouldn't even talk to me at first. All I had were our pictures and memories. It was hard Jewels. I mean all I kept seeing was the look on your face the night you dumped me. I couldn't even get it out or look in your eyes, you remember, all I could say was, 'Baby I'm sorry' and kept dropping my head. I said that like three times, then I saw your facial expression change and was like, 'She knows what I'm about to say'.

After that, you stood up, did not say a word, just walked to your door and opened it. I stood there like thirty minutes holding back tears, hoping you would come open it and talk to me. Finally went to my car, put it in reverse, and had to put it back in park because the tears started flowing and I could not see. I was probably crying in your driveway close to an hour. Baby, that was a whole new experience for me."

He shakes his head at himself, "Baby, I'm in the car crying, like, 'Dang she ain't go off on me or nothing'. I rather have had that then silence."

She giggles and he says, "Jewels, why is this funny?"

"It is not. I giggled, because I played this, Lately by the group Divine a lot as well. I can't believe we were both listening to the same song. I really can't believe you even knew it existed. I saw you in my driveway too. I didn't realize you were crying though, but yea after you kept saying sorry, I knew what it was.

It actually took three times for me to get it. Usually, I would have caught on right away, but I truly believed you would not do anything like that to me. I was pretty shocked. And then I kept hearing Kellie's voice in my ear saying that you were going to eventually do that...I had no words."

He shakes his head at himself, "Baby, I couldn't believe I was that stupid either." He rubs her cheek then says, "Sorry baby", she rolls her eyes but smiles as he says this. He then holds her hand, and says, "But dang baby, we were listening to the same song and didn't know", he chuckles. "Yea, and I first heard it in college. This girl in our dorm played it non stop. It used to irritate the heck out of me, but when you left I finally understood what she was going through. These words and melody hit different when you experience that lost." He glances at her and continues to hold her hand while saying, "And baby, I couldn't even get the words out. I was so mad and disappointed in myself. Then seeing the look on your face just did it for me."

She pinches his cheek, "I guess I am just emotional because these words always hit me deep, well about ninety percent of Rhythm and Blues hit me to the soul. I mean have me in my feelings for no reason."

They both laugh and Tony continues to drive, when Lenny Williams' I love You, begins to play. Tony looks at Jewels and says, "Dang baby, I have not heard this in forever. I need to add it to my playlist", he pulls over to the side of the road and begins singing it to her with all of his soul as their son continues to sleep through it all. As he sings to her, he kisses her during pauses, but points to her with every loving lyric being sang. He can barely hold a note, but to Jewels, he sounds better than Luther, Gerald, and K-Ci.

They finally make it home, prepare for bed, and for tomorrow.

The next day comes. Tony takes his wife and son to her parents' house. Mr. Lowd is up waiting for Jewels. He waves bye to Tony, plays with his grandson for a few minutes, looks at his daughter, and says, "Baby girl, lets get to work. I am taking you to breakfast first."

"Okay daddy, I am ready and can we go to a place that serves omelets please?"

"Sure baby girl."

As they eat breakfast, her dad is full of questions. He first asks, "Jewels, you have been married for two years and now you are a mom, how are you liking this new life?"

Smiling, "Dad, I am actually enjoying every minute of it."

"That is great. How is Tony treating you?"

Blushing with her eyes brightened as she answers, she says ,"Great dad. I have no complaints. I do not want to jinx it though because we are still honeymooning and he swears we will be honeymooning for life." She pauses and smiles some more as she thinks of Tony, "Dad, he is really good to me. I really appreciate him and he keeps me smiling the way you keep momma smiling. I really did not believe that type of love I saw growing up still existed. And dad, he really takes pride in making sure our household is running smoothly and that we are happy and safe. I truly love and respect him dad."

Her dad laughs and says, "Your mom and I never stopped either, even with our kids growing up. And I am glad to hear this. I knew he would be good to you and for you", he laughs. "Baby girl, I always hoped you would end up with him too. I knew I would have nothing to worry about. When you two broke up, I was like dang, now I have to watch out for these other men. Now I still have to watch out, but I know Tony is on point too."

"Yea, I love watching you two too. It is sooo cute and adorable and I understand dad."

He smiles, then puts on a serious face, "But Jewels, what is going on with Jesse? Is he following you and has he ever threatened you?"

Shaking her head, "No dad. I do not know what it is, well he said he wanted closure and I gave it to him again. I am not afraid of him or anything, but Tony is not comfortable at all."

"I understand Tony. He had no right blocking you. When you told him to move, he should have, but baby girl lets finish breakfast so we can get to work. It is better to be safe than sorry."

Jewels nods in agreement. They finally finish breakfast and makes it to the gun range. Her dad is satisfied because Jewels' aim is still impeccable. She hits the areas to stop a threat, that are usually not life threatening, but is able to hit those life threatening areas as well, if they are needed. After his satisfaction is met, they leave, where they both spend the rest of the day playing with Zion and Tony's parents soon join them.

As they play with Zion, Kellie stops by with a gift for him. She walks up to Jewels and hands her a Tablet, "Hey Jewels, this is for my godson."

Laughing, Jewels says, "Keep that. We are not getting him electronics like that. He will use a computer where he is monitored when he is of age, and what would he do with that now anyways Kellie? And you know he has no godparents, stop that", she laughs and so does Kellie.

Kellie continues, "Jewels I hear you, but he cannot survive in this new world without it. And I am his god mom, it is just the natural order of things. You and Tony are not going to stop that."

Bending over in laughter, Jewels tries her best to stop laughing to say, "I bet Tony's ears are ringing right now! You are about to lose, 'play' auntie status with that talk. Zion is our child, so what we say goes. You are funny though."

As she continues to laugh and Kellie looks at her, not pleased, she receives a text message from Tony. Looking at her cell phone, Jewels says, "See, I knew his ears were ringing. This my baby texting." She continues to laugh as she opens the message to read it. It reads,

"Hey baby. I am just checking on y'all. How's your day going?"

"Aaaaawwwweeeee, hey baby. It is going fine. Zion has slept most the day. How's work?"

"<smiles>, work is fine. I am ready to get off though, lol. Baby, I've been looking at houses too for us. I saw one I think you may like, here is the link to the house, <attachment>"

He text messages a link to a house that is not far from where they live now. Jewels responds,

"Baby, I love it, but isn't 400k to much for us?"

"Not at all baby. We paid off the rest of your house when I sold mine, with extra remaining plus the savings from Cali. We have not touched it and you know I have been adding to it. The city also has programs to help with down payments, closing costs, and stuff like that. I was not even aware of them when I bought my first house. Baby, you know I do not live beyond my means either."

"Okay baby, I hear you and will love to see it in person. But I don't want you overworking yourself either."

"Okay, but I am still looking too, this is one I thought you may like. But as you look, remember we can do this amount and live just as comfortable as we do now baby and that is with Zion's expenses as he grows. We are good baby. I have been looking at this full-time position here as well. So when I take that, we will be even better."

"<smiles>, okay baby, I love you."

"I love you too, <kiss>."

Jewels ends her conversation and sees that Zion is still up. Kellie and his grandparents are entertaining him and he cannot stop laughing. Jewels walks over and Kellie says,

"Seriously, Jewels, he needs tech. He can't live in this new world without it."

"Yes he can Kellie, but he will not either. We will teach him how to use them, when he is of age, but he just will not own one in that sense. Even some of the developers of those electronics keep their children from them or give them very little time with them, so why would I want to immerse my child with it. It is a no for us."

Kellie laughs and finally gives up as she continues to play with Zion.

Later, after Tony gets his family, they make a grocery store trip. Jewels realizes she needs an onion and a bell pepper to complete their dinner. As Jewels searches the produce area, Tony and Zion go to the seasoning aisle. While looking at the seasonings a familiar voice says, "Hey Tony, I have not seen you since California."

Dropping his head without looking and taking a deep sigh, he says, "Hey Tika."

As he continues to look at the seasonings while holding his son, she says, "Well, is it like that Tony? You can't even look at me? I am not mad at you. I understand why you asked me to leave."

Shaking his head, "Tika, I spoke. What do you want?"

As she is about to respond, she hears the baby and says, "Oh, wow, Tony I did not realize you were holding a baby. Is it yours? I had no clue you had a child."

He finally looks at her with Zion in his arms and says, "Yes, he is Jewels' and I son."

Nodding, she says in a shocked voice, "Oh you two are still together?"

"Yes we are, for life, Tika what do you want? We have nothing to talk about."

She tries to rub Zion's back and say something, but Tony quickly moves his son out of the way saying, "Tika, you know me better than that. Why even try that? You know you should not try and touch my child. We are not cool like that."

"My bad Tony, I thought we were friends?"

"Friends? Jewels and I are together and you thought we were friends? You do not even like my baby, Tika stop it, but I need to get back to shopping---"

As he says this, Jewels walks up and says, "Hey Tika." She looks at Tony, "What is going on here?"

Tony says, "Nothing."

Looking at Jewels, Tika says, "Hey Jewels. I saw him and spoke, but congrats on your marriage and the baby."

"Thanks", Jewels says sarcastically.

"You're welcome", she responds. She waves and finally walks away.

Shaking her head she looks at Tony, "That girl knows she does not like me, but saying congrats. Tony, I hope she did not touch my child?"

Laughing, he says, "Your child, don't you mean ours? And you know I ain't allowing that."

Laughing, "Well in this moment he is mine, until your ex's aroma leaves this space. Look, Zion even looks bothered."

"He is. She kept trying to talk as I tried to ignore her. I know he felt my vibes", he laughs and kisses Zion on the forehead.

Jewels laughs, and says, "Whatever, Tony."

He bursts into laughter, kisses Jewels' cheek, and says, "I love you too baby."

They finish their shopping. Tony drives pass the house he messaged Jewels earlier and she likes it even more. They drive pass a few more houses and notices a new housing development, where the model house is being built. They stop and notates that the homes are starting at three hundred thousand dollars. They add this development to their home prospects.

They finally make it home. Jewels finishes dinner as Tony showers. Tony ends his shower as Jewels completes dinner and he prepares Zion for bed while Jewels bathe.

CHAPTER SEVEN

AT HOME MOM, DAD'S WORK VISIT

Zion is quickly approaching his one year anniversary of being on Earth. Tony has decided to finally pick up the full time position at his job, because he is looking to purchase a new home for his family as soon as possible. One day, it is a bright and sunny day filled with singing birds all over the neighborhood. It is so bright that the house is shining as though the sun is sitting in the living room's ceiling. The air condition has been running non stop and their ceiling fans are in constant rotation. Her roses, she has by the window, are seemingly dancing to all the sunlight shining on them.

Jewels is happy and singing, because Tony and her parents are now okay with her staying home while Tony is at work. She cannot stop singing Kirk Franklin's Smile, as she does chores around their house. She adds in a few more feel good tunes as well as she gets their house in order. She has it smelling lemony fresh, with a hint of lavender.

As she prepares dinner she watches their son in his designated play area. She watches as he continues to try and stand as long as he possibly can. At one point she laughs because she sees him lie on his back. While he is down there, he seems to try and stretch his legs as though he is prepping them to stand again. She thinks to herself, "Not only does he looks like Tony but he seems to act like him already, just full of determination", she smiles thinking of this as she continues their meal.

She has an alphabet recording playing that he pretends to listen to at times. Every time the recording stops, he claps twice but continues to work on his standing.

He has a sketch book sitting in there that Tony bought. She laughed hysterically at this while saying, "Baby, he cannot even hold a pencil yet so why are you getting this?"

Laughing he responded, "Baby I know, but I know he will be an artist like his dad. So I want him to start looking at this stuff now, you know, getting him ready."

She watches him as he crawls over the tablet and looks at it, trying his best to figure out what it is. She continues to prepare dinner, which includes; red beans and rice, buttered biscuits, and chicken, seasoned with basil, curry, and lemon pepper. As she continues, she glances at Zion and sees him take his first step. Screaming in shock and excitement, she grabs her cell phone to record him saying,

"Zion! Zion, you are stepping. Wow you are just ten months, your dad is going to be so happy." She smiles and starts chanting, "Go Zion. Step baby, because you are a great little prince."

As she records him walking and him laughing at her screams, she decides to surprise Tony at work. She wants to show him his son's accomplishment. She decides to make a crock pot meal, so the dinner can cook while she and Zion are out. The red beans and rice are done. She puts the chicken in the crock pot and will bake the biscuits when she comes back.

She takes her chicken breast, she has already cleaned and places them in the crock pot. She adds the seasoning, of lemon pepper, basil, and curry and lets the chicken cook. She decides to make lemon aide before she leaves so it can begin to cool.

She finally makes sure Zion is not wet. Packs his diaper bag. Makes sure her home is secure, picks up Zion, and begins the journey to Tony's job. As she drives she plays a number counting recording and sings along with it as she glances at Zion through the rear-view mirror.

Once there, she decides to surprise him. As she enters she puts her finger over her mouth, asking his co-workers and the receptionist not to say anything. As she approaches, she sees Tony standing to his desk talking to a woman. She stops in her tracks and watches. She notices Tony looks annoyed, but the woman is very flirtatious. She cannot stop laughing and she continuously places her hand on her chest with every laugh. Jewels sees Tony shake his head a few times, while resting his left hand under his chin which shows his wedding band.

The woman in his office continues to laugh and flirt. At one point, Jewels tilts her head and places one hand on her hip when she sees the woman touch Tony's arm and her chest at the same time while laughing. Tony moves his arm and looks at her with a face, saying, 'stop touching me'. She seemingly gets the message, because she stops.

As she continues to watch, one of his co-workers passes her and whispers, "She's our new boss."

Jewels nods and shrugs her shoulders to this, but says, "Thanks for informing me."

Not caring who she is, Jewels continues to look on. Finally, Tony looks out of his office's window and smiles joyfully when he sees Jewels and Zion. Jewels can tell he looks at his boss and asks if they are done. His boss finally leaves, but first, she tries to hug him, but Tony extends his hand for a handshake.

As she leaves, Jewels walks to his office shaking her head. As she enters, he closes his office's door and closes the blinds to the window then gives Jewels a huge hug but she does not hug him back. He steps back and asks, "Baby what's wrong?"

She whispers while squinting her eyes, "What was she doing in here and why did she keep touching you?"

Looking shocked at her questions, he picks up Zion, kisses him, and walks to his desk. Holding her head back, because he did not answer right away she sees him take out a note pad and pencil. He starts writing then hands her the note and it reads,

Baby, she is my new boss. You know there is not much privacy around here, so I am trying not to talk, but we can talk more at home. Are you saying I am cheating on you?

After she reads the note, she tilts her head, shrugs her shoulders, and asks with a straight face, "Are you?"

Shaking his head, he sits Zion back in his stroller, takes the note and shreds it. He stands Jewels up, sits in the seat, and guides Jewels to sit in his lap. With hurt in his eyes he whispers, "Baby no, why would you even think that? Baby, you are all I want and need, you know this."

Whispering back, she replies, "Yea, whatever, but you need to keep that woman up out your face. I don't care who she is."

Surrendering with his hands up, "I will do my best."

Still whispering, Jewels responds with a straight face, "Naw, you better just do it."

Laughing, "Baby you got it, but don't get mad when I am jobless."

"I won't, rather jobless than wifeless."

Smiling as he kisses her cheek, "You are right about that. I can find another job, but not another Jewels." He rubs her cheek, "I love you baby."

"I love you too."

They end that conversation and he continues in a regular voice, "But baby, what brings my two favorite people by today?"

Jewels stands and gets Zion, "Well we wanted to show you something. I caught your hardworking son doing this."

She stands him up so he can show off his skills. She takes a few steps back, smiles, and quietly claps as Zion stumbles to her, laughing with every step he takes. Seeing this, Tony smiles proudly and picks Zion up saying, "My boy, my boy is walking." He pinches and kisses his cheek, then stands him up again to let him walk some more.

They both quietly cheer him on as he continues to take steps. They watch him fall on his butt a few times. Each time, Jewels rushes to get him and Tony stops her saying, "No baby, let him get up on his own. He can do it. I don't want you to 'handicap' him."

She reluctantly stands back and watches as he rises to the occasion each time. Seeing this, she says to Tony, "You know naming him Samson was right because your son is pretty strong. I was holding him talking to Mrs. Mary, and he gripped my necklaces and ripped them off my neck like it was nothing."

Laughing, "Yea baby, you remember how tight he gripped my finger at the hospital."

They both laugh and Zion wobbles to his mom. Jewels checks the time and says, "I think your son is hungry."

Tony walks to his window and makes sure his office blinds are completely closed then stands at the door because there are no locks on it and watches as Jewels breast feeds Zion. After he finishes, she burps him and sees that he went to sleep. She changes his diaper, looks up and sees Tony watching and smiling. After the changing he gives her some wipes and sanitizer for her hands, kisses her, and says, "Thank you baby."

"For what?"

"Just for being you."

She blushes and he kisses her again, then says, "But baby, I think it is time to stop breast feeding him."

Looking up at him, she asks, "Why do you think that?"

"Two reasons, he is now starting to walk and baby, I ain't gone lie, I miss them."

She bursts into laughter, "Not, 'Mr. basketball team', missing them? What will you do if I keep having babies?"

Laughing, he responds, "I will manage, one baby at a time, but Zion's time is up", he laughs as he kisses her cheek.

Nodding and laughing with him, "Baby, I was thinking it was time to stop too though."

He smiles at this as he checks his time, then says, "Baby, I am going to end my work day and come home with my babies. I was just sitting here working on some designs anyways before my boss walked in."

Smiling, she says, "Okay baby, and you know he usually sleeps a few hours after he eats too."

Grinning, he slaps her behind and says, "I know."

She laughs as he turns off his computer and office lights to leave. He stops at the front desk and tells the receptionist he is leaving for the day. Also, to let her know to place any messages for work on his desk and he will get to it tomorrow.

When they make it home, Tony places Zion in his crib as Jewels waits for him in their bedroom.

∽∽∽

A week later, Tony is out with Jewels' brother. They are at a local park playing a football game with some friends, mainly for exercise. They decide on a flag football game instead of tackle, to prevent any hospital visits. Their last tackle game resulted in Tony breaking his wrist. Which cost him a little income, but luckily he was still able to design work on the computer. Where he was able to use his non dominant hand to create designs.

As Jacob hands Tony his belt for his waist he says, "Lil' bro, I think we are sticking with these for now on. You know what happened last time."

Laughing while nodding in agreement, Tony replies, "Yea, my baby took good care of me though. We had just started dating too", he smiles thinking of this memory, "my baby took off from work and everything. Man I appreciated her so much for that. My momma kept calling and I'm like, 'Ma I am good. Stay home, my baby here with me'."

Laughing at this, Jacob says, "Yea man, I remember. She calling me talking about, 'Jacob, how y'all let this happen? You know that is how he earns a living? He needs his arm'."

They all laugh at this memory and continue to prepare for their game.

Tony and Jacob are on opposing teams, but do not take it light on one another and play as well as they normally would. The other team members include classmates from their high school and old friends they grew up with. Some played college football and are now coaching high school teams.

Their game has brought on some watchers who are enjoying every minute of it. Some of them cheer on both teams in laughter. With Jacob's team scoring the final touchdown. They end their game with Jacob's team as the victors, happy and feeling good from a nice workout. After the game, Tony and Jacob talk a little while still at the park. They watch as parents and coaches arrive to start football practice for the boys who are participating this season.

Tony looks at Jacob and asks, "Why aren't you coaching this season?"

"Scheduling. I will not be able to dedicate the time needed. We are still signing your nephew up after his physical for pee wee football."

Nodding, "I was wondering when he would start playing. I know he will be as good as you too."

"Better, I hope." He laughs and continues, "Speaking of sons, Tony, how is parenthood and married life treating you? You and my sis has been married two years now, right?"

Smiling thinking of his family, he responds, "Man, bro, great and yea, two years. I still can't believe my baby is my wife now. I look at her sometimes and just think about our childhood. She thinks I am joking when I tell her I knew she was my wife when I first saw her at eight. And Zion, man, I just look at both of them and count my blessings."

Jacob smiles hearing this as Tony continues, "Did I ever thank you?"

"For what", Jacob asks?

"For talking to Jewels when she was still in D.C.. She said that talk helped her realize how much she missed me and us, man thank-you."

"Man, you do not have to thank me for that. I was just being a big brother. You know she can be a little stubborn sometimes, but I am always going to give her the facts even if she don't like it. Tony it was written all over her that she still liked you", he looks at Tony, sees him cheesing to this statement, and laughs at him then continues, "but she was to stubborn to believe it. When y'all first broke up, I really thought she was done with you. But when she came to get me from the airport and your name came up, I saw it all over her. I didn't say anything until the next day when I took her to lunch", laughing, he continues, "but speaking of D.C., is Jesse still a problem?"

Still smiling from hearing the first part, Tony responds, "Yea man, before I left for Cali I saw it." He laughs at that, stops, and says, "He has not tried anything, but I am still watchful. I know he still likes my baby and I do not know what he is capable of. Jewels says he was never violent, but I do not care, I do not trust him. But I am more comfortable with her at home while I am at work now. All our neighbors know too."

He becomes quiet and shakes his head, Jacob asks, "What's up? Why you looking like that?"

"Man speaking of him made me remember something. Do you know your sister thought I was not only cheating on her, but with my new boss? Man,----", he pauses and waves at some people who passes them to sign their children in to begin football practice, and continues, "Maaaannnn, Jacob, it hurt so bad when she asked me that because she knows how much I love her. I know what happened in the past, but she knows the circumstances around that. I was not mad at her for asking either, but it hurt."

He looks at her brother who is looking to the sky shaking his head, and continues, "I understand, don't get me wrong. When we first got back together we talked about it. I mean a real talk too. I wanted to make sure we both were pass it in a way. I didn't want it to cloud our relationship. She told me how it did affect her, maaannn bro, it hit hard listening to her too. Like, me, of all the people is responsible for this? My job was always to make her smile and I messed up my perfect record."

Shaking his head at himself, he continues, "She told me how it hurt. How there were times she needed something done and her first instinct was to call me. But as she dialed she would remember that she was done with me and hang up then figure out how to do it herself. I am dropping my head, so disappointed in myself but telling her, 'You know I would have came'. She said she knew, but just did not want me there."

He shakes his head, and continues, "She really let it all out too. She told me whenever I touched her, her skin crawled. That is why she did not want me hugging her." He shakes his head at himself and repeats, "She said her skin crawled Jacob. Saying it did because all she could think of was me touching another woman. Man it was a hard pill to swallow, but I did understand, because if she cheated I would not touch her for a minute too", he laughs and looks at Jacob who laughs too.

Jacob finally says, "Man, I get it Tony. My wife and I been married a decade and to this day, when we are out and a woman stares at me she asks, 'Are you sexing her'? I am starting to think it is something she will never fully get pass. She does not hold it over me or hold grudges, but I can tell it is something she will never forget."

Shaking his head, "Man, I think you are right. Jewels doesn't either." Smiling, he continues, "You know I love my baby though, even with her accusations." Laughing a little, he continues, "Man your sister even looked at me and said, 'Tony, that belonged to me, but you allowed another woman access and it was just to much for me'. I am looking at my baby, like dang, just like that, like I am a piece of meat? She did laugh and assured me it was not meant that way."

They laugh hysterically at this and Jacob says, "Dang, my baby sis a little possessive. I didn't know."

They both laugh, and Tony says, "Yea, she is a little. I love her though."

Jacob then asks, "Hey I keep forgetting to ask this, but what did you whisper to Tika that day we were at your place? I mean, she hopped up, ain't even say bye, and stormed out."

Tony laughs and says, "Bro, I thanked her for stopping by but I told her I need you to leave because I need to check on my baby."

"Dang Tony. You said it like that. I am shocked she did not key your car when she left."

He looks at Jacob with a serious face and says, "Man she knew what was up. I talked about Jewels constantly to her. Before she came inside I told her Jewels was there, but she came in anyways. She dumped me in high school because of my baby, so she knew what the deal was."

They laugh hysterically again and decide to watch a little bit of the childrens' practice before they finally leave. As they watch, some of the parents walk over to them. They notice, they are old high school teammates and they begin to chat. The parents point to their children as Jacob and Tony pulls out their cell phones to show them their children. Some of the moms join them as the parents stay to monitor practice. Not comfortable with the conversation, both Jacob and Tony finally leaves.

Shaking his head as they walk to their cars, Tony says, "What is up with some of these women? It is like some of them are forever throwing themselves at men, married or not."

Laughing at him, Jacob says, "Lil' bro, that is how temptation works. Just make sure you do your part and move out of the way."

"You got that right."

They give each other a pound, then leaves.

A few days pass, Tony and Jewels are out on their monthly date night. They have ordered a few different chicken wing flavors, from barbecue, buffalo, sweet and tangy, and fried. They sit the baskets of chicken wings in the center of the table so they can share in them as they please. They also order onion rings with peach tea as her drink and black tea as his.

While eating at Jewels' favorite restaurant on the beach, Tyrone's, Tony asks about her friend Justice.

"Baby, how is your friend doing, you know the one whose wedding we attended?"

Shaking her head, "Not good Tony. I talked to her a couple of weeks ago and she told me there is a warrant for her husband's arrest as a suspect in her cousin's murder."

Looking shocked, he shakes his head in disbelief, and she continues, "I know Kellie went to visit her, but she never gave me an update."

Shaking his head, "I am not surprised. And speaking of her, you know I ran into Brandon the other day and he told me they are not together any more."

Jewels drops her mouth and says, "What!? I had no clue, but did he say why? How long have they been broken up?"

Looking at her with a straight face he says, "He caught her with another man", he claps with each word he says as he continues, "in their bed Jewels." He stops clapping and says, "Baby I am still surprise he didn't catch a charge that day! In their bed Jewels. I told you she is trifling, I do not trust her at all baby. She will probably bring a man around you she knows is lusting after you and risk our family." Shaking his head, he continues, "I think he said it has been a month, but she has not been interrupting us so I bet she has another man already. Baby, you really need to set some boundary rules with her. I know we all grew up together, but just as she likes spending alone time with her man with no interruptions, I love doing the same with you. She don't even call before she stops by."

"Baby I have and I think she has listened." Jewels sits back and tilts her head, while saying, " Annnnndddd, whatever Tony, you know I do not even get down like that."

Laughing, he responds, "Baby I know, but I am talking about my freedom."

She drops her head in laughter and says, "Baby no, we need you home."

He smiles and nods in agreement, "But Jewels, when he told me I looked at him like I am not surprised. You knew who she was. We all grew up together and you saw how she got down. I know he went to a different high school, but he knew the stories."

Trying to defend Kellie, Jewels says, "But baby, they were together for eight years and he did not marry her. I guess she got tired of waiting."

Smirking, while looking at her, "Naw, your friend is just trifling and no man in their right mind will wife her unless she does a one eighty. All these hotels in Jacksonville and she chooses their bed. Baby, I walked around with your ring for four years, just scared to ask. I didn't think you were ready, but I knew I was going to ask. It def does not take nearly a decade. He was not going to ask, so you are somewhat right, but your friend is trifling." He laughs, "But I did tell him, that is what you get for allowing that extra woman in y'all's bedroom. He thought he was winning the lottery when she asked for a threesome."

Jewels drops her mouth and says, "Tony, you had my ring for four years!?!?!? I had no clue you hid it that long, but a threesome, wow!?"

Smiling, he responds, "Yea baby, I was walking around with it trying to build up the courage. You know I was ready to be your husband from day one." He laughs at himself and blows her a kiss then says, "But baby you didn't know about the threesome? You mean, your friend kept that from you?" Shaking his head while laughing, "I do not know how them dudes enjoy that, especially with your girl? The only person I want kissing and caressing you is me."

"No, I had no clue. I am glad I didn't though and I agree with you! It took me three years to get pass you touching another woman while we were together, but the same bed, oh heeeeeeeck NO! Especially one touching me, I am not into that. To each their own though", she laughs and shakes her head at this.

He nods in agreement with a smile and continues to eat. He takes a sip of his drink and says, "Baby, are you ready to get back to planning our wedding? I know giving birth to Zion threw us off a little."

"I am and I actually have. I was going to talk to you about it, but you seem tired when you come home from work so I don't bother you about it. I have been talking to Zee about it though and she knows I want her here for it."

Smiling, "Baby you know you can't bother me. I can talk whenever. Do you want a planner?"

She smiles hearing this and says, "No, but do you have any suggestions?"

"Baby, you know I want it on our childhood block. The first place I laid eyes on my baby, my love. When we set a date I will get the permit from the county to block off the road for the weekend and start setting up. I just want it to be a joyful occasion, with our family and friends. Just all of us having a good time like we did growing up."

Smiling, she responds, "I agree Tony. It really does not have to be traditional to me either. I just really want to have fun and celebrate our union with those we know who loves us. I am actually thinking of a yellow dress and not white. Zee is against it, but I think I am going with it."

"It sounds good to me baby. Wear what you want and speaking of attire, you know I have decided to stop getting tape ups and edging my face like I usually do. I am going to keep it groomed, but cutout the other stuff. I am glad, I finally Loc'ed my hair too."

"Baby, you know you are handsome and do not need to do all that anyways, but what made you decide on this?'

Smiling with cockiness, he jokingly responds, "Thank you baby." He rubs his beard and laughs, "I knew all this sexiness pulled you. I used to see you looking at me growing up", he laughs and blows her a kiss.

Laughing too, Jewels replies, "Whatever, cocky man."

Still laughing, he continues, "But baby, my dad been told me to stop, but you know I study the Word more and some of what I have read has prompted me to do this. We are raising Zion now, you know, I want to be the best example of a man he sees. I already see him trying to copy me. I had him on the pot the other day and had to go myself. Do you know your son stood up and tried to go like me? Made a huge mess and all I could do was laugh."

Laughing hysterically, "Where was I", Jewels asks?

"I think you went to the grocery store. And baby you know every time I am out, if I see flowers I am getting you some. If I have him, he always points to flowers when he sees them now, smiling too Jewels."

Smiling, "Awwwwweeeee, but he does not do that with me. He plays in the dirt when I work in the garden. I wonder why? He barely pays attention to the flowers."

Laughing, "He is your son baby. I have no clue."

They laugh and begin to flirt with each other a little, while still conversing. They finally finish their meal and their waiter brings their bill. After Tony pays, they begin to leave to watch a movie from the early two thousand's, Love and Basketball.

As they pass a table on their way out, Jewels notices Kellie is there and stops to greet her. Kellie seems nervous and a little afraid. She barely speaks to Tony, but Jewels says, "Kellie. Hey, how are you? I haven't spoken with you in a few weeks."

Nervously speaking, she responds, "Hey Jewels", she waves at Tony and continues, "I have been a little busy and had some changes. But I am fine."

Jewels nods, then says, "Oh, I understand, but I see an extra cup and assume you are on a date so I will talk to you later. Enjoy your night."

Kellie says nothing, but waves bye. As Tony and Jewels walk off, they hear a male's voice say to Kellie, "Sorry about that, that was my son calling."

Thinking she recognizes the voice, Jewels turns to look at the man, who quickly says, "Jewels is that you?"

The man tries to give Jewels a hug, but Tony quickly pulls her behind him and says, "Jesse, didn't I tell you to never touch my wife again", he looks at Kellie as he says, "you with this dude now? You dating someone your friend dated? Dang, you just don't care, do you?"

Kellie says nothing, but looks a little ashamed when Jesse says, "I am not here to cause any problems. You and Jewels are together now and I am actually happy for you two. You have nothing to worry about."

With an angered face, Tony says, "Dude, I know I have nothing to worry about in that aspect so don't flatter yourself. But do not ever come around my wife. If you see her, turn your head and walk the opposite direction."

Jesse nods and takes a seat. Tony takes Jewels' hand to turn and leave. As they walk away, Jesse watches Jewels with a smile, until he cannot see her anymore. He tries to hide it, but Kellie catches it and asks, "Why are you looking at her like that? Do you still like her?"

Shaking his head no he says, "No I do not. It is just that we ended so abruptly, I never had a chance to say goodbye and seeing her just now brought that memory back. I did love her at one point, but I have moved on and happy she has too."

Kellie nods her head to this, but does not fully believe him either.

As they drive to a beach a county over to watch the movie Tony has on his Tablet, Tony says, "Dang baby, just when I started feeling comfortable leaving you and Zion at home he pops up. Baby, I know you do not want to, but you and Zion are going back to our parents' house while I am at work. I do not trust him. I know he is just using Kellie too, to try and get close to you. He's not slick. I wonder if he is who Brandon caught Kellie with." He pauses and looks at Jewels, "Baby, you okay? Why are you looking like that?"

"I am fine. I am just still in shock about what just happened. Like wow, first she came at you, now him. Wow, I am just a little shocked. But as I remember, she did talk about how sexy and fine he was when she first saw him."

Looking at her, while still trying to focus on the road, he says, "Jewels, I know you ain't just low key call this dude sexy while talking to me?"

In a shocked and apologetic voice, "No Tony, never. I was just remembering how she talked about him. You know I only have eyes for you."

She rubs his back and continues, "Baby, I just want to forget what just happened and continue to enjoy our night."

"Baby we are, but I know Jesse will be a problem. Kellie can play dumb all she wants, but Jesse still likes you. He couldn't even stop looking at you and I had you behind me."

Sitting in silence the rest of the drive, they make it to the beach. Tony first, surveys the area for any strange behavior. Everything looks okay. He notices they are not the only ones there and he sees a police car parked with the headlights on. He parks and sets up his Tablet to begin the movie. As he does this, Jewels reaches in the backseat for a blanket and some candy. He finally sits the Tablet on the car's dashboard and they begin the movie while snuggled under each other as the waves flow to soothe them.

During the middle of the movie Jewels realizes Tony has stopped caressing her arm and nibbling on her cheek. She looks at him and sees he is asleep. She laughs and lets him rest until the end of the movie.

They finish their night on a happy note. They pick up Zion from Tony's parents' house and drive home. After they put Zion to sleep, Tony and Jewels just holds each other until they fall asleep.

The next morning, as Jewels feeds Zion, Tony makes phone calls to their parents and Jacob to tell them what happened. He lets the Lowds know that Jewels and Zion will be coming to their house Monday morning. They agree, but is concerned as well.

As Tony talks to Jacob, Jacob asks, "When y'all gone let me spend some time with my nephew? Y'all always take him to his grandparents. I need to bond with my nephew too."

Laughing, Tony says, "Whenever y'all are ready for him. We did not know you were ready for him. I know you are usually busy and didn't want to bug you."

"I hear ya, but we are free next weekend. He can come over and spend the weekend with us. He and his cousins can get to know each other better."

"Okay bro, next weekend it is."

They end their call. Tony walks to Jewels and says, "Baby, Jacob is going to get Zion next weekend so we will have the weekend to ourselves", he smiles and kisses her cheek.

Smiling while nodding her head, she says, "Okay baby."

Later that day, they decide to take a walk around their neighborhood. Tony stops and plays a quick basketball game with some of the boys out playing, while some of the girls run over to Jewels to play with Zion.

As Tony plays and talks with them, he asks how school is going? Holding the basketball, Tony looks at them and asks, "How are y'all's grades looking?"

They all nod saying that they are good, Bernard adds, "Mr. Tony my grades are really good. Right now my GPA is 3.8, but they are really getting on my nerves with all this assessment testing for graduation. I am just ready to take it and move on. It is like their only focus."

Laughing, Tony responds, "Man, I remember those days and was ready to get it over with too", he looks at Lenny and notices he keeps looking at the girls who are with Jewels. Noticing this, Tony asks, "Which one of those girls you like Lenny?"

Laughing, Lenny responds, "I don't like none of 'em."

Smiling with laughter, Tony says, "Yes you do and I think it's Tisha."

He drops his head as Bernard and their other friends say, "He does like her, but she has a boyfriend so all he can do is look at her", they burst into laughter and jokingly point at their friend.

Another friend adds, "She used to like him in middle school, but Lenny thought she was to nerdy. Now he can't stop looking at her."

They all burst into laughter with Lenny dropping his head again.

Tony cuts in and says, "Well, you need to respect her relationship and if she becomes single you better approach because you really like her."

Lenny looks up and asks, "How you know that Mr. Tony?"

"I used to look at Jewels like that growing up." He looks at her talking to the girls and continues, "Dang, I still look at her like that and you see she is my wife now. I know what's up."

Lenny laughs as he drops his head once more. He looks back up and says, "I respect her relationship. She is still my friend too, but when she finally dumps him I am approaching. This clown she is with don't deserve to be with her anyways. He tried to fight me one day because I bought her lunch in the snack line because she forgot her lunch money. And he got real mad when I told him, 'If you bought it I would not have the opportunity to so step your game up. We grew up together and if my friend is hungry and I can feed her I will'."

Shaking his head in laughter, "Dang man, I think y'all been around me to long. I would have done that in high school with Jewels too. None of her boyfriends liked me, but y'all pops ain't with it either though", he laughs and shoots a few more shots.

He laughs harder as he sees the boys nod in agreement with him.

As Jewels continues talking with the girls, she notices one of the girls, who Jewels tutored before, keeps looking at Tony. Jewels jokingly says to her, "I see you are still crushing on him."

The girl drops her head and blushes, then says, "No ma'am."

"It is okay baby. You just have a school girl crush, but you have good taste too", Jewels laughs.

One of the other girls say, "Mrs. Jewels, she has always had a crush on him too. We will try and double dutch but she sees Mr. Tony and starts smiling. She would interrupt our whole rhythm. And she now has a boyfriend at our high school."

In a shocked voice, Jewels asks, "What!? I did not know you were allowed to date and now you also you have a boyfriend. What is his name? What are his future plans? Are you kissing, because my momma and her friends always told me, 'You can get pregnant from kissing'."

Laughing at her last statement, Tisha says, "How can you get pregnant from kissing, but my parents have met him and my dad does not want me dating? He says ninth grade is to young, but he and my mom came to a compromise. I think my mom reminded him, how she was not able to date, but they snuck around with each other and she did not want me sneaking. And his name is Russell."

Laughing, "I asked the same question to them. Never got an answer, but I agree with your mom."

They all laugh and notices Zion fell asleep. They talk a little longer with Jewels and sees Tony coming, so the girls finally run off to finish practicing cheers. They run back over to show Jewels and Tony one of their cheers. They are both truly impressed with their skills. All their toe touches are high and well executed with pointed toes. Their voices are loud and clear, where every word they shout is clearly heard. They show off a few more of their jump skills, back flips, and splits before leaving.

When they finish, Tony looks at Jewels and says, "Baby, didn't you write that cheer?"

"Yep, that is one I wrote. To this day, I do not think those girls know they were performing cheers I wrote. You know they thought I was just quiet, shy, and nerdy, but their coach came to me for help. I was not into that stuff at that time."

She laughs, as he smiles, and continues, "Yea my 'nerdiness' and shyness is a huge reason your little high school ex and her friends could not understand why you and I were so close. You know, they were prom queen types, I wasn't into that. I was in the book club and student government, but I had skills too, just lost interest in high school. And you, on the other hand, you played almost every sport and was very popular. So they just could not understand our friendship."

Laughing, he responds, "Baby, you know I couldn't care less what others think. I am my own man, but they were jealous. Especially when I used to get your lunch or take you home." Laughing at the memories, he continues, "I remember your lil' corny boyfriend getting heated because I made you smile and he couldn't. Baby, I laughed so hard, after I whispered in your ear as I passed you and kept walking when I saw you smile. His whole face dropped."

Dropping her head in laughter, "Yea baby, you always know how to put a smile on my face, even if I do not want to." Laughing some more, "Tony he asked me for like for a week, repeatedly, what did you say, but I never told him."

Laughing harder, Tony says, "He was trying to steal my technique, but he needed to learn his own. Learn your lady", he laughs some more, "he would've been real mad if you would've told him. Just two words, I still remember, 'Smile beautiful', and the blush appeared."

Laughing hard, she says while patting Tony's back, "Yea, only you could do that with those words though. I knew it was genuine."

"It was baby."

Laughing, Tony and Jewels finally continue their walk. As they walk Jewels says, "You know, lil' Tisha has a crush on you?"

Shaking his head filled with laughter, "No I did not, but I think Lenny likes her. He could barely play trying not to look at her. You know I had to mess with him", he laughs some more.

Laughing with him, Jewels says, "Yes baby, she does. I saw it a few years ago. After we broke up. Her mom asked me to tutor her in Algebra, and I was shocked because she never made lower than a B in math. But one day I was tutoring her and you stopped by. We were on the patio, and you know, during that time I would stop you in my entryway. As I am talking to you and dodging your hugs, she started walking up their showing her answers.

Before you stopped by, she acted like she was having a hard time with this equation. But as I am talking to you, she all of a sudden got it and made it her business to keep coming to me to show me each answer. I noticed she kept looking at you each time so I just sat back and observed. Walked you to my kitchen where she could see you from the patio, and was like, yep, she is crushing on Mr. Tony, because she stop coming to show me her answers."

She laughs and continues, "Baby, I had to sit her down though, and let her know my time is valuable. I have no problem tutoring you if you need it, but not just for you to come over to see Mr. Tony. She apologized and showed me her A grade when the semester ended." Bursting into laughter, she asks, "Tony what is it about you? You have girls around here crushing and women are continuously lusting."

He laughs, shrugs his shoulders, and says, "Baby, I have no clue. I am just me, who only wants you. You sexy too baby", he smiles and hugs her.

Laughing she continues, "Yea, and why was your boss in your office grinning like she won the lottery? I didn't forget."

Shaking his head, "Baby, I am still not clear. I am sitting to my desk working on this logo design and she walks in. I spoke, using her last name and she turned that into a convo saying how she prefers for me to call her Taylor. I told her, 'No, I am not comfortable with that'. She goes on and on, still trying to get me to call her Taylor. She even brought up how she knows we called our last boss by his first name.

Then she started low key flirting. I'm thinking, 'Will this female get out my office'. I stop her and show her the picture of us and the picture I have of you on my desk. She couldn't care less. Baby I was so happy when I looked out the window and saw y'all so she can leave my office and she has a husband!"

Shaking her head, "Yea, you better make sure you keep her out of your face. I do not deal with disrespect to well and she is beyond disrespectful. She didn't even speak when she passed me."

He hugs her from behind, kisses her cheek, and says, "Baby I am, but you know I don't want no one but you." He continues to hug her from behind as they continue to walk and nibbles on her cheek while attempting to sing, If I Ever Fall In Love by Shai. Jewels blushes the whole time at his off key singing, while Zion sleeps.

CHAPTER EIGHT

THE REACH OUT

On a Saturday afternoon, Tony and Jewels decide to take a trip to their local outlet center. This day is cloudy, but it is hot. Though the sky is filled with clouds, there is no signs that rain will come. Before they leave, Tony washes one of their cars as he waits for their lawn crew to finish. He truly takes his time cleaning the car. He cleans it just as well as Jewels cleans Zion. Watching him as he cleans, Jewels says to him,

"Baby, I am a little jealous. You are treating this car like it is your woman. I mean, you are taking your time making sure it is shining and scratch free."

Smiling, while listening to Jewels, he says, "Don't be, I always take my time with you."

She laughs, as he continues, "But you know we gotta ride in style."

Still laughing, she says, "Whatever Tony", she stops and listens. She hears Zion cry and walk inside to check on him with Tony following. They see he has awaken and just needs to see his parents' faces. Tony picks him up and plays with him. He walks outside with him and sits in the car. While holding him and watching the boys as they finish the yard work, he turns on the radio then stands Zion up to playfully dance with him. Zion laughs the whole time as he tries to do a two step his dad is guiding him to do. As they are outside, Jewels remains in and puts some slices of chocolate cake on a plate she made two days ago. She packs it for the yard workers and cuts an extra slice for herself to eat.

As she begins to eat her slice, Tony walks in holding Zion and helps her. He kisses her cheek and says, "Baby this cake is delicious. I think this is your best one yet. Almost as good as your momma's."

"Thanks, but just almost? I thought I had made it to her level by now?"

"Baby you almost there, but you know your momma went to school for this. I ain't gone lie to you. But it is delicious baby."

Laughing, she responds, "I appreciate your honesty, but how is the yard looking?"

Kissing her again, "They are finishing up now. That is why I came in, to get their payment and I know you were packing them something."

"Okay. I will take a shower then we can head to the mall."

"Baby, I have to take one too. So I'ma join you after I pay them."

"Well, who is going to keep an eye on Zion?"

"The play pen. He can't get out."

She laughs and heads to the shower, but she beats Tony before he joins. As he sees her getting dressed, he says, "Dang, Mrs. Dubois came over and started talking and I missed our shower."

Laughing, "Yep, but we will have this coming weekend to ourselves. Is Mrs. Dubois okay?"

"Yea, I know, but she is. She was just checking on us. Asking if we needed anything and seeing if Jesse is still a problem. You know she is like the entire neighborhood watch." Laughing at this, he continues, "Baby she wouldn't stop talking. I kept looking back at the house thinking, 'Dang, I am going to miss Jewels, come on Mrs. Dubois, get it out. I am trying to get to my baby'."

Laughing, Jewels pinches his cheek saying, "Baby, I know." She stops and checks herself in the mirror, then asks Tony, "Baby are these jeans to tight? I am wearing this shirt with it", she shows him a white fitted tee shirt.

He examines her by holding her waist, twirls her around, and says, "No baby. They are fitting just right. You look just as delicious as your cake tastes."

"Thanks, what are you wearing? I will lay it out for you."

"The blue jeans you bought me last month and whatever shirt you get", he laughs, "and thanks baby."

"You are welcome", he kisses her and heads to the shower.

As he showers, she cleans Zion and dresses him for their outing.

An hour and a half later, they make it to their local shopping center and it is pretty packed. It has not been busy like this in years. More people have been indulging in online shopping. Today, everyone has decided to get some fresh air and shop the old way.

This center is where there childhood friends own a shoe store. Their store sales athletic shoes, jerseys, and athletic shorts. While there, they decide to buy shoes for all of themselves. While looking around at the shoes, on this cloudy day, an employee walks out to assist them. He is no more than fifteen years old, but is quite the polite gentleman. He engages in a short conversation with Tony, while giving him some advice on the best shoes for Zion. Taking his advice, they decide to get the pair he suggests. They tell him that they are still looking and will let him know when they are completely ready.

Jewels sees an all black pair of sneakers for Zion, that are apart of the series the employee suggested as Tony finds himself an all white pair. He looks at Jewels and asks, "Baby, you don't see anything?"

"No, I do not. I will just let my boys shoe shop today."

"Okay baby, let me know if you change your mind." He walks over, kisses her cheek, and whispers in her ear, "And Jewels, you mean your boy. I ain't been a boy in nearly two decades", he laughs and playfully pinches her cheek.

Jewels laughs and shakes her head. They call the employee over and shows him the shoes they want.

As they wait on the employee to bring their shoes, their childhood friend, who is the co-owner, walks in. He immediately sees Tony and Jewels, grins, and says, "Lil' Tone and Ju' Ju', what's up? I haven't seen y'all in a minute and I am still waiting on my wedding invitation."

As they stand to greet him, Tony says, "Hey Kenneth", while shaking his hand. "Yea man. We have been busy. We had some changes, but we have made online orders. You know we only get our shoes from you."

Kenneth nods as he hugs Jewels, who smiles while hugging him back. Tony clears his throat and says, "Alright Kenneth, you hugging my baby to long."

Kenneth and Jewels bursts into laughter as Kenneth responds, "Well, I see not much has changed. You still don't want no one touching her. We friends too Tony."

Laughing, Tony responds, "Whatever man. I know y'all friends, still though, keep your hands to yourself."

They all laugh, as Jewels checks on Zion because he made a whining sound. As she picks him up, Kenneth gasps and says, "Man, is this y'all's son? No one told me you two had a child." Looking at him, he continues, "Tony he looks just like you too."

Kenneth holds him and asks, while playing with him, "What is his name?"

Smiling, Tony says, "Zion. Man, he is why you have not received an invite yet. When we found out he was coming things began to shift, but your invite coming."

As he continues to play with Zion, the employee walks out with their shoes and says, "Hey dad. I see you know our customers?"

Tony looks at the young teen and Kenneth then shockingly asks, "Dad? Kenneth, I did not know you had a child this old?"

Laughing, as he plays with Zion and pats his son on the back, "I did not either, until five years ago."

Tony nods as he waits for his son to walk to the cash register and whispers, "Do we know the mom?"

Nodding his head yes, Kenneth says, "His mom is Mona."

Looking shocked, Tony gives Jewels the payment method so he can converse with Kenneth more as she pays. As Jewels walks away with Zion, Tony whispers, "Mona? Man I did not know you two dated. I thought they moved to Georgia."

"Yea, her fam did, but when she graduated she attended college here. She came through looking over her old neighborhood and I saw her and hollered. It did not last long. I think her fam thought I was not good enough and she finally caved, but he made it first."

"Not good enough? Her dad has three different baby mommas and we all knew all her mom's children did not belong to him, but you were not good enough."

"My dad said the same. She even told me I was the best boyfriend she ever had, but she let them get in her head. I think it was really her mom though and sisters, her dad was cool and bros didn't care either way. Now when I get my son she flirts non stop, but I am a happily married man and do not want her. She missed out. I think her fam was stuck on that hard time we went through when my dad lost his job, because he became ill, but I was not even bothered. Her loss and my gain because I found my wife a few months later."

Shaking his head, listening to this, Tony says, "I think her mom was always like that too. I remember how she used to frown at us growing up."

Kenneth is about to say something else, but Jewels and his son walks up.

They talk a little longer as Kenneth gets to know Zion while Tony and Jewels gets to know his son.

After, they continue to walk the mall some. They pass a clothing store, The Secret, and Jewels decides to go in to purchase a few scents along with maxi dresses. As she goes in, Tony says, "Me and Zion will be in the store next door."

They kiss and part ways. Nearly thirty minutes later, Jewels walks to the store next to her looking for Tony but does not see him. So she walks out, has a seat by a play area, and calls him. He does not answer, but calls back, "Hey baby, you ready?"

"Yes, but where are you? I walked in the store you said you will be in and did not see you."

By this time, he is standing behind her and says, "I had to change Zion's diaper."

They finally leave the mall, buys dinner, and travels home. Jewels prepares Zion for bed then feeds him. As she does this, Tony prepares dinner for them. Zion is wide awake, so they give him some learning toys to play with as they eat. After, they begin to clean the kitchen, Jewels says, "Baby, I got it. Take your shower."

He kisses her cheek, "Thank you baby."

After he showers, he sees Jewels playing with Zion. He walks over and gets him so Jewels can bathe. After her bath, she walks out smelling like coconuts, and sees Tony walking back and forth rocking Zion while telling him the tale of Samson. Jewels walks over and sees that Zion is asleep. She kisses his cheek as Tony kisses her forehead then takes Zion to his room.

When he comes back, he sees Jewels sitting on the couch watching an old comedy special they watched as kids. He hears her laughing hysterically at the comedian and watches some of his routine with her. He laughs too while massaging her shoulders. When a commercial comes on he stands in front of her, blocking her view. Jewels laughs and asks, "Why are you blocking me?"

Laughing, he grins and says, "You know why."

Laughing while shaking her head, he stands her up and starts giving her loving smooches on her cheek. At one point he stops and holds a gold necklace with a heart pendant in front of her face saying, "Jewels, Zion and I bought this for you today while you were shopping for clothes. I know he popped your other ones, so we decided to start replacing them for his momma."

Grinning with shock, love, and appreciation, she says, "Tony, baby, thank you, but you do not have to keep buying me things. I appreciate you for you."

Laughing and kissing her forehead, "Baby I know, and I appreciate you too. This is one way I show it."

She constantly smiles as he places the necklace around her neck and continues to kiss her.

~~~~~~

A week passes and they take Zion to Jacob's house. Zion is happy to see his uncle and his cousins. He cannot stop smiling as Jacob plays with him. He continuously throws him in the air saying, "Hey, uncle's big boy. Are my sis and bro treating you good? You know, you can call your uncle if they don't. I got you nephew."

Listening to this, Tony, Jewels, and Jacob's wife cannot stop laughing. As they laugh, Jacob's children walk out. They hug Tony and Jewels then begins to play with Zion. As they play, Jacob, his wife, Tony, and Jewels talk. His wife looks at them and asks, "How have you two been doing?"

Smiling, Jewels responds, "Fine. How are you two, and my nieces and nephew?"

"We are fine", she looks at Jacob, "but your brother wants another child. I told him he has his boy and I have closed up shop."

Laughing listening to his wife, he says, "Yea sis, she will not give me another one. I am hurt."

His wife replies, "No you are not, those labor pains hurt. If you felt those pains you would stop at one."

Jewels laughs, but agrees, "Those pains are no joke. I understand you completely."

Laughing at them both, Jacob asks, "Well what do you two have planned this weekend since you are baby free?"

Tony says, "We are catching a movie when we leave here, but we plan to just 'chill' and 'relax' some."

Nodding with laughter, Jacob says, "I understand that."

As he nods, Tony says, "Did you know Kenneth and Mona has a fifteen year old son?"

Looking shocked, Jacob says, "What!? Who we grew up with? I always thought Mona's family thought they were to good for us. Well her dad was cool, but the rest was stuck up. I never thought Kenneth would not only date her, but she had his child. I know her mom hit the roof when she found out."

"I bet she did too. Growing up, Mona used to like me too. I used to tell her to leave me alone."

Shocked, Jewels says, "I did not know she crushed on you. Now I know why she came around me so much, she was trying to get close to you."

Laughing, Tony says, "It was not going to happen for many reasons. The only girl I wanted in that neighborhood was you, I did not like her family, and her attitude was too stuck up for me. If she did have a chance, she really messed up becoming your friend. I know she knew I liked you too." Laughing at himself, he continues, "I remember she thought she was the baddest girl in our neighborhood. I used look at her like, 'You alright. Not my taste, now stop trying."

Laughing, Jacob says, "Tony you just don't hold back do you?"

With a serious face, Tony responds, "Maaannn, life is to short to beat around the bush especially with those types. She really thought she was something special----", Zion walks to him and he stops talking. Picking him up he asks, "What's up lil' man? You tired?"

He lies his head on his dad's chest and Tony rocks him to sleep. After he falls asleep, they all talk a little more. Then Jacob's wife takes Zion and places him in his sleeping area. They move on to a new subject about parenting techniques.

Jacob then changes the subject and asks, "Are you two still looking to buy a new home?"

Tony says, "Yea, we need more space. I want at least four bedrooms, just in case we have more kids. I keep letting your sister know I can handle it financially. She thinks I'ma over work myself."

Jewels looks at Tony and says, "Baby, you know you are a hard worker. I just do not want you wearing yourself out and I do like to spend time with you."

He kisses her cheek, "Baby I know and I am not. You know Cali put us in a better financial position. And you def know, I will always have time for you, always baby."

Jacob finally says, "Well I was asking, because I was looking at the empty lot in our parents' neighborhood. You know the one that has been empty since we were kids. I have been talking to some people and am really thinking about purchasing it. I am thinking about putting three houses on it. Y'all think y'all will be okay moving there? I am trying to get Zee to move back home too, I think she is ready to come home."

Tony says, "Man, keep us posted and let us know. That sounds like a great idea. What do you think baby?"

Nodding her head, she says, "I agree."

They discuss that more then kisses Zion goodnight as he sleeps. Finally, Tony and Jewels leaves to catch a movie.

\\\

Nearly three months have passed since Jewels saw Kellie and Jesse. Jewels has blocked Kellie, but it does not stop her from coming to Jewels' house. Jewels ignores her and eventually one of her neighbors will ask Kellie to leave. One day while at her parents' home, she is out front playing with Zion. Her mom is inside cooking dinner for her home, Tony's and Jewels' home, the Ellison's home, and Jacob's. She is doing it with a smile and singing a melody of gospel tunes. Some of the artists include, Yolanda Adams, Tamela Mann, Marvin Sapp, and more. Sometimes she gets so loud and filled with Praise from her singing, Zion stops playing and dances to his grand mom's voice.

As she is outside with Zion, she helps him as he walks in circles for a moment trying to figure out what to get into. At some points he tries to dodge Jewels and run out of the yard. Each time, Jewels catches him and he laughs as though he is playing the best game ever created. As she plays with Zion, she sees Kellie pull up and quickly grabs Zion to go inside.

Kellie rushes out of her car and says, "Jewels please don't go in. Can we talk?"

She says nothing, but walks to the front door, calls her mom, and hands her Zion. Her mom waves at Kellie who waves back then walks back in to finish their meal. She places her grandson in a playpen, Tony and Jewels bought for each of their parents' home. As she sits her grandson in it, she says, "Sorry grandma's baby, but I have to put you in baby jail for thirty minutes so I can finish up this meal. I love you", she kisses him then continues cooking her meal.

While outside, Jewels looks to the sky for a moment. She finally stops, looks at Kellie, and annoyingly asks, "What?"

Crying, Kellie says, "I am sorry."

Rolling her eyes, Jewels responds, "For what? Kellie, this is the second man that I was attached to that you went after and you think I want an apology from you?"

Looking confused, Kellie asks, "What do you mean second?"

Shaking her head, Jewels sighs and says, "I know about you coming on to Tony in high school knowing how he felt about me, but you did not care. I gave you an excuse then because Tony and I were just friends then and I know you suffer from self esteem issues. But I no longer care. You seem to be trying to hurt me and I will not give you the chance anymore. I have a family to focus on now. So have fun with Jesse and let him know I do not want him, so do not come at me in any way."

Wiping tears, she says, "Jewels can I explain? I saw him at the reception and we became Friendbook friends. He started contacting me through Messeged and we decided to go out, it just happened."

Poking out her lips as she rests her eyeballs to the top of her eyelids, Jewels sarcastically responds, "So you mean to tell me, after I told you why we left the reception you thought becoming his Friendbook friend was appropriate? This is also, after, your requests he turned down when he and I were together. Yea I know about those, but now you think he wanted to be Friendbook friends with you solely because of you? You cannot be this delusional." Jewels laughs and continues, "But Kellie, I do not think you are hearing me correctly either. I do not care. Enjoy him now and cry later once you see he is only using you. Not my problem, but this friendship is over." Jewels sees Tony driving up and smiles. Looks at Kellie and says, "You need to leave, bye."

Kellie stares at her with shame in her eyes, when Tony walks up shaking his head. Kellie speaks to him, but he walks pass her. Hugs and kisses Jewels, then says, "Hey baby. You good?"

She kisses him back and says, "I am fine, just waiting on Kellie to leave my parents' property."

He kisses her again, then walks inside to thank and give her mom some, 'thank-you' cash for looking out for his family while he is at work. They always take the cash and spend it on Zion, buying things he does not need with a smile on their faces.

Kellie finally leaves feeling sad, disappointed, and ashamed. Tony, Jewels, and Zion sit outside and wait for the food to finish. Mrs. Lowd completes the meal and comes out to tell them. They go inside and make to- go plates, kisses Mrs. Lowd goodbye, and show their appreciation. Then they leave for home.

On the drive home, Tony asks, "Baby what did she want? Was she trying to apologize for her trifling behavior?"

Rolling her eyes, "You know she was. But Tony, I have had enough from her. This was the last straw and I let her know this friendship is over. So stop coming by our house and my parents'."

Looking annoyed, he responds, "What!? You mean to tell me out of all the stuff she has done interfering in our relationship, both as friends and a couple, you finally draw the line at Jesse? I can't believe this Jewels, do you still like him?"

"No", she says in a shocked voice. "I could not care less about him in that way. It is the fact that she knows what went down in Miami and how it has your alerts high, but yet she thinks it is okay to date him and go to one of my favorite restaurants at that. That was just the final straw, not the person, but the act. I have remained friends with her in spite of, because I know she lacks self esteem and I do love her as a friend. But I can no longer deal, her disrespect has finally hit the wall with me."

He begins to say something else, but checks his rear-view mirror and stops. He looks at Jewels, still a little mad, and begins to play an alphabet and number counting recording that they made for Zion to listen to, with Tupac's song Changes added as the background beat. Jewels looks in the backseat and sees that Zion is paying attention to them as though he understands the conversation being held. She blows him a kiss, then turns around and rides home in silence. Only the recording is playing. She tries to rub Tony's cheek at one point, but he moves his head and glances at her to stop. Jewels is taken aback by this gesture and folds her arms while shaking her head. Tony glances at her as she does this and shakes his too.

Once home, Tony places Zion in his playpen after giving him some of daddy's love. He then takes Jewels' hand and walks to their bedroom. They sit on the foot of their bed and Tony says in a low voice, "Jewels, baby, be real with me, do you still like him? I mean, out of all these years of Kellies disrespect and interference with us, you finally draw the line at this man. Why?"

Shaking her head, "Tony no! It is not the man but the act. Why are you even asking me this?" She drops her head, "Baby, it is just that, I know some things she has been through. She has experienced some serious stuff Tony. I was trying to be understanding of it, but I no longer can. She needs to get some help and refuses. I finally see she wants everyone unhappy like her and I am done. I pray she gets the help she needs because I do still love her."

Shaking his head as he looks and listens to Jewels, he responds, "Baby, I know you. You were with him for three years, sharing your body with him. You do not get pass stuff like that so quickly. And on top of that, I know he was not pleasing you correctly so I know you really liked him at one point Jewels. I am not saying you love or want him, but do you still like him in some way? And Jewels, you cannot save someone who does not want to be saved. We all have a story baby, why was hers so important that you were willing to risk us?"

Holding her forehead she responds, "Tony, no. I do not like him at all." Shaking her head in disbelief, she continues, "I can't believe you even think this. Do you remember me showing up at your doorstep? You knew it just was not to work on our friendship. Tony, I really missed you, I was ready to be back with you, Tony, YOU", still holding her forehead, she pauses.

Tony then says as he smiles, "Yea baby, part of me did know, but it wasn't confirmed until you left my patio."

As he talks, he notices Jewels' demeanor is a little off and asks, "Baby, what is it? What's wrong?"

Jewels shakes her head and continues, "Tony, do you remember the story of the little girl who was raped on our elementary school's playground?"

With a serious face, he responds, "Yea, I remember that. Our parents had the neighborhood locked down after that. I remember all the neighborhood dads walking the neighborhood constantly armed. They were ready for war after that, until the cops finally caught the rapist. They would not let us out of our yards to play. I remember they started blocking off streets to keep outsiders out and to determine if the rapist lived there, or came from somewhere else. Man, they had us living in a whole other universe until the rapist was caught." He looks at Jewels, "But baby, why did you ask me about that?"

Jewels says nothing, but shakes her head. Tony drops his and says, "Dang baby, was the little girl Kellie? Oh man. I never knew. Dang it explains a lot. Wow, dang, I am sorry for that."

Wiping a tear, she finally responds, "Yes, baby it was her. Baby she was just eleven and everything, but her physical life was taken in that moment. But that is why I put up with so much from her, but I can't no more baby."

Holding Jewels, he kisses her forehead and says, "I understand baby and I do pray she gets the help she needs." He kisses her forehead again, stops, and listens, then stands to walk to Zion. Jewels stands too and he says, "I got it baby, you had him all day. Rest."

She smiles at this and sits back on the bed. Tony comes back laughing and says, "Your son threw all his toys out of the playpen and is sitting there crying looking at them", he kisses her cheek and continues, "I have a feeling he is going to give us a lot of stories to tell."

They both laugh and Jewels asks, "Are you okay now Tony? I love you baby."

"Yea baby, I love you too. I just needed to be clear."

Jewels looks at him and says, "But, I do have a question."

"I am listening", he responds while rubbing her back.

Laughing, she asks, "Tony, why do you believe I was not being pleased correctly? I think this is like your second time alluding to this."

Laughing, he looks at her and asks, "Did I lie?"

Dropping her head she responds, "No, but how do you know? I do not talk about that stuff."

Pinching her cheek, "Baby, I know you. I heard it in your voice. I know the difference, just wasting all your time and energy with this dude when you had me ready to love you and love you correctly."

She laughs and he continues, "Baby, remember I realized that I was your first orgasm. I had to have a talk with you on that one though. Like, you mean to tell me, you laid down with your ex and he did not do his part? What did I tell you about that when I realized you were having sex? I know you remember our convo? You got this man seeing the heavens and you barely seeing the clouds. But knowing these clowns you dated he probably thought he was doing something", he laughs and rubs her cheek.

Laughing hard, Jewels responds, "You are a trip, but I do remember our convo. You got really real with me too. I am glad you did and gave me condoms and all."

Laughing as he rubs her cheek, he responds, "Of course. I had to make sure you knew to protect yourself. And to not trust or depend on him with it."

She laughs, "I appreciated your talk too, but it was also funny. The whole time I'm thinking, 'He really thinks he is my dad and not my friend'."

Laughing at her he says, "Whatever Jewels, I was being a friend and you know I always thought I was your man. You just didn't know."

Bursting into laughter, she checks her time and asks, "How was work Tony?"

"It was fine baby, not much happened. I am starting to get the feeling that no one likes our new boss though because she is to 'friendly' with married men. Baby, even with the clients. One client has already called the corporate office about her, like I am here for business and nothing else. I have a feeling she is not going to be there long."

He looks at Jewels and sees her shaking her head, "But baby I saw my old boss when I was out for lunch a few days ago. He told me how they wanted him to take a pay cut, he declined, and left. I do not blame him. Y'all want him to work the same workload, but cut his wage. I would've quit too. I remember when I talked to him about coming back. I told him how I want to, but I do not want to cut my Locs so I am looking at other places too.

Baby, he gave me the whole run down when he was off and told me all the steps I needed to take to keep my Locs. I was so thankful for his help, because he did not have to do that. Emailed me some paperwork and all. But he was always cool like that and he always had side hustles too, like me. My dad always told me to have more than one stream of income, especially now I have my babies to take care of. You know I love putting smiles on y'all's faces."

"Baby, I am glad you do, but you know I am not a material girl."

"I know Jewels, but I want to make sure you want for nothing either. You never ask for things, but it is just natural to me to give to you though baby, you know."

She kisses him, then they look at each other and runs to Zion. When they get there, they see he is sleep and Jewels says, "I know he was way to quiet and had to make sure he did not get out and doing something he should not be doing."

Tony laughs, looks at Jewels, and asks, "Baby you bathe him at your parents' house right?"

Jewels nods yes and he continues, "You fed him too, right?"

"Yes, Tony why are you asking me this?"

He looks at her, kisses her forehead, picks up Zion, and takes him to his crib. Comes back, picks up Jewels, and carries her to their room, "Tony, I have to finish the laundry."

Kissing her he stops, "Baby you are good. I will help do the laundry."

She smiles and says, "Alright baby", and kisses him back.

The next morning, Saturday, the sunlight wakes Jewels. She turns over and sees Tony is not in bed. She rises, and sees a small brown teddy bear sitting on her nightstand holding a purple tulip. She smiles as she gets the teddy bear and sees that it is sitting on a note. The note reads,

"Good morning baby, I decided to go old school and leave a note instead of text. I love you. I got Zion too. I am getting breakfast for us and I will ride him around a little. He woke me up at Seven and we decided to let you rest. Oh, I turned your phone volume on silent, so it will not disturb you, so turn it back it up when you wake. Oh, one more thing, your flowers are blooming beautifully, the tulip is from your garden."

She smiles as she reads the note, checks her time and sees that it is Nine Thirty in the morning. She talks to her Father before she exits their bed then walks to the bathroom to start her day.

Monday morning arrives. Jewels takes dirty laundry with her to her parents' home to complete a load. A load they were not able to complete during the weekend. As she goes through Tony's pants and jacket pockets, to make sure nothing is in them, she finds a business card in one of his blazers. She sits it to the side with the other things she found to throw in the trash.

After all of his clothes are loaded, she takes the pocket trash and walks towards the garbage.

As she walks, Zion runs to her and holds her leg, which causes the business card to drop. While asking Zion what he wants, she notices the name on the business card. She picks the card up, shaking her head, and it reads:

La'Tika Samuels

Janitorial Services

We cater to small and large businesses

Phone:9045556000   Fax:9045556001

Email: samuelsjan@services.com

Shaking her head some more as she reads the card, she sees what Zion wants. He wants nothing, but only for his mom to hold him. She walks to the front porch to hold him while kissing his forehead and singing the alphabet to him. Her dad walks out and says, "Jewels put him down. You are always holding him. I am surprised he started walking so early. He needs to get down, play, and get dirty. You are going to make him to soft."

Laughing at him as she kisses Zion's forehead, she responds, "Dad, I am not, but you are starting to sound like Tony. He just needed some of his momma's love because I have been in the wash room all morning."

Laughing at his daughter, he takes his grandson from her arms and walks to the park with him. After they leave, Jewels takes out the business card, takes a picture of it, and text messages it to Tony. He responds thirty minutes later,

"*Baby, why are you texting me this? I don't want her services.*"

"*<Rolls eyes>, whatever Tony. I can't believe you are even trying me like this.*"

"*Like what baby? What are you talking about?*"

"*I guess you are playing dumb Tony. I found this card in your blazer's pocket. Why do you have it?*"

"Baby, I do not know how it got there, but I never took a card from her. I do not even talk to her when they are here."

"???????????????????, What do you mean, when they are here???????"

"Baby, her cleaning service begin cleaning this building like a week ago. I did not know it was her cleaning service, but a few days ago she was here walking the building with the owners and my boss and that is when I realized her business had the contract to clean our building. I never took a business card from her or even held a conversation with her. She passed my office and waved. I threw my hand up and closed my office door."

"Whatever, why didn't you tell me?"

"I was, but forgot, it slipped my mind. Baby I do not want her and you know this."

"Whatever Tony."

"Come on baby, why are you acting like this?"

Jewels stops responding. An hour later he sends another text message.

"Baby, why did you stop responding?"

She ignores his text message so he calls a few minutes later. Jewels does not answer and sends him to her voicemail. Close to forty minutes later he is parking at her parents' curb. He gets out of their car looking at Jewels, but looks around for Zion also. As he begins to walk towards Jewels, she stands and walks inside her parents' home. Quickly following her, he takes her hand as she enters her childhood's bedroom and asks, "Baby, what is wrong?"

Jewels says nothing, but hands him the business card. He looks at it, then says, "Baby this is my first time seeing this card. I do not know how it got in my pocket."

"Whatever Tony. So it just magically appeared?"

"Jewels, baby, come on now. She must've put it there hoping you find it and act like this. You know I do not want her or any other woman, dang baby, you know I don't." Shaking his head at this moment, he continues, "Jewels I did not even touch her when she used to come to Cali, she tried to too, but I do not want her at all baby. "

Jewels says, "Whatever Tony", and tries to leave the room. He holds her arm and says,

"Jewels, you need to think clear. She had to do this on purpose, out of spite. Remember, I made her leave to comfort you. Baby, I love you and I only want you."

She says nothing, but he finally lets her go when he hears Zion's voice. He walks to them to greet his in-laws and kisses his son. He walks to the laundry room, where Jewels is and helps her with the rest of the clothes so they can travel home to finish talking.

After they finish the laundry, they make a to-go plate of food Mrs. Lowd cooked and travels home. Once home, they prepare Zion for bed, first starting with a bath. Tony feeds him and lies him down for bed. He waits for Jewels to join him in the dining room for dinner, but she never does. He walks the house looking for her. As he gets closer to their patio he hears Confessions Part I by Usher playing. He drops his head while shaking it as he hears this song play thinking, "Lord, Lord, my baby, Your child, really thinks I am creeping." He finally makes it to the patio and sees her eating her dinner while in deep thought.

He walks in the patio to talk to her, but she stands to leave. Holding her arm, she looks at him and says with a straight face, "Tony, let me go."

He does not, but asks, "Baby why are you acting like this?"

"Like what? Like my husband is cheating on me with his ex?"

"Baby, I am not. Why do you keep accusing me of this?"

She looks at him out of the side of her eyes, but says nothing. He is about to speak, but pauses for a second when he hears, A Thin Line Between Love and Hate, H-Town's version begin to play. He shakes his head again, thinking to himself, "Dang, my baby has a whole cheating playlist playing and I ain't even do anything."

As he holds her, he finally says, "Jewels, baby, I love you. I am not doing anything. Baby why don't you believe me?"

She looks at him with a straight face, and says again, "Tony, let me go."

He reluctantly does and she turns to walk away. He says, "Baby please don't walk away mad. Nothing is going on."

"I am not mad", she says as she continues to walk away.

He shakes his head while scratching it, as he watches her walk away. He turns the music off feeling disappointed, sad, and irritated when he notices the next song is, When A Woman's Fed Up by R. Kelly.

After they both shower and prepare for bed, Jewels looks at him and says, "You need to leave."

Looking confused at her, he asks, "What?"

"I said you need to leave?"

"This house?"

"Yes."

Shaking his head he says, "Baby, I know you are upset, but I am not leaving our home."

"Whatever Tony, you need to sleep on the couch then."

"Baby, I am not doing that either, especially over something that did not even happen. You are my wife. I take my vows seriously. I love you. You are just mad right now, but we cannot start this sleeping apart stuff, especially in anger baby. We can't start that baby. We can't go to sleep angry either baby. If we have to talk all night, so be it."

"Tony, I am not mad at you. Why do you always think it's that emotion?"

"Baby, that is what it feels like when you are not happy with me."

Shaking her head, but still not happy with him, they finally hug and lie down to sleep.

In the middle of the night, around Two, Tony rolls over and feels that Jewels is gone. He sits up and sees the bathroom lights are off. He quickly stands, searching their home making sure everything is okay. He checks on Zion, who is sleeping peacefully with a smile on his face. He then walks their home more looking for Jewels and sees her asleep on the living room's couch.

He shakes his head while looking at her. He turns the television off, but first notices, Waiting To Exhale, is playing. He stops the movie then joins Jewels on the couch. He lies behind her, kisses her forehead, and falls asleep.

Hours later, their alarms goes off at Five in the morning waking Jewels. A song by Tevin Campbell, Can We Talk, is the tune that wakes her. She stops the music, while her eyes are still closed, but soon wakes. She opens her eyes, but shakes her head when she sees Tony has her wrapped in his arms. She stands and wakes him by saying, "Tony! Tony! It is time to get up."

He wakes yawning and says, "Thank you baby."

Jewels says nothing, but walks to Zion's room who is still asleep. She walks to their bathroom and sees Tony is in there. She waits for him to finish before she enters. As he brushes his teeth, he looks out of the door for Jewels because she usually joins him in the bathroom to brush her teeth as well.

He sees her sitting on the bed waiting for him to finish and shakes his head. After he leaves the bathroom, Jewels enters and dodges him as he tries to kiss her cheek. He takes her arm and kisses her anyways saying, "Good morning baby, I love you."

Rolling her eyes, she responds, "Good morning Tony and I love you too."

He shakes his head as he smiles at Jewels and continues to get ready for work. After Jewels washes up and gets dressed for the day, she walks to Zion's room to wake him to get him ready. He is not there, but she hears Tony talking to him. She walks to the kitchen and sees that Tony has dressed him and is now feeding him. She walks over and kisses Zion's forehead, while saying, "Good morning my little Prince. I love you."

He smiles, while reaching for his mom to pick him up. She does, as Tony looks at her in disbelief because she is still ignoring him. After she lovingly plays with her son for a few minutes, she gives him back to Tony so she can prepare his lunch for work. As she walks to the refrigerator, he says, "Baby, I made my lunch. I packed Zion's bag too."

She says, "Thanks", and turns to leave the kitchen.

He follows her, while holding Zion and asks, "Baby, are you still upset?"

She looks at Zion and says nothing. Tony turns to sit Zion in his playpen, then walks back to Jewels, "Baby, are we starting our day like this? Nothing happened or is going on. Baby she is playing you. This is what she wants."

"Whatever Tony." She checks her time, and asks, "Are you ready to leave?"

Still in disbelief, he nods yes. They take a quiet ride to the Lowds' home. Tony walks them in and kisses them good bye. Jewels turns her head trying to avoid the kiss, but he gets one in anyways, and says, "Baby, I love you."

Rolling her eyes, she responds, "Yea, whatever, I love you as well."

He drops his head at her response, but kisses her forehead, then leaves for work.

As he sits at a stop sign that is in front of hlis parents' home, he sends his father a text message reading,

"Good morning dad. Are you up?"

He sits his cell phone down and continues to drive to work. As he travels his dad calls. Tony answers quickly,

"Hello", Tony says.

"Good morning son, I saw your text. Do you need anything?"

Sitting at a red light Tony responds, "Good morning dad. I need your advice."

"What is it? Is everything okay with you and Jewels?"

"No dad."

"What is wrong?"

Tony sighs, then says, "Dad, I just don't know what to do. My baby thinks I am cheating on her----."

His dad cuts in and asks, "Are you Tony?"

In a shocked voice, Tony responds, "Dad no! Why would you think I was? I love my baby. I don't want these women."

"Tony, I have to make sure so I can respond correctly. But why does she think you are cheating?"

Shaking his head, Tony responds, "Because Tika trifling behind put her business card in my pocket and Jewels found it. Dad I did not even know she did that. I do not even talk to her. Dad I just do not know what to do because Jewels really believes it. She even wanted me to leave our home last night. Dad, I'm hurting right now. I do not know if I am about to lose my baby over this and I ain't even do anything."

Listening attentively, his dad finally responds, "Tony, Jewels just has to calm down. You have cheated before and that is probably replaying in her mind now. When you talk to her you need to remember you are speaking with someone you did cheat on once, to help you better understand where she is coming from. You know Jewels loves you and I doubt she believes it, but her emotions are just taking over right now."

"Dad thanks. I just got to work so I'ma talk to you later. I love you. Give momma a kiss for me please."

"Alright son, I will talk to you later."

They both say goodbye and end their call.

Tony sits in the parking lot for a few minutes looking at pictures of him and Jewels. He calls his boss and tells her he will be late. She is okay with it. Tony leaves and drives back to the Lowds' home.

Jewels' parents are still asleep. She lets them know that she and Zion are there. Then, she decides to sit out front with Zion. As she sits out playing with him, Tony returns an hour later. Looking confused, she asks as he exits the vehicle, "Why aren't you at work?"

He walks up to her and whispers in her ear, "Baby, I can't work like this. I called them and told them I am coming later. We need to talk."

She whispers back, "About what?"

He looks at her with his head tilted, but does not respond to that question. He then asks, "Where are your parents?"

"Sleep, why?"

"My dad is up. I'ma take Zion there and we are going home to talk."

"Whatever Tony."

He shakes his head at her as he picks up Zion to take him to his parents' house. As he walks Zion to his parents' house, Jewels goes inside to tell her parents she is leaving and that Zion is with Tony's parents. As he drives, Tony tries to hold her hand, but she moves it. He glances at her and rubs her cheek as he continues to drive. Once they make it home, Tony says after they enter the house, "Baby, seriously, why do you even believe this?"

With a serious face, she responds, "Really Tony? You act like you haven't done something like this before."

Looking to the ceiling shaking his head in disbelief as he rubs his hand over his face, he finally responds, "Baby that was a mistake. A stupid mistake that happened years ago and is not gone happen again Jewels. And you know it isn't, that is why you married me. You know there is no way you would have married me thinking that, that was a possibility."

Bobbing her head back and forth, with her hands on her hips as she listens, she responds, "You are right, but I am not a psychic either."

Folding his arms he says, "Really baby? So not only do you think I am cheating, but with her of all the people?"

She looks at him and shrugs her shoulders, as he continues, "Baby, if I am cheating with her, why would I put her business card in my pocket when I know you do my laundry? Jewels, you know if I wanted her I would be with her. I am where I want to be. I talked about you the majority of the time we hung out in L. A..”

Standing there with her hands still placed on her hips, she shrugs her shoulders while saying, “Maybe you forgot it was there. And you talking about me changes nothing.”

Tilting his head as he looks at her out of the side of his eyes, he says, “Whatever Jewels, you do not even believe that. And you know there is no way I would be talking about you if I was trying to get with her. I know you think I am cocky, but baby you have known me practically my whole life, and you know I have never had a problem with getting a woman. You are the only woman I had to put in work for. So you know I am where I want to be.”

She rolls her eyes and walks off. He follows her, hugs her from behind, and says, “Come on baby, cut this out. You know there is nothing going on. You are my wife. You birthed our son. I love you to life baby.” He kisses her cheek, then says, “Baby, you know I only want you and these women can’t do nothing for me.”

Trying to wiggle out of his hug, but he holds her tighter and smooches her cheek, she says, “Whatever.”

Smiling and kissing her cheek again, as he squeezes her, he responds “That sounds like one of those, ‘you are right’, whatevers.”

Rolling her eyes, she pokes her lips out while responding, “Maybe.”

Laughing, while still holding her and nibbling on her cheek, he responds, “I love you baby.”

“I love you too.” She checks her time as he continues to hug her and sees that it is Eleven Thirty then asks, “What time is your job expecting you?”

Caressing her arms and smooching her cheek, he responds, “Whenever I walk through the door. What’s up?”

She tilts her head, “Well what time were you expecting to walk through there doors?”

Grinning, he releases her as he responds, "Baby, I didn't have one. My focus was us."

Smiling, she responds, "Well, baby you know it is pretty rare for us to have our house to ourselves lately."

He nods in agreement, still grinning, as he begins to kiss her and says, "Jewels, I love you baby", he squeezes her butt and smooches her forehead.

A few hours later, he takes her back to her parents' house. Smiling with love and joy, he kisses her cheek and says, "I love you baby. See you in a couple of hours."

"I love you too."

He watches until she enters the home then drives to work.

She walks in and sees everyone is at her parents' house playing with Zion. She begins to make dinner for her family while Zion is occupied. As she cooks, he runs to her holding her leg a few times. His grandmothers finally get him, to prevent any injury, but his grandfathers soon come to get him and takes him on a fishing trip with them, well more of a boat outing.

When they get back, they show everyone pictures. They actually gave Zion his own fishing pole and in the pictures, he is holding the pole as though he is an expert fisherman. She texts messages Tony the picture and he laughs hysterically.

CHAPTER NINE

Nearly a year passes since Jewels has ended her friendship with Kellie. During this time, she and Tony plans to attend a wedding and the groom is Brandon. They meet his fiancé before the wedding who is a very lovely women and has a career as a nurse. She seems to be the complete opposite of Kellie. She has two children from a past relationship. She seems to enjoy the home life and not hanging out much.

They have never seen Brandon so happy. He now has local work and does not work his life away. His entire demeanor is more energetic and he cannot stop smiling or touching his fiancé.

"Hey Brandon", Tony says while also waving at his fiancé as she and Jewels walk off to converse. Both he and Jewels notices she is someone from their high school who is closer to Jacob's age. Brandon and Tony talk privately, while Jewels speaks with his fiancé.

Smiling, Tony says, "Brandon, I see you have finally found your wife. I am happy for you man!"

Cheesing, Brandon replies, "Yea man, finally. I had to let baggage go first, then man she walked right into my life and I went extra hard at her. I even go to plays with her and you know that bores me, but I watch them with a smile." He laughs at himself, "It still blows my mind how I met her too."

He pauses and looks at her, then continues, "I am out of town working and saw her at a gas station and introduced myself. Come to find out, she is a traveling nurse, well was, but is from and lives here. I am still shocked on that one", he laughs. "I never worked that hard in my life to get a woman either, but I will do it all over again. I understand your smile now man and it feels good too."

Still smiling for his happiness, Tony says, "Yea man, I will do it all again too for my baby." He smiles more and says, "But y'alls' wedding is a month away. Are you ready?

"Yes I am. She is too. She was planning non stop without a wedding planner. She planned everything herself, I helped a little too, but she is really into that stuff." He looks over at his fiancé and Jewels, then asks, "How are you two? Do you two still want a wedding?"

Looking at Jewels, Tony smiles and says, "We are great and I enjoy every moment of us. And yes, we still will have one. She knows it is pretty important to me. It is just that when we had Zion our priorities begin to shift, but she has gotten back to planning. You will receive an invite, soon, I hope. You know her and", he stops and looks at their women talking to make sure they are still occupied with each other, and continues, "her and Kellie aren't friends anymore so she does not want any brides maid, just a maid of honor and to keep it really small and cozy."

Brandon shakes his head when he hears Kellie's name, looks at Tony, and walks outside. Tony follows, knowing he wants to continue talking. Once they make it out, Tony looks back making sure Jewels is still talking and Brandon says, "Man, do you know she showed up to my job three months ago, knowing I am an engaged man. I know one of our mutual friends told her and they had to tell her where I work too, crying and apologizing. But get this, her and Jesse are still together. I'm looking at her like, I really do not know how I ever loved you. She is just really selfish and scandalous."

Listening without an ounce of shock, Tony responds, "Man it took Jewels nearly thirty years to see her for who she is so I get it, a little." Thinking for a minute Tony asks, "Is Jesse who you caught her with?"

Shaking his head as he rubs his chin, he responds, "Yea man, it was him. I could not believe it. I was really shocked. Not only are you cheating, but in the bed we share and with your friend's ex. Tony, my dad was so happy when I told him I finally left her. He told me she never, 'complimented' who I am and that she was just a 'leach'. He never trusted her, but man I really did love her at one point."

Tony tries to say something else, when Jewels comes to get them and says, "Our table is ready."

He looks at her, smiles, and takes her hand saying, "Okay baby."

They all go in and enjoy dinner with a delightful conversation. They all tell Brandon some old stories from high school that he finds hilarious.

```````````````````````````````````````````````````````````````````````````````````

A few months have passed.  Zion is steadily growing and is a fast learner.  Jewels spends a lot of time teaching him. He is starting to count and say some letters.  To their surprise, he is able to recognize colors and names them without hesitation.  Tony always looks at Jewels and says, "I told you he's going to be an artist.  That is why he is picking up on colors this easy", and laughs each time.

Both, she and Tony decides to home school him once he reaches that age.  With Jewels being the main teacher.  They have also been spending time teaching him about the Daughter's of Zion.  They want to make sure, as he grows, that he fully understands the meaning behind his name.

Their fourth year anniversary is approaching.  They spend the whole month waiting for their day while singing to each other non stop.  So much so Zion tries to sing with them.  Some of the songs they sing are from artists like, Jagged Edge, Babyface, The Temptations, and The Isley Brothers.  As Tony sings, Just My Imagination by The Temptations to Jewels, he stops and says,

"Baby, you were at one point, but now you are my reality."  He smooches her lips and continues, "Ummmm baby, a sweet reality too.  I looooovvvveee you."

Blushing, she smooches him back, "I loooovvveeee you too."

Tony begins singing again as she looks around their home and can barely see straight through.  Tony has their entire house filled with flowers, balloons,
```````````````````````````````````````````````````````````````````````````````````

candy, and personal cards he designed himself. One of the cards, which Jewels loves the most, is pretty simple and straight to the point. The front of the card is a picture of them on their wedding day at the courthouse he sketched.

The sketch is of them giving each other their first kiss standing at the alter, after they said, "I do."

On the inside he wrote,

 *FOR LIFE*

She continues to look over there house smiling at all the gifts. It is so much, Jewels has to hide the chocolate to keep Zion from getting to it. One day, they caught him hiding in the corner eating some Turtles Jewels forgot to hide. All they could do was laugh at him sneakily eating the chocolate, but enjoying every bite. He has also popped a few balloons.

Every time he pops one, Tony picks him up and says, "Zion, didn't I tell you to leave these balloons alone. They are for your momma."

Finding it funny, Zion laughs each time and as soon as Tony sits him back down he makes his way back to the balloons to play. Finally, Tony gets smart like Jewels, and places the balloons where Zion cannot reach them. Jewels laughs when she finally sees this, and says, "I see you have finally had enough?"

Laughing, Tony responds, "You got that right baby because he is popping all my money away."

They both laugh and Tony walks over to hug her. While holding her, he says, "Baby, we have been legal almost four years, but you know we been loving each other nearly thirty years. Well I know I have been loving you that long."

She laughs while responding, "Yea, you are right. I can't believe we have even known each other this long. It feels good."

He kisses her cheek, "Yes it does baby." He squeezes her butt and continues, "I love you baby."

"I love you too", he begins passionately kissing her and Zion starts crying. Tony stops kissing her and laughs as he says, "I do not think he wants any siblings.

Every time he sees me kissing you he does that." They both laugh and Jewels says, "Naw, he thinks you are hurting his momma", they continue laughing.

Tony picks up Zion then takes him to his room where he has an area he put together that keeps him both safe and entertained. He comes back, smiling, and holds Jewels, "Now he does not have to see me 'hurt' his momma", he kisses her and caresses her while constantly stopping to profess his love to her.

Everyday at work he text messages one love song to Jewels accompanied with a photo of them, ranging from their childhood to adulthood. He always adds a message to it that correlates with the picture of them. Jewels does the same until the day of their anniversary arrives.

Today is a sunny day where there are barely clouds. Jewels is at her parents' house doing nothing. Her mom and Mrs. Ellison comes to her and they all walk to a local park to let Zion play. Jewels sits and watches as their moms push Zion on a swing. They help him slide down a sliding board and lets him run freely in the deep green grass. Jewels notices at one point, he stops running and walks to some flowers. His grandparents walk with him and he tries his best to pluck them, but is unable to. The pieces that fall in his hands he gives to his grand moms with a smile. He tries to pluck some more and brings them to Jewels.

She smiles, kisses his cheek, and says, "Oh thank you Zion. Mommy loves you. You are a gentleman already and your dad will be proud."

He smiles as though he understands everything she says. Jewels spreads the petals on the table top she is sitting to, takes a picture of them, and text messages it to Tony saying,

"Baby, look at what your son plucked for me and his grandmoms. <smiles>, I know he gets this from his dad. He is a little gentleman already."

Tony replies a few minutes later,

"My boy, already learning how to put smiles on y'all's faces. That's what I'm talking about."

"Yes he is and I'm still smiling."

"<smiles>, love you baby."

"Love you too. See you soon."

"<smooch>"

After she finishes her text conversation, their parents walk to her. They walk back home and Jewels continues on the front porch.

While sitting there, Tony text messages her a photo of them. It is of them in their high school's hallway, standing by her locker. It reads,

"Happy anniversary. Do you remember taking this junior year? You opened your locker and saw the card I made for you, while you were at a tutoring session and I waited for you in Team Higher Up to drive you home. When you saw the card sitting on your books, it surprised you and made you smile and your hug made me smile. I love you Jewels. <smooch> <attachment>, Shai, Comforter."

Jewels blushes non stop as she reads it and listens to the song. An hour later, she replies with the picture of the card attached. It reads,

"Of course I remember this picture and here's the card. Your words on the front, 'The greatest friend ever', still brings a smile to my face to this day. I never got rid of it. It is in my teen photo album here at my parents'. Here, also, is a picture of us when you tried to teach me how to box. You kept laughing at me as you held the punching bag and I had to remind you, that I was only eleven and a girl. I need more time, lol. You did not give up on me though, and worked with me until I got better, <heart eyes>, <smooch>. I love you. <attachment> Dru Hill, These Are the Times. Happy anniversary."

Responding right away, he replies,

"Never will I give up. <smiles>, see you soon baby."

"<smiles> <grins>, I love you."

<hr />

A few days passes and they decide to spend their evening sitting out on the front porch. Some of the neighborhood's children run over to play with Zion. Some of them challenge Tony to a basketball game and he takes the challenge.

On this bright and semi windy day, Tony jogs down his steps full of energy. He stops in their driveway first to stretch a little. At one point during his stretching, he stops and laughs because he notices Zion is trying to stretch like him. He takes off his watch, hands it to Jewels, and kisses her for good luck.

As he walks to the street to begin the game, one of the opposing players jokingly says, "Lets go old man, but are you sure you can play because we don't wanna hurt you?"

Laughing but ignoring his statement, Tony checks the basketball to him. They play for five minutes then Tony calls a timeout. Shocked at how well their skills have evolved, Tony has to stop and actually make sure his tennis shoes are tightly secured and takes off his shirt. When he takes it off, Jewels claps and says in a playful voice, "Ohhhhh, ohhh, oooohhhh. My, my, my, look at that handsome man." All the children laugh hysterically, while Tony smiles and blows her a kiss as he prepares to continue to play against three teens, who are all starting players on their high school's basketball team.

During the years, their high school basketball team has been ending the season undefeated from the other schools in the county. Sadly, they always get knocked out of the playoffs by a school in another county. Some of those schools have tried to recruit one of the players who Tony is now playing, but he declines every time and stays loyal to his other teammates.

Once, he came to ask Tony for advice. Tony said to him, "Lenny, you have to do what will make you happy. What has your parents said about it?"

Responding to him, Lenny said, "Both my parents said what you said, but I really think my mom wants me to stay. She thinks the other school is to far and just wants to use me. She does not think they really care about my future. Our coaches here, has already got us looking at Universities and the business side of things. We are learning a lot from them and not just basketball."

Nodding in agreement, Tony replies, "Yea, they have always focused on our overall achievements. But it sounds like you are where you want to be, so stay."

"I think I am. I came to talk to you because I know you turned down sport's scholarships for an academic one. What made you do that?"

Laughing, he asks, "Who told you that?"

"Our coaches."

Tony smiles and continues, "Yea I did. But I knew my goals and an athlete was not one. And I def was not about to make them money, just for a scholarship when I have other options. It was not a big deal to me. Remember to always have options though. You do not want to be stuck in a situation with no way out."

He thanked Tony for the talk and decided once and for all to remain at his local high school.

As the street game continues, Jewels is cheering Tony on non stop. Cheering him on enthusiastically, she looks at Zion who is doing the same. Smiling with pride, she watches as Tony is holding his own against these magnificent players. She laughs as they all call fouls on each other, for the smallest reasons and playfully talk trash to try to throw off each other's game. Their game has brought the whole neighborhood out to watch and enjoy.

Their neighbors stand on sidewalks cheering on the players. Some become 'sidewalk' coaches, yelling techniques the players needs. None of the players listens to them. Mrs. Dubois brings bottled water for them to drink and sits the water by Jewels as she continues to watch the game. Mr. Dubois becomes the score keeper as he cheers all the players on. At one point, Tony calls a timeout to catch his breath. While resting his hands on his knees, he looks at Jewels and says, "Baby, they are really working me this evening. I gotta get back to the gym."

Jewels smiles and says, "Baby you are looking good out there! You got this! You are up by five points and it is three against one. You know your skills are the best baby."

He smiles and walks to her, kisses her cheek as he says, "Thank you baby and I appreciate that. Now I am going to finish this. I need five more points and it is game", he rubs Zion's afro and walks back to continue the game.

As he walks away, she slaps his butt, "You got this", Zion claps as his father walks away as well. They continue their game, with cheers coming from the whole neighborhood. As he bounces the ball in front of Tony, Bernard says, "Mr. Tony, I never saw you sweat like this before. You getting old", he laughs as he bounces the ball between his legs and continues to talk trash to Tony. Tony laughs at his trash talking, but focuses on the ball the entire time. He steals the ball from Bernard and dunks it. He turns and laughs saying, "I ain't that old Bernard, remember, I taught you what you know."

Bernard laughs as Tony checks the ball to him, and says, "You right Mr. Tony, but you still sweating heavy though."

They all stop and laugh as they hear Jewels scream with cheers saying, "That is my baby. Y'all see how he stole that ball. Y'all don't see him. My baby got game", she giggles as she bankhead bounces while trying to show Zion how to do it.

Tony laughs some more at Jewels, and says, "Thank you baby." He looks at his opponents and says, while glancing at all three of them, "I am about to end this game."

They laugh, but Tony hits a three-point shot, that does end the game with Tony as the victor. They all shake hands, laughs, and talk a little. Tony, jokingly wags his finger at Bernard, and says, "What I told you about doing all that talking while you are in control of the ball. You were talking so much, stealing it was a breeze." He looks at all three and continues, "I gotta make some of y'alls' games. Let me know the schedule when it is ready."

He pauses, and they all stop talking. They look at Jewels and laugh some more as they hear Jewels continue to cheer and celebrate Tony's win. Smiling, Tony says, "Y'all see how my baby cheering me on and was hyping me up the whole time? Y'all better make sure y'all get a winner like her. She smart and sexy too."

He smiles, gives the opposing players the basketball, and walk towards Jewels.

They nod in affirmation to it all as Zion walks up and the teens begin showing him how to play. Tony walks over to Jewels, they sit on the curb, and Tony smiles as he watches them try and teach his son what he taught them.

All the watchers give a round of applause for their game, then they go back to doing what they were previously doing. Jewels leans over and kisses his sweaty cheek saying, "Baby, you did so good."

He smiles and whispers to her as he holds his bottled water, "Thank you baby, but your man is TIRED." He laughs and continues, "I really got to get back to the gym and on the court more. Playing with our brother and our friends didn't help." He laughs some more, "And baby I make love to you constantly, so I do not know why I am so tired", he drops his head then looks to the sky. He leans in closer to Jewels and says, "Baby, I hope I haven't been slacking. Have I?"

She drops her head with laughter, looks at him as he eagerly waits for an answer and says, "Not at all."

He kisses her cheek with a smile. As they both smile, they continue to watch as Zion is being coached and is trying his best to act like he is one of the big kids. They laugh as they see Zion running in circles trying to grab the ball Lenny is keeping from him. As they continue to watch they see Zion trying his best to hold and bounce the basketball, but his hands are not big enough yet.

\\\

Finally, their anniversary arrives. Tony has taken off the entire week using vacation time he has accumulated. Their parents share in the babysitting of their son, so Tony and Jewels can share their week with each other. To thank them for this, they have decided to send their parents on a vacation. Their parents decide on a cruise, so Tony and Jewels book it for them. It is a quick day cruise that leaves out of Orlando, but they plan to stay in Orlando the entire weekend.

They spend their week mostly snuggled up under each other. They study The Bible as well. They spend a lot of time in the Book of Genesis. Studying how it all begin. From the making of man and the gift The Creator gifted him after putting him in a deep sleep. While studying that part, Tony looks at Jewels and jokingly says, "Ummmmm, baby, that gift is the greatest ever", he slaps her on the butt as they both laugh.

They go on to study how they were kicked out of the Garden and Jewels says, "Y'all men have been letting breast and thighs get you in trouble since the beginning", she laughs while shaking her head.

He laughs too and says, "I guess baby….."

They continue on and stop where Joseph's brothers sell him to the Ishmaelites, who took him to Egypt.

As they prepare for the day of their anniversary, they go on a date every night this week. Every date night, Tony constantly says, "Baby I plan to date you for life and we are not stopping honeymooning either."

Jewels smiles and nods in agreement each time.

One of their date nights includes them making a meal at home and they indulge in it at a local park that has the view of a popular river in Jacksonville. After they finish the meal, Tony sits next to her as they relax watching the water as it sits calmly. Tony cannot stop kissing her cheek and rubbing her arm. At one point he says, "Dang baby, you know I can't keep my hands off of you. I hope I don't annoy you with it."

"Of course not. I love it and you but if you ever stop giving me this affection I will be annoyed."

Kissing her forehead, "Never. I love you too baby."

They spend another hour relaxing at the park then drives home.

Their anniversary day is finally here. The day is rainy, but the sun never disappears. Jewels wakes and listens to the rain for thirty minutes. As she listens, she closes her eyes and meditates on her life. She remembers her struggles, her aches, her pains, both physically and mentally. She remembers her friendship with Kellie, but begins to smile when she remembers all of her joys and successes. Both personally and professionally. She smiles harder as she remembers how Tony was always there to give a listening ear and provide a shoulder to lean on.

She hums an uplifting tune, Smile by Scarface and Tupac Shakur, then proceeds to start her day. She spends her day singing and dancing as she lays out dresses to wear. She skips with every step she takes around their home, stopping to smile at each picture of her and Tony she passes. She finally decides on a black fitted dress, that drops just below her knees. When she bought this dress, she saw Tony's eyes light up after she tried it on. Even Zion clapped when she walked out of the dressing room to ask Tony for his opinion. She will accompany the dress with black and gold stilettos she purchased a week ago. She never forgets her gold cuff bracelet either. She decides to let her two strand twists hang, so she is going earring free. She also decides to wear a solid gold chain that drops to her chest, with a heart pendant attached.

As she enjoys her day, she receives three phone calls. Each call is not accompanied with a name so she does not answer. She thinks it is someone who is trying to sell something, an annoying telemarketer, so she ignores them happily. The third time she does answer, making sure there is no emergency, but the call ends when she says, "Hello."

To be sure all is okay, she text messages Tony, her parents, Tony's parents, Jacob, and her sister Zapphire. Everyone responds and let her know they are fine. Tony calls her as well, checking to make sure she is fine.

As Jewels gets ready at home, Tony gets dressed at their favorite beach front hotel to come over to pick up his love. He has been there before the sun rose. He decides to wear blue jeans accompanied with a black buttoned shirt that has a lion on it. He has his Locs pulled into a low ponytail and his beard is fully grown out. He will wear a pair of all black sneakers that are ankle length, that he purchased from their friend's shoe store a week ago. The shoes lean more on the casual side, but is a tennis shoe none the less. The whole time he gets dressed he listens to a Rhythm and Blues playlist with a few Rap songs sprinkled in.

After he showers and before he gets dressed, he sits on the bed with his bath towel wrapped around his waist. He holds his cell phone and remembers the journey he and Jewels traveled before they finally reached the alter. He holds his head down and shakes his head at himself remembering the day Jewels broke up with him.

He finally unlocks his cell phone and looks through his photos. He smiles as he sees pictures of them running track and playing flag football. He laughs, when he sees five different pictures of them where he constantly tries to kiss her cheek but Jewels moves her face each time. He thinks to himself while laughing at the photos, "My baby was always running from this good loving. We finally got it right though", he laughs some more at this thought. All of the photos are at different stages of their lives, from elementary school to adulthood. He finally comes across a photo of them on the day they became engaged in California. He smiles non stop at this picture then sends Jewels a text message,

"<smooch emoji>, I love you."

After he sends the text message, he gets dressed. After he is dressed, he places rose petals on the bed and places a card on top, after he sprays it with his cologne to give it a scent. Before he leaves he calls her, but gets no answer. He finds it suspicious, but tries not to worry. Once in his car, he sends her a text message reading,

"Hey baby. I am on my way. I called you but no answer. Are you okay?"

He begins to drive, but she never responds. Becoming a little worried he picks up speed, but as he gets closer she calls, "Hello", Tony says in a relieved voice.

"Hey baby, sorry about that. I was soaking in the tub."

Smiling, he says, "Okay baby, I was just letting you know I was on my way."

"Okay, I should be ready when you get here. Love you."

"Love you too."

He continues to drive with soft music playing the whole time. He begins to sing The Isley Brother's tune, For The Love of You. Singing along to the tune, he pulls over to the side of the road and text messages a link of the song to Jewels. She immediately replies,

"<hearteyes smile> <heartbeat>, I love it and I love you, <kiss> <kiss> <kiss>"

Smiling at her reply, he sits his cell phone down and continues his drive. As he turns on their street he notices an unfamiliar car parked at the corner of their block, but pays it no mind. He brushes it off thinking that the car belongs to a friend of their neighbor. He is just ready to take his wife out. As he parks at their house, Jewels calls, he answers, but the call ends. Thinking it is a butt dial, he happily gets out of his car. He retrieves a bouquet of yellow roses he has for her and places a gold necklace around a few of the rose's stems. He bought the necklace for her as an anniversary gift. He places a small card with it as well. He does this while humming, It's Our Anniversary by Tony Toni Tone.

When he pulls up, Jewels sees him through their bedroom's window. She walks to their front door to greet him, but freezes when she sees Jesse standing at it. Frozen in shock, she hears Jesse say with a smile, "Hey beautiful, are you ready to talk to me?"

He begins to walk to her and Jewels finally snaps out of shock. She turns and tries to run to their room, but Jesse catches her saying, "Jewels, you know I am not going to hurt you. I just want to talk. I miss you, my daughter misses you, but I can't even get you to talk to me."

Struggling away, she says, "Jesse, let me go."

"Jewels, I just want to talk. Where's your man and why is he leaving you alone? I thought he wasn't leaving you alone since I saw you in Miami? What happened, did he cheat again? And why don't you want to talk to my baby girl? You two bonded."

In a shocked voice she asks, "How do you know any of this? I never told you anything about Tony's and I past and I definitely have not talked to you since I left. So how would you know my husband's plans are not leaving me alone? And, YOU, are the reason I do not talk to her. I love your daughter and wish her nothing but the best. Now LET ME GO AND LEAVE OUR HOME!"

Still holding her against her will, he says, "Your friend, Kellie told me everything Jewels. I could not believe you left me for a cheater. That is the ultimate disrespect and you took him back after that." He pauses for a second, then continues, "I am still trying to figure out how you and her were ever friends. You are nothing like her. I mean, you are so reserved and keep personal matters to yourself. You would have never told me any of her business, no matter what, even if I asked, I know you wouldn't. But your friend, well ex friend, was telling it all and I did not even have to ask and I know she had to know I was still crushing on you, even when I denied it."

Ignoring his last statements, she continues struggling to get out of his grip. As she struggles, Jewels remembers she has her cell phone and tries to dial the police. He snatches the phone from her saying, "Jewels, I just want to talk. Why are you doing me this way? I thought you would be my wife, but instead you left me and married another man. A cheater at that. You had concerns about my ex, when I should've had them about yours. What did I do? Why did you leave?"

Still struggling, she responds, "You did and your interference of our friendship is part of the reason I left."

Still restraining her he asks, "What interference? Jewels I loved you, I still do---." He tries to kiss her cheek, but Jewels moves her head out of the way and he says, "Jewels, I am not going to harm you."

As he talks, she sees her cell phone in his hand and tries to grab it, but he throws it on her sofa. When he does this, Jewels finally starts screaming.

As Tony places the necklace around the roses as he leans on their car door, he hears Jewels screams and runs to their front door, dropping the gift. He unlocks it, but cannot get in. He bangs on the door frantically as he continues to hear her scream. DMX's upbeat song, Party Up (Up In Here), begins to play in his head and it gives him more momentum. Finally, he kicks the door in as their neighbors begin to run over.

When he enters he sees a man holding Jewels. He grabs the man and begins pounding on him non stop. The man tries to fight back, but Tony's punches are to swift and hard to handle. As he continues to punch and kick the man, as he is on the ground, one of their neighbors grab Tony as another holds the intruder at gunpoint until the police come.

The neighbor says to Tony, "Calm down. The cops are on their way."

Tony, still heated, forcefully says while pointing his finger at the intruder, "I knew your ass was going to mess with my baby again, but you came to my home! Where my wife and child lay their heads." Pacing back and forth, looking for an opportunity to evade his neighbor, Mr. Dubois, he continues yelling at Jesse as he pounds his fist in the palm of his hand, "Leave my wife alone! She don't want you! You were just a moment. I am her lifetime, but you have really crossed the line today and I'm gone whip your ass some more. And I ain't forget about them three years you kept my baby from me either, I'm whipping your ass for that too."

As Jesse finally stands, he says, "Forget you. You kept interfering in our relationship, now you can't deal with mine? You can try, but you do not scare me." He looks at Jewels and says sarcastically, while pointing at Tony, "This the man you let wife you?"

Tony continues to pace while looking for an opportunity to rush Jesse. When he hears this question, he stops, and says, "Jesse, I am not one to play with! I have told you to many times to stay away from my baby. I am done talking to you! And I didn't interfere in nothing, your insecurities did. You knew Jewels and I were friends from jump. If you couldn't deal with that you should've kept it moving----"

Jesse interrupts, and says, "Stop lying. You continuously called her, even when she was at my house. I am not dumb. You would call her while I am sitting next to her. She wouldn't answer so I knew it was you---"

Nodding his head in agreement, Tony interrupts, "She is my friend, now wife, of course I called. You were just a distraction because she was mad at me at the time, but you could never love her the way I do. Move on----"

Jesse responds as he looks at Jewels, "Is this true? Were you just using me until you were ready to take him back?"

Crying, while trying to catch her breath and composure, Jewels tries to say, "No, I would not do anyone like that."

Looking irritated, Tony quickly looks at Jewels and says, "Why are you explaining yourself to him? You don't owe him an explanation." He looks at Jesse again and says, "She's lying to you. You were just a distraction. She would not even move out of your guesthouse. We always slept and sleep in the same bed. Move on---"

Jesse smirks and says, "Now it's my turn to return the favor and interfere as a distraction to you."

Tony nods his head, while making sure his Locs are tightly secured in it's ponytail as he says, "Okay, I see you think this is a game." He nods his head some more and continues, "I haven't hurt you because of my wife and our child, but you have tried me for the last time----".

Jesse cuts in, and sarcastically says, "Child?" He looks at Jewels, "I forgot you had this cheater's baby? Are you sure you are the only momma of his kids? More importantly, are you sure you are his only woman? I know he likes to play around."

Hearing this enrages Tony even more. He points his finger at him as he tries to get to him again, but Mr. Dubois holds him, as Tony says, "Yes! Our son! And Jewels is my one and only and my baby knows this. I know Kellie slow ass telling you our business too. Y'all made for each other, but I know one thing, you will never touch my baby again, NEVER!"

Mr. Dubois says, as he restrains Tony, "Tony, calm down. He is trying to trigger you. You know Jewels loves you and don't want him."

"I know Mr. Dubois, but he has tried me to many times and I am putting an end to it today."

Laughing, Jesse says, "You ain't going to do a thing."

Jesse laughs some more as Tony is about to say something else but does not because he hears Jewels crying. After, Mr. Dubois asked him to stay calm, Tony begins pacing again. He stops pacing for a minute, looks at Jewels and watches as Mrs. Mary holds her and tries to console her. Jewels is sitting in a chair in their living room trying her best to stop crying and regain her composure. Tony watches as Mrs. Mary gives her tissue and hugs her, letting her know she called their parents and the police are on the way.

Jewels is constantly trying to catch her breath in between tears. Still in shock of what is occurring right before her eyes and wondering what would have happened if Tony was not outside? She fans herself with her hand as Mrs. Mary tries to help wipe her tears.

Seeing all the tears flowing from her eyes, Tony rubs his face and says, "Baby, I love you. It's gone be okay. Stop crying." He pauses and looks at Jesse, then back to Jewels and says, "Baby, I promise you he is not gone mess with you no more after this though."

After he says this, Jesse looks at Jewels and says, "Yes, it is going to be okay beautiful." He looks at Tony, smirks, then back to Jewels, "You are still soft and smells delicious too. I miss holding you."

Tony becomes enraged to silence after hearing this. Tony looks to the ceiling and rubs his face while taking a long deep breath, as he takes in what Jesse is saying. He stands still for a few minutes. As he stands there, Tony places his hands in his pockets, looks at Jesse with a straight face, and with his head tilted, as Jesse continues to talk to Jewels. Tony is hoping this will make Mr. Dubois ease up on his stance blocking him.

As Tony continues to listen, he hears Jesse say to Jewels, "Yes Jewels, I really miss holding you. I miss those days holding you in my arms while we rest in my bed talking about anything that crossed our minds.", as he continues to talk to Jewels he looks at Tony and smirks some more.

Tony continues to stand still and watches Jesse as he speaks. Tony's face is emotionless, but his thoughts are running through his head non stop as he looks at Jesse. He is thinking of many things and they are running through his mind as fast as an Amtrak train runs it's course. He is thinking, 'he is really trying me', 'when I get to him again I am not letting up', 'Mr. Dubois needs to move. I don't want to hurt him', 'when I get to him this time, he ain't gone want to hear Jewels name again', and more thoughts are going through his mind as he watches Jesse.

As Tony continues to stand calmly, hoping Mr. Dubois will drop his guard, he hears Jewels yell, "Shut up Jesse! Baby do not let him get to you."

Tony looks at Jewels with his hands still in his pockets, blows her a kiss, and says, "Baby, I am okay." He looks at Jesse and continues, "You might want to turn your head though."

Jesse says something that makes Mr. Dubois look in his direction. When he turns his head, Tony finally sees an escape, dodges his neighbors, and begins pounding on Jesse again, while saying in an angry voice, "Didn't I tell you not to touch my wife again! Boy, you have tried me for the last time and you got my baby crying. Stay the hell away from her!" Mr. Dubois tries to subdue Tony again, but cannot. Tony continues to hit him as he continues to speak, "I told you I am not the one to play with, especially when it comes to Jewels. You came in my home--."

Tony stops speaking for a moment because Jesse is able to get a couple of punches in this time, but Tony is not phased by any of them. Jesse finally falls to the ground and Tony continues to pound on him saying, "Stay away from my wife! Jewels is my baby and you will NEVER touch her again!"

Finally Jacob enters, before the police arrives, and helps Mr. Dubois pull Tony away from Jesse.

As they try and move Tony, Jacob yells, "TONY! TONY! Stop man. You beat him good enough. I know you are mad, but your wife and child need you home."

As they pull him away, their fathers arrive, and Mr. Ellison says, "Tony calm down before the cops get here and wants to arrest you too." Mr. Ellison looks at Jacob and says, "Get Jesse out this house so Tony can calm down."

Mr. Lowd walks to his daughter to check on her. He sees Mrs. Mary consoling her, but when Jewels sees her dad she stands and hugs him. As he hugs her, he asks, "Baby girl, are you okay", he releases her and checks for bruises?

As he checks for bruises, Jewels responds, "Dad I am fine, just a little shaken up. Where is mom and Zion?"

"At home. She and Mrs. Ellison have him trying to keep him occupied, but I think he senses something is going on. When your neighbors called all of our moods changed instantly."

Her dad continues to console his daughter, as Jacob removes Jesse by jacking him up. It took a minute for Jesse to stand, but once he does, Tony looks at Jesse forcefully saying, "Leave my wife alone punk! You better thank God they stopped me----", becoming upset again, he rushes Jesse, but his dad stops him. "Dad, please let me go. He came in my home dad. He really crossed the line this time and the things he said deserves another one...", still trying to get to Jesse, he pauses in his speak then continues, "I thank the Lord I pulled up in time. Ain't no telling what he would've done to my baby---."

His dad cuts him off and says, "Tony, son, I know you are angry, but I need you to calm down before the cops get here. You know how some of them can be. I don't want them trying to arrest you."

He listens to his dad and starts pacing back and forth while reciting a couple of Bible verses in his head from the Book of Proverbs, Chapter Seventeen. Tony calms down some more when he hears Jewels yelling, "Baby, no, stop. I do not want you in jail! Calm down, I am fine."

He finally walks over to Jewels taking deep breaths. When he gets to her, Mr. Lowd pats his shoulder and says, "Thanks for protecting my baby girl, but calm down. She does not need you locked up."

Nodding in agreement, Tony responds, "I'm calm, but Jesse has been asking for this for years. I was ready to do a few days today and send Jewels and Zion to y'alls' house. He came in our home Mr. Lowd and he finally got the beating he has been begging for. He ain't gone mess with my baby no more though", he looks at Jewels who is still crying and walks to her. He sits next to her, holds her, and says, "Baby, I am not going to jail. Stop crying. You okay? Did he hurt you?"

He kisses her forehead, as she says, "Baby, I am fine, he did not have time to do anything because you came."

Wiping her tears, he continues to hold her, and says, "I love you baby."

Shaking some she replies, "I love you too."

The officers finally arrives and talks to everyone. They try and separate Tony from Jewels to hear their accounts of the story separately, but Tony says, "I am not leaving her side. She is shaken up."

The officer fully understands and begins taking their accounts, starting with Jewels. She places her hands on her hips and says, "I am not sure how he even got in. But, I saw my husband arrive and started to walk to our front door to greet him and when I got to the hallway I saw him standing at the door. I tried to run to my room to retrieve my weapon, but he caught me. I had my cell phone in my housecoat's pocket, took it out, and tried dialing the police, but he snatched it from me. He eventually threw it and I just started screaming. The next thing I know, Tony was there, getting him away from me."

The officer asks, "Do you know him?"

"Yes, he is my ex."

Writing down her account, the officer then asks, "Do you need medical attention?"

"No, I am fine."

Tony rubs her back as she speaks and the officer looks at him, then asks, "What did you witness?"

"Not much. I was outside and heard my baby scream and rushed in. When I got in, I saw him holding her and I moved him."

The officer's partner comes to the door and motions for his partner to come outside. They all walk out and he says, "I am arresting this man. He admitted he broke in, but he claims that he was not going to hurt her. He just wanted to talk. I am arresting him and letting the courts handle this. The EMT's want to do a CT scan first just to make sure he has no internal bleeding." He looks at Tony and says, "You beat him pretty bad. I don't blame you, because I would have too."

Tony neither agrees or disagrees with the officer, but shakes their hands. They sit on their steps as they wait for the officers and the ambulance to leave. As they wait, Kellie walks up. Tony stands and says, "Kellie, get off our property!"

She tries to say something, but Jewels stops her and says, "You heard Tony, leave!"

She does as Mrs. Lowd and Mrs. Ellison walks up. Jewels stands and asks, "Ma, where's Zion? I thought you two had him to keep him away from this?"

Mrs. Lowd responds, "Mrs. Willis has him. We had to come check on our daughter and son. Are you two okay?"

"Yes ma'am. Still a little shocked, but we are."

Everyone walks over to them and they all hug. They all stand there watching the ambulance and police until they leave. After they finally leave, they talk a little and Jewels fills them in with more details of the night's events. Bernard's dad is there and says, as he shakes his head thinking of the night's event,

"Man, y'all know I had to hold my son off."

Lenny's dad is there as well and says the same thing. Bernard's dad continues, "I am sitting on my bed, trying to unwind from work and he runs in there saying, 'Dad! Dad! Do you hear that?' Putting on his tennis shoes saying, 'I think that is Ms. Jewels screaming.'

"I told him to be quiet and I listened. I was like that is her and it sounds like screams for help. Man I grabbed my pistol and ran to the door and Bernard is on my feet. I had to tell him to go in his room, get on the floor with your mom, and lock the door. I bet Jesse has finally showed up. Man Bernard was ready."

They all laugh a little and Tony says, "Man I am glad to know we have neighbors who are ready though. Thank y'all man and know I will do the same."

They nod in agreement and Bernard's dad says, "Man, we know."

They give each other a pound and walks back to their homes. Tony, Jacob, and their dads, then look over the home making sure everything is secure. As he searches the backyard, Tony notices a broken into window and realizes this is how Jesse got in. With the help of their dads, Tony secures the window with some plywood they have in their garage. They also secure the front door that Tony had to kick in and leaves out of the back door, where they are able to lock it.

Tony and Jewels decides to leave their home for the night and sleepover at the Ellisons' instead of the hotel. To help them try and celebrate the rest of their anniversary, their parents cook them a quick meal that includes sloppy joe on some toasted buns, lemon aid, and pound cake Mrs. Lowd baked two days ago. Appreciative of this gesture, Tony and Jewels give their thanks and enjoy their meal as though they are at a five star restaurant. Their parents smile, wish them happy anniversary again, and leave them two to eat amongst each other. They try their best to enjoy their dinner close to midnight. It is not easy to, but they manage to smile some.

As they finish and prepare for bed, Mr. Ellison comes to Tony to say, "Son, I am going to be a little lenient tonight", he laughs while patting Tony's back, "you can close your room door this time."

Grinning, he says, "You serious dad? Thanks, but I think I am just going to hold my baby tonight."

His dad nods, says goodnight to both Tony and Jewels, who is already in the bed preparing to go to sleep. Tony walks his parents' home, making sure all doors are locked and windows are closed. He enters his childhood's bedroom and sees Jewels is asleep. He says a prayer, then joins her by wrapping her in his arms, kisses her cheek, saying, "Goodnight baby."

Jewels responds, "Good night."

Shocked, Tony says, "Baby, you still woke? I hope I did not wake you."

"You did not. I am just lying here resting my eyes." She rubs his arm and asks, "Are you okay?"

"Yea baby, I am fine. How 'bout you", he asks as he rubs her arm and kisses her forehead?

Sighing, "I'm fine. I have finally digested tonight's event. Now I am just ready to get the legal process over with." She shakes her head and continues, "But I can't believe Kellie told him all of our business. I bet if we were still friends he would have known about our plans and planned his break-in better. I am glad I stop being friends with her. She is just trifling like you said." She laughs, "I can't believe I agree with you."

He kisses her cheek, "Yea, me too baby. But I am not shocked at all about Kellie though. You and Brandon were in denial about her. I always saw her for who she is. I understand better now, but her character is not friend material." He laughs, "Dang baby, he was real mad too, bringing up that old stuff. I know what he was trying to do, but I guess he forgot you are not a fool, but it did piss me off."

"Why?"

Shaking his head thinking of the moment, he responds, "Because baby, he was trying to plant seeds to make you not trust me and question my love and loyalty to you. Especially when he brought up 'only mommas'. I know Kellie told him about that situation. Jewels when I tell you I am done with Kellie, I am done. She better not even look at me if she sees me. She really went to far this time. I mean she knows I was not having that. Telling that man the most hurtful stuff of our past, knowing how it affected us at that time.

I do not know what you two's futures hold, but I want nothing to do with her and I def do not want her around Zion. Now you know why I never wanted her alone with him. She would probably ease in all types of negative things to our son."

Shaking her head, still in disbelief of Kellie, she responds, "Baby, you have a great point, but I am done with her. I can't deal anymore. So you do not have to worry about that."

He lies his head on her shoulder and rests as he continues to hold her while thinking over the night's events. Jewels lies there rubbing his arm, but examining his childhood's bedroom.

Moments later, she giggles. Hearing her giggle, Tony asks, "What's funny?"

Still giggling, she says, "Baby, I was just thinking about how weird it feels to be in your twin sized bed as full grown adults and I see you still have that Lil' Kim poster front and center."

He laughs, as he looks at the poster, "I forgot I even had that. I think every male my age had that poster growing up. She was the only women, who did not fit my physical type, that had me crushing. Baby, Kim was sexy." He laughs thinking of his childhood crush, rubs her arm, and continues, "It does feel a little weird, especially with me in the bed with you. You know, I would sleep on the floor and give you my bed."

Laughing, she looks at him saying, "Seriously, so you are going to call another woman sexy while touching me?" She smiles and continues, "Yea, and you always did give me your bed with a smile too." She pauses and continues with a giggle as she looks at his door, "And I see your dad let you close the door this time."

Laughing, he responds, "Baby she was, but you know your are the sexiest woman I have ever laid eyes on", still laughing, "I got the teen dreams to prove it too. I never dreamed about Kim", he kisses her cheek and laughs as he squeezes her in his arms saying, "you know what I mean too."

Laughing, she says, "Unfortunately, I do."

He chuckles and continues, "But Jewels you were crushing over Ginuwine. And I know he had to be soft. Probably wouldn't punch a grape in a fruit fight, but you had this man's poster in your dorm room." Still laughing and smiling, Tony says, "Yep, and my dad came to me and gave me permission baby."

Rubbing his arm wrapped around her, she bursts into laughter about his Ginuwine comment and says, "Yea, he was sexy." She laughs some more and proceeds to ask, "And permission, huh? Is it locked?"

He stares at her for a few seconds, rises, walks to the door to lock it. He turns to her and says, "It is now baby, what's up?"

She grins as he walks to her, "I love you baby. Happy Anniversary."

"I love you too, Tony. Happy anniversary."

The next morning the sun wakes Tony. Still hugging Jewels, he kisses her cheek then stands to go to the bathroom. When he opens his bedroom's door, he sees Jewels' gift hanging on the door knob. He smiles when he sees it, then notices a note tacked to the door left by his dad. The note reads,

Hey son. Your mom and I left to make a quick trip to the grocery store. We are going to make breakfast for y'all and the Lowds. Before we left the Dubois' stopped by with this necklace. They found it this morning, as they walked the street next to some flowers and assumed it belonged to you and Jewels. I told them it does. I was with you the day you bought it for Jewels as an anniversary gift. But you two can rest up, we will let you know when breakfast is ready, Jacob and his family will be here too.

Smiling as he holds the necklace, he looks at Jewels who is still sleeping. He walks to her and places the necklace around her neck. He then continues to the bathroom, where he washes up for the day. As he finishes, Jewels walks in, hugs him, and says,

"Good morning baby", she holds her necklace around her neck and continues, "thanks for my gift. I love you."

Grinning, he turns to her and says, "You are welcome baby. I love you too."

As she begins to brush, Tony says, "Jewels, my parents are cooking breakfast for us, all of us, your parents too. Jacob and his fam are coming over as well. I'ma call the hotel and extend our stay for a day, so we don't have to rush. And later, I am going to go by and get my things I left then check-out."

Jewels nods as she listens and he continues, "You know, I wouldn't mind if you come with me to help me get my things too." He hugs her and looks in the mirror at her, "I'm just saying, four hands are better than two."

Laughing, as she finishes drying her face, she says, "Whatever Tony, I know the real reason."

He laughs and kisses her cheek, then walks out of the bathroom. He notices his parents are still gone so he walks to their car to retrieve his Tablet. When he re-enters the house and walks to his childhood's bedroom, he sees Jewels getting dressed. He looks at her and asks,

"Baby, why are you getting dressed now? We have time. My dad will text when the food is ready."

"Tony, because I am not home. I do not feel comfortable just lying down all morning in someone else's home. You get up and get dressed."

Laughing, "Baby, I understand, but these are our parents. My dad left a note saying he will let me know when the food is ready so we are good baby. It is no disrespect. I got my Tablet so we can relax and watch a movie. What do you want to watch?"

Laughing, she says, "I guess Tony, but if they come knocking and regulating, I am letting them know you are to blame."

"I would not mind at all, but baby, stay comfortable. What do you want to watch?"

"I want to laugh. Do you have Friday on there?"

"Jewels, you know I have all the classics on here", he watches as she takes off her shorts and puts on one of his t-shirts, then takes her hand and leads her to the bed. He closes the room door and loads the movie to play. When the movie is ready he joins Jewels and they snuggle up to laugh at Smokey and Craig. After the movie ends, they join their families in the dining room and enjoy their breakfast that includes, eggs, pancakes, grits, and fish. Zion runs up to them first, hugging his parents like he has not seen them in a year.

CHAPTER TEN

WEDDING BLISS

Six months have passed since the intruder incident. Ending with Jesse being put on probation and a restraining order being delivered to him. During, one of the court proceedings his parents are there with his daughter. As they are leaving the courthouse, his mom approaches Jewels and Tony with Jesse's daughter.

She gets Jewels' attention and says, "Jewels, I am sorry for what my son has done. This behavior is out of character for him." She looks at Tony and says, "I am sorry, hello. I assume you are Jewels' husband? I am Jesse's mom", she extends her hand for a handshake.

Looking out of the side of his eyes, Tony reluctantly waves and says, "I am."

Understanding the non handshake, Jesse's mom continues, "Jewels, I just came over to apologize. Also, Elisha wanted to say hello too. She misses you."

Jewels finally speaks, saying, "Thanks for the apology Mrs. Flenderson, but it is not needed. You are not responsible for your son's behavior." She looks at his daughter and says, "Hey sweetie. I miss you too. How have you been?"

She hugs Jewels and says, "Ms. Jewels, I have been okay. I miss talking to you. I am even better at the piano now and even gotten a couple of paying gigs."

Before Jewels responds, she looks at Tony and can tell he is not pleased with the hug. She pats his back and says to Elisha, "That is good to hear. I miss talking to you too sweetie, but it just is not appropriate for us to talk. When you get a little older and enter into a real relationship you will understand."

She laughs and says, "My mom said the same thing."

They hug again and Tony says, "Baby, we are going to be late for our appointment. Are you ready?"

Mrs. Flenderson takes her granddaughter's hand and says, "Okay Elisha, we have to go now. Bye Jewels", she waves at Tony as Tony and Jewels wave back to them.

Once in the car, Jewels looks at Tony and asks, "What appointment Tony?"

Looking at Jewels with a straight face, he says, "The appointment to get away from your ex's family."

Jewels shakes her head when she hears this and Tony says, "You know you would have been ready to go too if the roles were reversed. Jewels, she is not your child. I understand y'all 'bonded', but baby, she belongs to another man. One you dated at that. You know I am not with that. I can overlook a lot of stuff, but you continuing a relationship with his child ain't one. Especially after his behavior."

Tony shakes his head thinking of this moment and continues, "And his momma thought I was going to shake her hand? I know how some of these parents are. If Jesse did not act up, she would be trying to ease in talking to you for him. I do not trust any of them."

Laughing, while shaking her head listening to Tony, she says, "But baby, what about me? You don't trust me? You know I would have never allowed that."

"Baby I know. But I also know you can get a little softhearted at times, especially when it comes to kids. I know Jesse realizes that too and you know I trust you baby."

She laughs at him and Tony starts to drive. While stopped at a red light, he laughs as Tupac Shakur's, Hit 'Em Up plays, and says, "Dang baby, this song would play after we leave the courthouse. I am glad the courts 'hit him up' though."

Jewels laughs hysterically at this, but begins to rap the lyrics of the song along with Tony as he continues to drive.

Weeks later, they receive documents from the judge. Jesse is now not allowed to come near Jewels, Tony, or Zion without the threat of going to jail. This order is good for five years, but can be extended if deemed necessary.

Meanwhile, Kellie has continuously tried reaching out to Jewels, who is still ignoring her. She has even gone as far as to having her mom reach out to Mrs. Lowd. Mrs. Lowd calls Jewels one day and says,

"Hey Jewels, how is it going?"

Smiling, Jewels responds in a cheerful voice, "Fine ma, how are you and dad?"

"Good." She sighs and continues, "Baby girl you know Kellie's mom stopped by the other day?"

"No I did not. What did she want? Is Kellie okay?"

"Yes, your friend is okay---"

Jewels interrupts, "Ma she is not my friend. Just a human who I happen to love."

Shaking her head at her daughter, she replies, "Okay Jewels, 'the human you happen to love', is fine. Her mom was just trying to see if you two can mend your friendship?"

Sighing, Jewels says, "Ma, I have no ill will towards her and wish her nothing but the best, but our friendship is over. She has done to many things. I am tired. I have a son to raise now and I do not want him thinking her behavior is okay."

"Yea, baby girl, I told her mom you were over the friendship." Her mom becomes silent and Jewels asks,

"Ma what is wrong? Why are you quiet?"

"Just thinking about some things her mom told me."

"What is it ma?"
Her mom sighs, "You know Jesse finally broke up with her."

Shaking her head, while squeezing her lips together, she sarcastically says, "I am soooooo surprised. When did this happen?"

"Her mom said it was the day before he broke into you and Tony's home. She said she cried all night too. He did her pretty dirty too, but I did remind her mom about how their relationship begin. I also asked if this is why she is trying to reconnect with you?"

Shaking her head, Jewels responds, "Well ma, I am not surprised. What did she expect? For him to treat her like a princess or queen when their whole relationship was based on peasant behavior? I mean she cheated on her, then boyfriend, with her friend's ex. What did he do, refuse to marry her and found another woman?" She pauses and continues, "Did her mom say if this is the reason she wants to be friends again?"

"Worse, in my opinion. You know she found out she was pregnant and he convinced her to get an abortion. Two days after the abortion he dumped her, but her mom also said that Kellie has been trying to mend her friendship with you before this. You will not talk to her though. Baby girl I laughed at that and was thinking, 'Did Kellie forget how Jewels ignored Tony?' You had that grown man walking around here looking like a sad puppy dog. He was sitting at his parents' house for hours on their porch hoping you stop by our house.

One day, I finally told him, 'Tony stop wasting your time. You know she is not coming, because she knows you and know this is exactly what you are doing. I bet you text her too while you are here?' Baby girl, he just dropped his head, because he knew I was right, hugged me, asked if I needed anything, and finally left. I told her mom, Kellie knows how you are."

Looking at the phone, Jewels chuckles at the Tony story and says, "Ma, Tony had himself walking around looking like that." She laughs some more then continues in a serious voice saying, "Ma, I am actually shocked at this. I know he wanted more kids, matter of fact he tried with me, but I refused. I mean he really wanted one and used to ask me all the time. Now that I think back, I believe that is another reason I got tired of him. I was not about to have his child and I made the right decision."

In a shocked voice, her mom says, "You never told me that."

"Yea, I know ma. I know you would have told Mrs. Ellison who would have told Tony and I know his tail would have hit the roof. I did not want to hear his mouth. He was already mad at me for not coming to Cali."

Her mom laughs while saying, "You right Jewels. I would have, but your dad would have not liked it either." She pauses, then asks, "But baby girl, are you ready for your wedding?"

Smiling with glee, she responds, "Yes ma'am. So is Tony. He has been walking around the house singing, Jesse Powell's You, for the last few days and I have been loving every terrible note." She stops and listens to her mom laugh, then says, "I will be to your house in a couple of days and he is going to Jacob's then his parents' house the day before. Our goal is to not see each other for a few days until our wedding day."

"Sounds good Jewels."

"Yep, and ma, I hope you did not tell her mom about it?"

"I didn't. I know you do not want her to know, but Jewels y'all will have the street blocked off the whole weekend and will hold celebrations the entire weekend. I am sure she will find out."

"I am sure she will too, but everyone knows she is not welcomed."

Her mom laughs and says, "Okay baby girl, but I was just calling to fill you in. See you in a couple of days. Love you."

"Love you too momma and see you soon."

She ends her call with her mom and walks to their front door, where she sees Tony teaching Zion how to hold a kid's baseball bat. Zion keeps banging the ground with the bat. Whenever Tony finally gets him to hold it correctly, including the correct stance, some children passes and it causes Zion to lose focus.

Tony stands and looks at his son while laughing as he shakes his head. He looks at their house, sees Jewels, and says, "Baby, I do not know where he gets this from? He is so easily distracted. I am going to have to teach him how to focus. None of us are like this."

Jewels laughs and says, "From his daddy. You notice those are girls passing and he's still looking."

Bursting into laughter, Tony says, "Whatever Jewels. I knew how to stay focus though."

Jewels laughs a little more at this and continues to watch Tony teach Zion. Finally, Tony ends his lesson with Zion and watches him as he runs around the yard. Tony secures their gates, then walks to the front porch to sit with Jewels. Sitting next to her, he looks at her while rubbing his beard, and says in a low voice,

"I walked in the house to get my cell phone and I overheard you tell your momma Jesse wanted a baby."

Jewels looks at him with her mouth open and asks, "Where you eavesdropping Tony?"

Laughing he responds, "Nope. Just walked in at the right time, and I would not have hit the roof either."

She looks at him not believing his words. He laughs and says, "Baby, if I would have known that, that would have been the final straw though. I would have been to busy booking flights to have hit the roof. The next time you would have talked to me, I would have been standing at Jesse's front door with your dad and brother in the car like, 'Jewels, lets go. You are going back to Jax. today'."

Jewels laughs so hard at this, she bends over on her knees and wipes a tear. She sits back up trying to stop laughing as she watches Zion, then looks at Tony and says, "Just like that? You really think you could have got me to leave because you asked?"

Shaking his head no, Tony responds, "Nope, not at all, but that is why your dad and brother would have been there. They would have accomplished it. They were not feeling him like that after a couple of years. I know they ain't want you having his baby either. But baby, the whole time I would've been booking the flights, my mind would've been repeating, 'Ain't no way you are going to be a stepdad to his child, naw, not about to happen'."

Shaking her head in laughter, "Tony you just knew we will be back together, huh? Just cocky."

Laughing with her, he kisses her cheek then says, "Baby, I just wasn't in denial. I knew I still loved you and I knew you still loved me, baby we are meant for each other. You know it's true. We just hit a bump in the road, but our car still functioned. You just needed some time."

He leans over and kisses her cheek again as Jewels nods in agreement while blushing. They sit and watch Zion as he runs over the yard until the sun begins to set. They finally go in, eat, and prepare for bed.

A week later, Tony and Jewels awakes in separate beds for the fifth morning. This is something they have not done since the day they became husband and wife. Tony text messages her at Five in the morning saying,

"Good morning baby. The sweetest woman I know. I loooooveee you and can't wait to see you. <heartbeat>, <smooch>, <attachment, Case, Happily Ever After>"

"Good morning handsome and the greatest husband ever. I love you too and I am sooooooo ready to see you and Zion. This will be a lovely day. <heartbeat>, <blushes>, <attachment, Jesse Powell, You>"

As she sends her text message, her sister Zapphire walks in the room and says, "Good morning! Sis, your day is finally here. Are you ready?"

Smiling, "Yes I am Zee. How does the street look?"

"Beautiful sis. This was a nice idea for you two to walk the street where you and Tony first met."

"Thanks, it was his idea too and I loved it. Are the waterfalls okay?"

"Yes they are. Everything is fine. The DJ is setting up now, then he will leave to get dressed and come back. Our mom and Tony's have been cooking all night too. I tried to get a caterer, but they wanted to do it. I guess as a wedding gift to you two, but they were up singing and dancing all night at the Ellisons' house. Zion swear he was cooking too. Tony had to snatch him up so many times until Mrs. Ellison said, 'Tony leave our grandchild alone and let him think he is cooking."

Jewels laughs hysterically as Zapphire continuess, "Yea, Tony laughed too as he surrendered with his hands up and slowly backed away then went back to sketching a photo of the three of you. Sis, he is one talented man. He sketched the photo fast, but it is still an award winning work of art." She smiles at her sister, and continues as Jewels agrees, "And sis, ma made you a beautiful cake. It is four layers too. She has roses all over it too, because she knows Tony always gifts you roses. She made a separate box like cake too. I think you will love them. You know Tony helped with some cake ideas too", she laughs.

As Jewels smiles, Zapphire says, "Sis, that man really loves you. I know my husband loves me, but I have noticed his eyes still light up just hearing your name, like they did when we were kids. I am so happy I, not only have the chance to witness the wedding, but partake in it as well. Thanks for waiting for us to come home."

"Awwweee, sis, you know there was no way I was doing this without you here and I really love my baby too."

They hug and her sister says, "Well, I will let you rest another hour, then we will start getting ready. Three will be here in no time. I checked the weather and it will be a sunny day."

Jewels smiles and nods as her sister leaves the room. She lies back down for thirty minutes. She spends some time meditating and the rest going through her cell phone looking at old pictures of them. As she looks, Tony text messages her a picture and the text message reads,

"*Baby, here we are on our first official date as a couple. Look at those smiles. I love you baby, <attachment, Jagged Edge, I Gotta Be>*"

Jewels replies, "<heart eyes smile>, <smooch>, I love you Tony and see you soon."

It is finally time for Jewels and her sister to get ready. They spend their time laughing then their mom and Mrs. Ellison joins them. Jewels thanks them for cooking and they help her with her dress. It is a beautiful powder yellow mermaid fitting dress. It is embellished with gold rhinestones all over it. She has her hair pulled up into a bun, that Mrs. Ellison did. Her ears have gold stud diamonds in them, that were a gift from her dad for her wedding. Her wrist is decorated with the gold cuff bracelet, Tony gifted her yeas ago that she wears daily. Every time she puts it on, she sees Tony smile.

As they get ready, there is non stop slow jams playing in the background. Most of it is jazz.

Meanwhile, the men, are playing a mixture of Rhythm and Blues with some old school rap songs included. Their rap artists includes, Tupac Shakur, LL Cool J, Biggie Smalls, Nas, and more. Each of them take turns free-styling to some instrumentals or when one of their friends beat-box or pound a beat on a nearby table. One of their childhood friends, who is also married to the shoe store co-owner, does Tony and Zion's hair for them.

After she leaves, Jacob looks at Tony, and says, "My bad about last night. I had no clue they were doing that. I thought we were just going to hang and play cards. Stuff like that."

Laughing, Tony says, "It is cool and I know you ain't know. And you know your sister would go off on me", laughing, "heck, she probably would have threw my clothes in the yard and changed the locks on the door."

He and Jacob laughs, as Tony continues, "I'm thinking, why are y'all even trying me like this? They know I ain't even into strippers. I probably been to a strip club three times and that was only for parties and stuff. I am not into a woman, 'dancing' for me, just to go and 'dance' for another man. Coming to me smelling like three other dudes. That ain't for me."

He laughs some thinking of his night and continues, " I am having a good time too. Enjoying the game that is on. I am happy too because I have not seen this recording in a decade. I forgot y'all even had it. I was on point that night too, hitting all my shots. I am just enjoying it while thinking about those days and seeing my baby cheering me on in the stands. I am laughing at myself blowing kisses at her and laughing at your dad holding his fist up to me. Then I see myself laughing at Tika giving my baby a unit while trying to cheer." They stop and laugh at this, then Tony continues, "Then this stripper comes out and stands right in front of me. Blocking my view. I'm looking around irritated and confused, like, 'Get this woman out of my face'."

Laughing hysterically, Jacob says, "She was really trying to work too and I hear them in the background saying, 'This is your wedding gift for your bachelor's party'." Still laughing, Jacob continues, "Tony you stood up so quick, looking at her, like, 'Move woman', and looked at them saying, 'I ain't been a bachelor in four years. Y'all gone have me in divorce court crying and begging my baby not to leave me while telling the judge, 'She can have whatever she wants', at the same time. Y'all know Jewels ain't with this. I'm out. I had fun though'. Tony we were rolling, but I was like I am out too because I am not about to get caught up with y'all."

Laughing, Tony says, "Yea, they tried it last night. I had to text Jewels and make sure her friends did not pull those stunts. She was so confused with our conversation, but I got my answer though." Laughing at himself, he continues, "Bro, I just text her, 'Hey'. Jacob, Jewels text back, 'Uhhhh, hey to you too', with side eyes and asked, 'you okay?' I am looking at the phone, like how can I respond? I don't want her to know I am spying. I finally respond, 'Yes, just saying hey to y'all.' She responds, 'Everyone says hi, but baby why are you texting like this? Are you okay?'

I'm like, 'Baby I am fine, bur I am 'bout to go to sleep and wanted to check on you.'

She finally says, 'Baby I am fine. We are just sitting here watching movies and I am about to call it a night myself.' Jacob, I smiled when I read that, like, 'Okay ain't no men been in your face. I'm good now.' I text her, 'Goodnight baby, I love you.'" He says this while still laughing.

Jacob bends over in laughter saying, "Tony, you are a whole trip. I bet you can't take a man staring at my sis."

With a serious face, Tony responds, "You got that right because ain't no telling what they are thinking looking at my baby. Maaaan", he looks at Jacob, still with a serious face and continues, "she is your sister so you can't see it, but my baby is SEXY."

Jacob continues to laugh as he shakes his head at Tony.

They continue to get dress and jam to the music playing in the background. They laugh at Zion as he tries to two step to the beats.

Down the street at the Lowds' house, Jewels finishes getting dressed. At one point, she stops and checks her cell phone, after receiving a text message. She does not recognize the number, but the text reads,

"Enjoy your day Jewels. I wish you and Tony nothing but happiness."

Jewels responds,

"Who is this?"

"Kellie."

Rolling her eyes and shaking her head, Jewels does not respond but blocks the number.

She looks at her sister as her sister asks, "Are you okay Jewels?"

Jewels says, "Yes, that was Kellie just texting me from another number. She really has some nerve. Zee she told that man all of our business and she knows how Tony is. I am so happy our neighbors were there to hold him off. The look my baby had on his face after that man mentioned my touch and scent scared me for a second, and this heifer has the nerve to message me on my wedding day. She tried it, but back to my happy occasion." She smiles and looks at her sister, "It is almost time. Is everyone ready?"

"Yes sis, she did. I am still in disbelief of her actions. But we are going to enjoy this day! Everyone is ready too sis, we are waiting for you."

Smiling, Jewels stands and says, "Okay, I'm ready to see my babies. Lets go." She dances as she walks outside.

Jewels and her sister stand behind a purple and yellow makeshift curtain set in her parents' driveway. It will open for each of them to walk out separately to the road. The road has a purple roll out mat with gold trimming embellished with jewels. Each side of the road, including the sidewalks, have chairs for their visitors. There are also chairs towards the end of the street that are blocked off with more makeshift curtains to provide a little privacy. Behind where Tony and Jewels will recite their vows are seven waterfalls, all placed behind small rose bushes planted in gold pots. The roses vary in colors from purple, yellow, and deep red.

As the song, Love by Musiq Soulchild plays, Zapphire walks out. The ring bearer, who is Zion, is already standing to the alter with his dad and uncle.

The flower girl, who is the child of a friend, walks, well skips the aisle while dropping the flower petals one by one. The guests finds this entertaining and cannot stop laughing.

Finally, it is Jewels' turn. As Jewels begins to walk out with her dad, she smiles at the beautiful scenery. The guests laugh some more because Zion yells, "Mommy", as he stands to the alter with his dad and uncle then tries to run to her. Tony quickly stops and holds him as he smiles watching Jewels walk to him.

Standing next to his dad as Tony holds him, Zion holds a pillow bearing Jewels' ring smiling as he sees his mom gets closer. As the tune, Loving You by Minnie Riperton, continues to play, Jewels notices Tony holds his head back trying to stop his tears from flowing.

As she walks, she cannot take her eyes off of Tony. He has on an all white tuxedo with a yellow bow tie accompanied with a yellow handerkerchief in his tuxedo's jacket pocket. His Locs are braided into five cornrows. His full beard flows neatly with his goat tee that has naturally formed, but he let his bone grow out. She glances at her son, who Tony is still holding, and sees that he is a miniature version of his dad. Also wearing white with his hair braided in corn rows and a yellow handerkerchief in his pocket. They both went casual for their footwear and are wearing yellow sneakers with a white embellishment that showcases the designer's sign of the maker of the shoe.

Finally, Jewels makes it to their make shift alter. Her dad hands her to Tony and Tony mouths, "You look beautiful baby."

Blushing she mouths back, "Thank you handsome."

The pastor begins to speak and the couple cannot take their eyes off of each other. At one point, Zion touches his mom's hand and says, "Mommy don't cry." The crowd collectively says, "Awwwweeeee", as Jewels pats her son's head and says, "Mommy's okay."

Tony rubs Zion's head smiling, and says, "That's my lil' man. Making sure your momma is okay."

Hearing this, Jewels blushes and blows Tony a kiss.

After they recite their vows, Tony says, while holding her hands and smiling, "Jewels baby", he drops his head for a second then looks at her again, "I have loved you since I first laid eyes on you. I always knew you were my wife, always baby." He smiles at her and continues, "Baby, I vow to continue to love you the way Christ loved the church. You are a special gift He created for me, and I will love and take care of His gift for life. Baby, you bring so much joy to me. I love you and I will continue to love you unconditionally. I could not have dreamed of a better wife. I just thank you for being you baby."

Trying to hold back more tears, Jewels says, "Baby, you know I love you too. I thank God, The Most High, for putting such a loving and courageous man in my life. I have also loved you from childhood. And I thank you for not giving up on us---." She stops, wipes his tears, and smiles when she sees him mouth, "Never."

Jewels continues, "Baby, I wake up smiling when your arms are wrapped around me. Feeling loved and protected. Baby I don't know if I say it enough, but I truly appreciate you, as a man, husband, and father. I love you."

After she finishes, the pastor says a few more words to them. The pastor smiles and says, "Tony, you may kiss your bride."

Grinning, Tony pulls her to him and passionately kisses her. He bends her backwards, like they see couples do in old television shows. As he stops, he smiles and gives her little pecks all over her face while saying, "I love you baby", with every kiss. He finally stops when he hears, Brian Mcknight's Back At One, begin to play.

Instead of holding her hand to walk down the aisle, he hugs her from behind and walks with her singing the song to her while kissing her cheek in between lyrics. With every step they take, Jewels continuously blushes. Zion is standing to the side with his granddads and watches his parents walk away filled with love and joy.

Later that evening, they turn the street into a block party that is their wedding reception as well. Tony and Jewels changes into more comfortable clothes. They want to really be able to dance and enjoy themselves. Jewels changes into a yellow maxi dress with gold sandals. Tony and Zion, both wear khaki cargo shorts, a yellow and blue polo shirt, with white loafers on their feet. At one point Zion has to use the bathroom. As Jewels takes him, Zapphire walks by and helps Zion to the bathroom for her. Tony sees this and takes Jewels' hand then walks back to his childhood's bedroom, where they changed.

He closes the door and says, "Dang baby", he pulls her to him, while squeezing her butt, "I missed you and I ain't been able to kiss you like I want to since I have seen you." He laughs as he continues to squeeze her butt and jokingly says, "Come here woman and give me them lips."

Jewels laughs and he begins to passionately kiss her. He stops, smooches her lips, and says, "I love you Jewels Ellison."

She smooches him back saying, "I love you too."

As they continue to smooch, they hear a knock at the door and Zapphire says, "Hey, we are waiting on you two. You two will be home in no time for that."

They laugh and say, "We are coming Zee", give each other one more smooch and exit. They walk to the street, turned dance floor, to have their 'first' dance. They begin to slowly dance to, K-Ci and JoJo's All My Life. As the song plays, Tony sings every line to her while smiling with every note. He twirls her and nods in agreement with every lyric he sings. When the music stops, they hear their guests, the ones in their age group, all cheer and start dancing themselves when they hear the first sentence of the song. Tony and Jewels begins to dance harder. They both laugh as Jewels attempts to jokingly twerk.

After a minute, Tony stops her and says, "Alright baby that is enough. Your twerk skills are for my eyes only. I don't want to have to hurt one of these men."

Jewels bursts into laughter, but stops. They laugh even harder when they see confusion on their parents' faces because they have no clue what this song is. They have no clue that it took over the end of the nineties' and the start of the two thousands'.

After their dance break, everyone sits to eat. Their moms have baked and fried chicken. The baked chicken is seasoned with basil and lemon pepper, which they notices has their guest licking their fingers. They also made macaroni and cheese with honey baked carrots for the side dish. As they eat, Zapphire and Jacob give toasts to their brother and sister as Zion sits with his parents to enjoy his meal. Zapphire goes first,

"First, congrats. It feels good seeing your friendship blossom into your marriage. Sis", she looks at Jewels and smiles, "I told you Tony was going to get you one day. You thought it was a joke, saying, 'We are just friends. He does not like me in that way and he probably sees me as a sister'." Laughing some more, "I was always like, 'Nope sis, brothers do not look at their sisters like that. Just remember I am helping plan the wedding when the day comes'." Tony looks at Jewels and says, "Right", and kisses her cheek.

She continues, "You always laughed at me Jewels, but now we are here. And you are smiling non stop, as his wife and the mother to his son. I am so happy for the both of you and I wish nothing but happiness to you. I love you both."

They smile and raise there glasses to her.

She blows them a kiss, then Jacob speaks, "Whew." He shakes his head, "Y'all know this has been a looooonnnnngggg time coming." The crowd laughs at this and one of their childhood friends shouts, "Toooooo long", the guests laugh again.

Jacob laughs and continues, "Tony you have always been like a little brother to me, but I had to always keep a watchful eye out for you when it came to my baby sis. I remember dad stopped me one day, as I was on my way outside, and said, 'Jacob, come here and let me show you something.' I think y'all were like ten, he continues, 'You see your sister and little Tony out there playing?' I nodded my head yes and dad was like, 'Now pay attention to how he looks at your sister. He likes her and I need you to make sure it stays there.'

I was like, 'I got it dad, he ain't going to touch her'." He laughs, "Now you are my brother in law and the father to my nephew." He looks at his dad and laughs, "I tried, but they fell in love. Seriously though", he turns back to the bride and groom, "you two are great together. I love y'all and wish you nothing but the best. Tony, continue to make my sis smile and sis, I know you will do the same."

Tony nods at Jacob, while raising his Champagne glass filled with sparkling water, and says, "I surely am and y'all know I was not going to cross the line with my baby", he laughs along with the attendees and kisses Jewels' cheek again. As everyone laughs, Mr. Lowd stands and says, "I have a toast too."

Jacob hands him the microphone and steps back so his dad can speak. Mr. Lowd looks around their neighborhood, then at the bride and groom, and says, "Tony", he shakes his head, "I always thought I was going to have to shoot you. I used to tell my wife, 'He is going to be a problem with my baby girl'." He stops and laughs as the crowd laughs too and continues, "But I got to know your parents and you better. And I must admit, that I begin to hope that one day you and my daughter would finally date.

I am a father, and I did see you truly cared for my baby girl. I saw that you loved her and would protect her." Tony smiles, kisses Jewels' cheek as she blushes, and they continue to listen to Mr. Lowd, who continues, "I remember when you came to me asking to marry my baby girl", he pauses, looks at Jacob, laughs, and says, "the second time you came to me." Everyone bursts into laughter. Tony shrugs his shoulders and nods his head in laughter as he looks at Jewels saying, "Yep, I surely did ask as a kid and I will do it again", he kisses her forehead as Jewels laughs and they continue to listen to Mr. Lowd.

Mr. Lowd continues, "Tony I sat there and listened to everything you had to say, but the whole time I am thinking, 'He knows the answer will be yes. Why is he so nervous and babbling?' But Tony, you finally got it out, showed me the ring and everything. I looked at it, like, 'Jewels will love it', and you said, 'I know. She picked it out without realizing it.'"

Jewels looks at Tony in shock, who looks at her, and mouths, "You did, in high school."

Slowly remembering, she smiles, nods, and continues to listen to her dad, "Baby girl, you know my goals of raising my children were to always love, provide, protect, and guide. I pray we did a great job in that, now we can step back and watch you two do the same with Zion. I love you both and wish you two nothing but much success in your marriage."

Tony raises his glass again saying, "Thanks Mr. Lowd, for your words and for my baby. I love you too."

They end their toasts as jazz music begins to play. Tony and Jewels walks to their cakes and she sees the one with roses first. The other one is next to it and on it are two pictures. One is of her and Tony, on their first day of school as they prepared to walk to their elementary school. The second picture is of them at his house in California on the day they announced their engagement.

Seeing the engagement picture causes Jewels to blush. After she takes in the designs of the cakes, they cut their first slice and feed it to each other. Instead of using a utensil, Tony puts a piece in his mouth and gives Jewels the remainder as he tries to steal a kiss as well. After they take their slices, her dad comes to get her so they can finally have their father daughter dance. The song that plays for them is, To Dance With My Father by Luther Vandross.

When the song completes, Mr. Lowd walks his daughter to Tony as Usher and Alicia Key's My Boo, begins to play. He gives his daughter to his son-in -law with a smile. He shakes Tony's hand as he gives him a nod of affirmation as the right choice for his daughter.

Tony takes his wife's hand, grinning with joy and pride, walks her to the street turned dance floor, to dance with her to this song.

"I love you Jewels", he says as he holds her tight while swaying from side to side to this song.

As she holds him back, she responds, "I love you too Tony."

He chuckles and continues as they continue to slowly sway back and forth to the song, "You are, 'my woman', for life baby."

Laughing, she responds, "And I am proud to be her."

He smiles and caresses her as they dance. He squeezes her and sings some of the lyrics of the song to her. Maxwell's Fortunate, begins to play and Zion walks up to them. They hold his hand and dances along to the tune with him. Minutes later, Mrs. Ellison walks up and picks up Zion. She says to them, "It is almost his bedtime. We are going to take him in your parents' house Jewels, bathe him, and put him to bed. You two can continue to enjoy yourselves."

Smiling, "Thanks ma." Tony says as he kisses his mom's cheek and pats Zion on the head while saying, "Goodnight son, I love you." Jewels kisses Zion on the cheek and says the same.

They continue to dance as, This Woman's Work by Maxwell plays. As they dance Tony looks around their neighborhood. He notices everyone is occupied. They are either dancing, talking, or eating. Tony kisses Jewels' forehead and says, "Baby."

"Yes Tony", Jewels says while her head rests on his muscular shoulder.

He whispers in her ear, "I need you."

Confused, she asks, "Huh? Need me for what?"

He squeezes her butt and continues speaking in her ear, "Baby, you know." He kisses her cheek and repeats, "Baby, I need you."

Laughing at him, she says, "We can't leave our reception."

Smiling, he looks over the street again and says, "We can baby, no one is even paying us attention. They won't even recognize we left. I'ma dance you to my parents' house and we can ease in."

Shaking her head in laughter, "Tony, don't you think you are over stepping on your father's permission? He only gave us a one night permit and that was because of our unusual circumstance at that time."

As she says this, Tony slowly moves her to his parents' house, looks around again, and says, "Baby, we are good. My dad understands and he knows what's up. You think our parents got Zion for no reason? That was our permission baby."

She drops her head in laughter, as Tony looks around again and sees no one is still paying them any attention. He takes her hand and they sneak away to his childhood's bedroom. He closes and locks the door. Closes the blinds, then turns to Jewels and says, "I love you baby, for life." He chuckles as he walks to her and continues, "Now give me them lips woman."

She shakes her head while laughing at him, but gives him her lips to embrace in a passionate kiss.

Forever My Jewels

www.ingramcontent.com/pod-product-compliance
Lightning Source LLC
Chambersburg PA
CBHW071509170626
46811CB00007B/2785